The Blessing

Books by Jude Deveraux

Published by Pocket Books

Jude DEVERAUX

The Blessing

POCKET BOOKS

NEW YORK LONDON TORONTO SYDNEY TOKYO SINGAPORE

POCKET BOOKS, a division of Simon & Schuster Inc.
1230 Avenue of the Americas, New York, NY 10020

ISBN: 0-671-89108-1

First Pocket Books hardcover printing November 1998

10 9 8 7 6 5 4 3 2 1

CHAPTER ONE

"I OUGHT TO KILL YOU, YOU KNOW THAT? JUST OUTRIGHT murder you," Jason Wilding said, looking at his brother from under straight black eyebrows that were topped with a lion's mane of steel gray hair.

"What else is new?" David asked, smiling at his older brother, giving that smile of such great charm that people trusted him with their lives. David Wilding, or Dr. David as he was known to the people of Abernathy, Kentucky, picked up his glass of beer and drank deeply, while Jason sipped at his single malt whiskey.

"So what do you want?" Jason asked, arching one brow. It was a look that had made many a business-man's knees quake.

"Now what makes you think I want anything?"

"Years of experience. The rest of this one-horse town

may think you're ready for sainthood, but I know you. You're up to something and you want something from me."

"Maybe I just wanted to visit with my illustrious older brother and the only way I could get you to come home for Christmas is to tell you that Dad was about to die."

"Cheap trick," Jason said with tight lips. He began to look in his suit pocket for a cigarette, then remembered that he gave them up over two years ago. But there was something about being in a bar in the town where he grew up that brought out the good ol' boy in him.

"It was the only thing I could think of," David said in defense of what he had done. He'd cabled his rich, overworked brother in New York that their father had suffered a heart attack and probably had only days to live. Within hours Jason's private jet had landed in an airfield fifty miles from Abernathy, and an hour later Jason was standing in their living room. When Jason had seen his father drinking beer and playing poker with his buddies, for a few minutes, David had feared for his life. But, as he well knew, Jason's bark was worse than his bite.

"I'm not staying," Jason said, "so you can get that idea out of your head."

"And why not?" David asked, trying to sound innocent. It had always been a family joke that David could get away with anything while Jason got blamed for everything. It was their looks. David had blond hair and blue eyes and a pink-and-white complexion. Even at thirty-seven he looked like an angel. And when he had on his doctor's coat, a stethoscope about his neck, every person who saw him breathed a sigh of relief, for any man who looked as divine as he did had to be able to save lives.

On the other hand, Jason was as dark as David was fair, and as his father had often said to him, "Even if you didn't do anything, you look like you did," for Jason was born with a scowl.

"Let me guess," David said, "you're booked for four weeks in Tahiti and you'll be bedding three women at once."

Jason just took a sip of his whiskey and looked at his brother archly.

"No, no, don't tell me," David said. "I really can guess this one. Maybe it's Paris and you're having an affair with a runway model. One of those tall, cool creatures with plastic breasts."

Jason looked at his watch. "I have to go, Leon is waiting."

David knew that Leon was his brother's private pilot and, in cases like this trip, he doubled as his chauffeur. David also knew that Jason's staff served as his family, since he never bothered returning home and he'd always been much too busy to create a family of his own.

Jason gave his brother a look, then finished his whiskey and rose. "Look, you know how much I'd love to stay here and listen to you make fun of me, but I have—"

"Let *me* say it," David said heavily. "You have *work* to do."

"Right, I do, and I would imagine that just because it's Christmas people don't stop getting sick, even in charming little Abernathy."

"No, and they don't stop needing help, even in Abernathy."

At that Jason sat back down. David asked for help only if he really needed it. "What is it? Cash?" Jason said. "Whatever you need, if I have it it's yours."

"I only wish that were true," David said, looking down at his beer.

Jason signaled the waiter to bring another single malt, and David looked up at him in speculation. Jason wasn't much of a drinker. He said it dulled his brain and he needed his wits about him if he was going to work. And, of course, work was Jason's be-all, end-all of life.

"I'm in love," David said softly; then when his brother was silent, he looked up and saw one of Jason's rare smiles.

"And what else?" Jason asked. "She from the wrong

side of the tracks? Are the biddies of this town up in arms because their precious Dr. David is no longer available?"

"I wish you didn't hate this town so much. It's a great place, really."

"If you like small-minded bigots," Jason said cheerfully.

"Look, what happened to Mother—No, I'm not going to get into that. I like this town and I plan to stay here."

"With your new ladylove. So what's the problem with this girl that you think you need me? What do I know about being in love?"

"You know about dating. I see your name in all the society columns."

"Mmmm. I need to network at those charity functions . . . and it helps to have a woman on my arm," Jason said without much feeling.

"It's nice that the women you escort happen to be some of the most beautiful women in the world."

"And the most avaricious," Jason said, this time with feeling. "Do you have any idea how much jet fuel costs? If you did, you'd get on with whatever has happened to make you lie and connive your way into getting me here."

"I figure one trip costs less than an EKG machine."

Jason didn't miss the hint. "You got it, so stop begging and get on with it. Who are you in love with and what's the problem? You want me to pay for the wedding?"

"Believe it or not," David said angrily, "some people on this earth want something from you other than that money that seems to be your life."

Immediately, Jason backed down. "I apologize for the insinuation. Just tell me about this woman and how in the world I can be of help to you."

David took a deep breath. "She's a widow. She's . . ." He looked up at his brother. "She's Billy Thompkins's widow."

At that Jason gave a low whistle.

"She's not like that. I know Billy had problems, but—"

"Yeah, the three *d*'s: drugs, drink, and driving."

"You didn't know him in his last years. He settled down at the end. He went away on some job across the river, and he came back two years later with Amy, and she was four months pregnant. He seemed to have turned over a new leaf. He even bought the old Salma place."

Jason raised an eyebrow. "Is that heap still standing?"

"Barely. Anyway, he bought it with his mother's help. She co-signed the mortgage."

"But then who in Abernathy would lend Billy money?"

"Exactly. But it didn't matter, because he died four months later. Plowed into a tree doing about eighty."

"Drunk?"

"Yeah, drunk, and his wife was left alone except for Mildred. You remember her? Billy's mother?"

"I always liked her," Jason said. "She deserved better than Billy."

"Well, she got it in Amy. She's the sweetest person you ever met."

"So what's your problem? I can't imagine that Mildred is standing in your way. Don't tell me Dad—"

"He loves Amy almost as much as I do," David said, looking down into his beer, which was already half empty.

"If you don't get on with it, I'm leaving," Jason threatened.

"It's her son. I told you that Amy was pregnant when she came back with Billy. Well, it was a boy."

"You deliver it?" Jason asked, one eyebrow arched.

"No, and don't start that again. It's different when you're a woman's doctor."

"Mmmmm. What about her son? Is he like his father?"

"Billy had a sense of humor. This kid is . . . You'd have to meet him to see what I mean. He's ruthless. Utterly without conscience. He is the most manipulative, conniving little monster I have ever met. Jealous doesn't begin to describe him. He completely controls Amy."

"And she has no idea what the kid's doing, right?" Jason said, his lips tight. He had been in David's position. Years before, he'd met a woman to whom he was more than just physically attracted. After one date he had begun to think that maybe there could be something between them. But then he'd met the woman's thirteen-year-old son. The kid was a criminal-in-the-making. He used to rifle through Jason's coat pockets and steal whatever he could find. Once he took Jason's car keys, which forced him to leave without his Jaguar that night. A week later the car was found at the bottom of the East River. Of course the kid's mother didn't believe that her son could do anything like that, so they had broken up. The last Jason had heard, the kid was now working on Wall Street and was a multimillionaire.

"You've had some experience in this area?" David asked.

"Some. You can't get any time with her unless the kid gives permission, right? And the mother dotes on him." There was bitterness in his voice.

"Like you've never seen in your life. She never goes anywhere without him. I've tried to persuade her to let me hire a baby-sitter, but she's too proud to accept my help, so the kid goes with us or we don't go. And it's impossible to stay at her house." David leaned halfway across the table. "The kid doesn't sleep. I mean it. Never. He's either a freak or a spawn of the devil. And of course Amy gives him one hundred percent of her attention all the time he's awake."

"Drop her," Jason said. "Trust me on this. Get away from her fast. If you did win her, you'd have to live with that kid. You'll wake up one morning with a cobra in your bed."

"He'd have to fight Max for space."

"The kid is still sleeping with his mother?" Jason said in disgust.

"When he wants to."

"Run."

"It's easy for you to say. You've never been in love. Look, I think I could handle the kid if I could just win over his mother. But the truth is, I have no time alone with her." At that, David looked up at Jason in a way he'd seen a thousand times before.

"Oh, no, you don't. You're not getting me into this. I have engagements."

"No, you don't. How many times have I heard you complain because your employees want to take time off at Christmas? So this year you can stay here and help me out and give that secretary of yours some time off. How is that gorgeous creature, by the way?"

"Fine," Jason said tightly. "So what is it you want?

You want me to kidnap the kid? Or maybe we should be done with it and have him murdered."

"The kid needs a father," David said, his mouth in a grimace.

"You do have it bad, don't you?"

"Real bad. I've never felt this way about a woman, and I have competition. Every man in town is after her."

"What's that, a whopping ten men or so? Or did old man Johnson die?"

"Ian Newsome is after her."

"Oh?" Jason said, giving his brother a one-sided grin. "Is that the boy who was the captain of the football team and the swimming team and also single-handedly won the state debating championships? The boy the girls used to throw themselves at? Didn't he marry Angela, the captain of the cheerleader squad, the one with more hair than brains?"

"Divorced. And he's back in town and he took over the Cadillac dealership."

"Must be making a lot of money there," Jason said sarcastically. There wasn't much call for Cadillacs in Abernathy.

"As a sideline, he sells Mercedes to the Arabs."

"Ahhhh," Jason said. "You do have problems."

"All I need is some time alone with Amy. If I could get her alone, I know I could—"

"Make her love you? That's not the way it works."

"Okay," David said, "but at least I'd like to get a chance."

"All Newsome has to do is send her over a red Mercedes convertible and she's his. Maybe you could give her free—"

"She's not like that!" David almost shouted; then when half the people in the bar looked at him, he lowered his voice. "I wish you'd stop joking. I'm not sure I want to live without her," David said softly.

For a moment Jason studied the top of his brother's head. David didn't ask for help often, and he *never* asked for help for himself. He had put himself through med school, refusing his brother's offer of a free education. "I won't appreciate it if it's handed to me on a platter," David had said. So now Jason was sure that David was still up to his neck in debt for that education, but he still wouldn't accept financial help.

But now David was asking his brother for something personal, something that didn't involve Jason's copious wealth. It had been a long, long time since anyone had asked Jason for anything that didn't have to do with money.

"I'll do what I can," Jason said softly.

David's head came up. "You mean it? No, no, what am I saying? You won't do what I have in mind."

Jason was by nature cautious, so now he said, "What exactly did you *have* in mind?"

"To live with her."

"What!?" Jason sputtered, again causing the patrons to look their way. He leaned toward his brother. "You want me to *live* with your girlfriend?"

"She's not my girlfriend. At least not yet, anyway. But I have to get someone in that house who can keep that kid away from her. And she has to trust him or she won't allow him to baby-sit."

"And then there's Newsome you have to deal with."

"Yeah, and all the other men who are after her."

"All right. I'll call Parker and she can—"

"No! It has to be you! Not your secretary. Not your chef or your pilot or your cleaning lady. You." When Jason looked at his brother in consternation at his vehemence, David calmed. "This kid needs a man's touch. You're good with brats. Look what you did with me."

Jason couldn't help being flattered, and it was true that he had been as much a father to his much younger sibling as he had been a brother. Their mother was gone and their father worked sixty hours a week, so they just had each other.

"Please," David said.

"All right," Jason answered reluctantly. In New York he was known to never give in on any deal, but then only David had the power to persuade him.

And, besides, there was part of Jason that wanted to replay one of the few battles in his life that he'd lost. A spoiled monster of a kid had kept him away from one of the few women Jason had ever thought he could love, and in the many years since then, he'd regretted not staying and fighting for her. Just last year he'd seen the woman again. She was happily married to a man Jason was doing business with and she looked great. They had a big house on Long Island, and they'd even had a couple of kids of their own. Now, at forty-five years old, Jason wondered what his life would have been like if he'd stayed and fought for the woman, if he hadn't let a thirteen-year-old con artist beat him.

"I'll do it," he said quietly. "I'll stay and see that the kid is occupied while you go out with your Amy."

"It won't be easy."

"I guess you think the rest of my life *is* easy."

"You haven't met this kid, and you haven't seen how attached Amy is to him."

"Don't worry about a thing. I can handle anything you throw at me. I'll take care of the brat for one week, and if you don't win this woman in that time, then you don't deserve her."

Instead of gushing with gratitude, as Jason thought he would, David looked down at his beer again.

"Now what is it?" Jason snapped. "A week isn't enough time?" His mind was racing. How many Little League games could a man attend without going insane? Thank God for cell phones so he could work while sitting on the bleachers. And if he got into a jam, he could always call Parker. She was capable of handling anything at any time, anywhere.

"I want your sacred promise."

At that, Jason's face grew red. "Do you think I go back on my word?"

"You'll turn the job over to someone else."

"Like hell I will!" Jason sputtered, but had to look down so his brother couldn't see his eyes. If the men he dealt with in New York knew him as well as his brother did, he'd never close a deal. "*I'll* take care of the kid for one week," he said more calmly. "I'll do all the things that kids like. I'll even give him the keys to my car."

"You flew; you don't have a car, remember?"

"Then I'll buy a car and give him the damn thing, all right?" David was making him feel decidedly incompetent. "Look, let's get this show on the road. The sooner I get this done with, the sooner I can get out of here. When do I meet this paragon of loveliness?"

"Sacred promise," David said, his eyes serious but his voice sounding as if he were once again four years old and demanding that his big brother promise that he wouldn't leave him.

Jason gave a great sigh. "Sacred promise," he murmured, then couldn't help looking around to see if anyone in the bar had heard him. In a mere thirty minutes he had gone from being a business tycoon to a dirty-faced little boy declaring blood oaths. "Did I ever tell you that I hate Christmas?"

"How can you hate something that you have never

participated in?" David asked with a cocky grin. "Come on, let's go. Maybe we'll be lucky and the kid will be asleep."

"Might I point out to you that it is two o'clock in the morning? I don't think your little angel will appreciate our dropping in."

"Tell you what, we'll go by her house and if all the lights are out, we'll go past. But if the lights are on, then we'll know she's up and we'll stop in for a visit. Agreed?"

Jason nodded as he drained the last of his whiskey, but he didn't like what he was thinking. What kind of woman would marry a man like Billy Thompkins? And what kind of woman stayed up all night? A fellow drunk seemed to be the only answer.

As they left the bar and headed toward the sedan where Jason's driver waited, Jason began to make up his own mind about this woman who had enticed his brother into wanting to marry her. The facts against her were accumulating fast: a drunken husband, an incorrigible child, a nocturnal lifestyle.

Inside the car, Jason looked across at his younger brother and vowed to protect him from this hussy, and as they rode toward the outskirts of town, he began to form a picture of her. He could see her bleached hair, a cigarette hanging out of her mouth. Was she older than David? He was so young, so innocent. He'd rarely left

Abernathy in his life and knew nothing of the world. It would be easy for some sharp-witted huckster to take advantage of him.

Turning, he looked at his brother solemnly. "Sacred promise," he said softly, and David grinned at him. Jason turned away. For all that his brother was often a pain in the neck, he had the power to make Jason feel as if he was worth what his accountant said he was.

CHAPTER TWO

THE OLD SALMA PLACE WAS WORSE THAN HE REMEMBERED it. It couldn't have had a coat of paint in at least fifteen years, and the porch was falling down on one side. And from what he could see by the moonlight, he didn't think the roof was going to keep anyone dry.

"See, I told you," David said eagerly, seemingly oblivious to the house's decrepitude. "The lights are all on. That kid never sleeps; he keeps his mother up all night."

Jason glanced at his brother and thought that the sooner he got him away from this harpy, the better.

"Come on," David said, already out of the car and halfway up the broken sidewalk that led to a fence that had half collapsed. "Are you afraid of this? If you are—"

"If I am, you'll double dare me, right?" Jason said, one eyebrow raised.

David grinned, his teeth white in the moonlight; then he half ran up the porch steps toward the front door. "Don't step on that, it—Oh, sorry, did you hurt yourself? The house needs some work."

Rubbing his head where a board from the porch had smacked him, Jason gave a grimace to his brother. "Yeah, like Frankenstein needed some fine tuning."

But David didn't seem to hear his brother as he eagerly rapped on the door, and within seconds it was opened by a young woman. . . . And Jason's mouth fell open in disbelief, for this woman was not what he had been expecting.

Amy was not a Siren luring men to her; she wasn't going to inspire sonnets written to her beauty. Nor was she going to have to worry about men falling at her feet in lust. She had long dark hair, which looked to be in need of a washing, pulled back at the nape of her neck. She wore no makeup, and her pale ivory skin had a few off-white-ish spots on her chin. Her dark eyes were huge, seeming to almost swallow her oval face; they certainly overshadowed her tiny mouth. As for her body, she was short and fragile-looking, and from the way her bones protruded from her clothes, she needed a good meal. The only thing of substance about her were her breasts, which were huge—and were marked by two large wet circles.

"Damnation!" she said as she looked down at herself; then she scurried back into the house. "Come in, David, make yourself at home. Max is—thank you God—asleep for the moment. I'd give you some gin, but I don't have any, so you might as well help yourself to the fifty-year-old brandy, which I don't have any of either."

"Thanks," David said brightly. "In that case I think I'll have champagne."

"Pour me a bucket full of it too," came the answer from a darkened doorway.

David looked at Jason as though to say, Isn't she the wittiest person you ever met?

But Jason was looking around the room. It had been a long time since he'd left what David referred to as his "house in the clouds." "You live so much in private jets and private hotels and private whatevers that you've forgotten what the rest of the world is like," he'd said too often. So now, Jason looked about the room in distaste. Shabby was the word that came first to his mind. Everything looked as though it had come from the Goodwill: nothing matched, nothing suited anything else. There was an ugly old couch upholstered in worn brown fabric, a hideous old chair covered in what looked to be a print of sunflowers and banana leaves. The coffee table was one of those huge, cast off wooden spools that someone had painted a strange shade of fuchsia.

The nicest thing Jason could think about it was that it looked like a place where Billy Thompkins would live.

David punched his brother in the ribs and nodded toward the doorway. "Stop sneering," he said under his breath; then both men looked up as Amy reentered the room.

She emerged from the bedroom wearing a dry, wrinkled shirt, and most of the spots on her chin were gone. When she saw Jason glance at her, she gave another swipe, removed the remaining spots, then gave a half smile and said, "Baby rice. If he got as much in him as I get on me, he'd be one fat little hog."

"This is my cousin Jason," David was saying. "You know, the one I was telling you about. He'd be really grateful if you'd let him stay with you until his heart mends."

This statement so stunned Jason that all he could do was stare at his brother.

"Yes, of course. I understand," Amy said. "Do come in and sit down." She looked at Jason. "I'm sorry Max isn't awake right now, but you'll get to see him in about three hours. I can assure you of that," she said, laughing.

Jason was beginning to smell a rat. And the rat was his little brother. The brother he had helped raise. The brother he had always loved and cherished. The one he would have died for. *That* brother seemed to have done a real number on him.

Long ago Jason had figured out that if he kept his mouth shut long enough, he'd learn everything he needed to know. Many times his silence had achieved what words could not, so now he sat and listened.

"Can I offer you some tea?" Amy asked. "If I can't afford champagne, I can afford tea. I have chamomile and raspberry leaf. No, that one's good for milk, and I doubt if either of you need that," she said, smiling at Jason as though he knew everything that was going on.

And Jason was indeed beginning to understand. Now he noticed a few things about the room that he had overlooked before. On the floor was a stuffed tiger. No, it was Tigger from *Winnie-the-Pooh,* and there was a cloth book against the edge of the sunflower chair.

"How old is your son?" Jason asked, his jaw rigid.

"Twenty-six weeks today," Amy said proudly. "Six months."

Jason turned blazing eyes on his brother. "May I see you outside?" He looked at Amy. "You must excuse us."

When David made no move to get off the old brown sofa, Jason dug his hands into his brother's shoulders and pulled him upward. One advantage Jason had was that wherever he went he made sure there was a gym available so he could keep in shape. David thought that standing on his feet fourteen hours a day was enough exercise, so now Jason had the advantage and he nearly lifted his softer brother into a standing position.

"We'll only be a minute," David said, smiling at Amy as Jason half dragged him from the house.

Once they were outside, Jason glared at his brother, his voice calm—and deadly. "What are you playing at? And don't you dare lie to me."

"I couldn't tell you or you would have run back to your damned jet. But actually I didn't really lie to you. I just omitted some details. And haven't you always said that no man should assume anything?"

"Don't turn this back on me. I was talking about *strangers*. I didn't think my own brother would—Oh, the hell with it. You go in there and tell that poor young woman that a mistake was made, and—"

"You're going back on a sacred oath. I knew you would."

For a moment Jason closed his eyes in an attempt to regain strength. "We are no longer in elementary school. We are adults and—"

"Right," David said coldly, then turned toward the car that waited at the curb.

Oh, Lord, Jason thought. His brother could carry a grudge into eternity. In one step he caught David's arm and halted him. "You must see that I can't follow up on my promise. I could look after a half-grown boy, but this is . . . David, this is a *baby*. It wears *diapers*."

"And you're too good to change them, is that it? Of course, the great and rich"—he sneered the word—"Jason Wilding is too good to change a kid's diapers. Do you have any idea how many times I have emptied bedpans? Inserted catheters? That I have—"

"All right, you win. You're St. David and I am the devil incarnate. Whatever, I can't do this."

"I knew you'd go back on your word," David muttered, then turned toward the car again.

Jason sent up a little prayer asking for strength, then grabbed David's arm again. "What is it you've told her?" he asked while envisioning his secretary flying to Abernathy and taking over the kid. No, the *baby*.

David's eyes brightened. "I told her you were my cousin and you were recovering from a broken love affair and it was the first Christmas you'd had without your lover, so you were very lonely. And that your new apartment was being repainted, so you had nowhere to stay for a week. I also said you loved babies and she'd be doing you a favor to let you stay with her for a week and take care of Max while she job hunts during the day." David took a breath.

It wasn't as bad as Jason had at first thought when he'd heard that "broken heart" remark.

David could see his brother relenting. "All I want is a little time with her," he said. "I'm mad about her. You can see that she's wonderful. She's funny and brave and—"

"And has a heart of gold, I know," Jason said tiredly as he walked toward the car. Leon was already out and had the back door open. "Call Parker and tell her to get here fast," he ordered. It felt good to give an order. David made him feel as though he were back in nursery school.

Jason turned back to his brother. "If I do this for you, you are never to ask anything from me ever again. You understand? This is the all-time, ultimate favor."

"Scouts' honor," David said, raising two fingers and looking so happy that Jason almost forgave him. But at least the good news was that now that David had lied to him, he felt free to do a little underhanded business of his own. He most definitely would get his competent secretary to bail him out of this.

David could see by his brother's face that Jason was going to do it. "You'll not regret this. I promise you."

"I already do," Jason muttered as he followed David back into the house. And once they were inside, it took David all of about four minutes before he excused himself, saying he had to get up early; then he left the two of them alone.

And it was then that Jason felt especially awkward. "I . . . ah . . ." he began, not knowing what to say to the young woman who stood there staring at him as though she expected him to say something. What did she want from him? A résumé maybe? Such a document might list several Fortune 500 companies he owned, but it wouldn't say anything about his ability—or in this case his inability—to change diapers.

When Jason said nothing, the woman gave him a bit of a smile, then said, "I would imagine that you're tired. The spare bedroom is in there. I'm sorry, but there's only a narrow bed. I've never had a guest before."

Jason tried to give her a smile in return. It wasn't her fault if his brother was in love with her, but, truthfully, Jason couldn't see what there was to love about the woman. Personally, he liked his women to be clean and polished, the kind of women who spent their days in a salon having every hair and pore tended to.

"Where are your bags?"

"Bags?" he asked, not knowing what she meant. "Oh, yeah. Luggage. I left it at . . . at David's house. I'll get it in the morning."

She was looking at him very hard. "I thought—" She looked away, not finishing her sentence. "The bedroom's through there, and there's a little bathroom. It's not much but—" She broke off as though she weren't going to allow herself to apologize for the inadequacy of the room.

"Good night, Mr. Wilding," she said, then turned on her heel and went through another doorway.

Jason wasn't used to people dismissing him. In fact, he was more used to people fawning over him, as they usually wanted something from him. "Right," he muttered. "Good night." Then he turned and went into the room she'd indicated. It was, if possible, worse than the rest of the house. The bed stood in the middle of the room, with a clean, frayed old red-and-white quilt spread over it. The only other furniture in the room was an overturned cardboard box with a lamp on it that looked as though Edison might have used it. There was a tiny curtainless window and two doors, one that looked as if it might lead to a closet and the other the bathroom. Inside that room was all blazing white tile, half of it cracked.

Ten minutes later, Jason had stripped to his underwear and was huddled under the quilt. Tomorrow he'd send his secretary to buy him an electric blanket.

It couldn't have been more than an hour later that he was awakened by a sound. It was a scraping noise followed by something that sounded like paper being crumpled. He'd always been a light sleeper, but years of jet travel had made things worse; he was now nearly an insomniac. Quietly, barefoot, he padded into the living room. There was enough moonlight that he could see the shadow outlines of the furniture and keep from bashing into it. For a moment he stood still listening. The sound was coming from the woman's room.

Hesitating, he stood outside the open doorway. Maybe she was doing something in private, but as his eyes adjusted he could see her in bed, see that she was asleep. Feeling like a Peeping Tom, he turned away to go back to his own bed, but then the sound came again.

Peering into the darkness, he saw what looked to be a cage in the corner, but as he blinked, he saw it was an old-fashioned wooden playpen and sitting up in it was what appeared to be a baby bear.

Jason blinked, shook his head, then looked again as the bear cub turned its head and grinned up at him. He could distinctly see two teeth gleaming in the pale silvery light.

Without thinking what he was doing, Jason tiptoed into the room and reached down to the kid. He fully expected the child to let out a howl, but he didn't. However, the baby did grab Jason's face and pinch in a way that made Jason's eyes water with pain.

After removing the little hand from his face, Jason carried the child back into his own room and put him down onto the narrow bed, pulled the quilt about him, then said sternly, "Now go to sleep." The baby blinked up at him a couple of times, then squirmed around so he was lying crosswise on the bed, and promptly went to sleep.

"Not bad," Jason said in admiration of his own accomplishment. Not bad at all. Maybe David had been right when he said that his older brother had a way with children. Too bad Jason hadn't used his firmest tone with that horrid boy so many years ago. Maybe . . .

He trailed off as he realized that he now had no place to sleep. Even if he turned the kid around, the bed was too narrow for the both of them as the child was as fat as a Christmas turkey. No wonder his first impression of him was that he was a bear cub.

So now what? Jason thought, looking at his watch. It was four A.M. and New York wasn't open, so he couldn't do any business. Ah, he thought, New York might be closed, but London was open.

After putting his wool suit on to protect him from the cold, he retrieved his portable phone from his coat pocket and went to the window, where the signal would be better, and dialed. Five minutes later he was being hooked up to a conference call with the heads of a major company that Jason had recently bought. In the background he could hear sounds of an office Christmas party, and he could tell that the managers were annoyed to be missing the fun, but it didn't matter to Jason. Business was business, and the sooner they realized that the better.

CHAPTER THREE

I DON'T LIKE HIM, AMY THOUGHT AS SHE LAY IN BED. FOR some odd reason, Max was still asleep; she could see the great lump that was him in the old playpen that had once been Billy's.

"I don't like him, I don't like him, I don't like him," she said aloud, then glanced anxiously toward the playpen, but Max didn't move. She'd have to wake him in a minute or two or she was going to explode from milk, but it was nice to have these few minutes just to think.

When David had proposed that she allow his gay cousin to live with her for a week, Amy had readily said no. "What will I feed him?" she'd asked. "I can barely afford to feed Max and me."

"He, uh, he . . . He loves to cook. And, well, I'm sure he'd love to have someone to cook for. He'll buy everything you'll need," David had said in such a way that Amy didn't believe him. "No, really, he will. Look, Amy, I know this is an imposition, but Jason and his boyfriend just broke up, and my cousin has nowhere to go. You'd be doing me a real favor. I'd let him stay with us, but you know how my dad is about gays."

Actually, Amy had met Bertram Wilding only once and she had no idea how he felt about anything except chili dogs (he loved them) and football (loved that too). "Isn't there someone else? You know everyone in town," she had wailed. David had been so good to her; he hadn't charged her a penny for either of Max's ear infections or the immunizations, and he'd sent over his nurse to help out when Amy was sick with the flu those three days. It wasn't easy being a single mother on a severe budget, but with David's help she'd been able to survive. So she owed him.

"You have a spare bedroom and you need him. You don't have anything against gays, do you?" he asked, implying that he may have misjudged her.

"Of course not. It's just a matter of space and, well, money. I can't afford to feed him much less pay him for baby-sitting services and—"

"You just leave that to me," David said. "In fact, leave everything to me. Jason will help you do everything, and he'll make your life much easier. Trust me."

So she had trusted him, just as everyone else in this

town trusted him, and what did she get? A six-foot-tall sneering man who made her want to run and hide, that's what. Last night, or actually, this morning at the two o'clock feeding, she had had to bite her tongue to keep from making a snide remark as she watched him look about the house, his upper lip curled in distaste. He was wearing a suit that looked as though it cost more than her house had and she could feel his contempt. Right then she wanted to tell David to take him away, that she wouldn't let him near her son.

But then she remembered all that David had told her about this poor man and his broken heart. But to Amy the man didn't look depressed as much as he looked angry: angry at the world, maybe even angry at her in particular. When he'd demanded that David go outside with him, Amy had almost bolted the door against the two of them, then gone back to her warm bed.

But she hadn't, and now she was going to have to spend a whole week with the jerk, she thought. One whole week of her life being sneered at. One week—

She didn't think anymore because through the thin wall came the heavy thud of something falling, and it was followed by Max's scream of terror. Amy was out of the bed instantly and into her boarder's room before he could pick up the child.

"Get away," Amy said, pushing at his hands, as she snatched up her baby and cuddled him to her. "Hush, sweetheart," she said, holding him tightly, her heart pounding. He had fallen off the bed. Had he hit his head? Was he all right? Concussion? Brain damage? Her hands ran over him, searching for lumps, for blood, for anything wrong.

"I think he's just scared," Jason said. "He fell on the pillow, and besides, he has enough clothes on that you could drop him off a building and he wouldn't be hurt." At that he gave Amy what she imagined he thought was a smile.

Amy glared at him. Max had stopped crying and was now bending at the waist as he moved his head downward, letting her know that he wanted to nurse.

"Get out," she said to Jason. "I don't want you here."

The man looked at her as though he didn't understand English.

"Get out, I said. You're fired."

She was having trouble holding on to Max as he jackknifed downward. "Take your . . . your telephone and leave." It was easy to see that he had been standing by the window talking on the thing while he'd left a baby alone on a narrow bed. She wasn't about to leave Max in the care of someone so careless.

"I've never been fired from a job before," Jason said, his eyes wide.

"There is always a first time for everything." When Jason didn't move, she tightened her lips. "I don't have a car, so if you want transportation, call David. I'll get his number."

"I know his number," Jason said quietly, still standing there looking at her.

"Then use it!" she said as she turned away, her arms around Max's squirming body. She stalked into the living room, put Max down on the two pillows on the couch, her hand behind his head, then angrily unfastened her nightgown to reveal her breast. Max made fast work of latching on, then he lay there looking up at his mother intently, obviously aware that something was going on.

"Look, I—Oh, excuse me," Jason said as he turned his back to her, and Amy could feel his embarrassment at seeing her breast-feeding. Pulling a baby blanket off the back of the couch, she covered herself and most of the baby.

"I'd like a second chance," Jason said, his back still to her. "I was in the . . ." He nearly choked on the word. "I was in the wrong to leave the baby alone on the bed. But I, uh, I meant well. I heard him, so I took him out of his pen. I just wanted to give you a couple more hours' sleep, that's all."

As far as Amy could tell, every word out of the man's mouth was a struggle. You'd think he'd never apologized before in his life. No, actually, hearing the wrench in his voice, you'd think he'd never done anything wrong in his life before.

"You're asking me to take a second chance with my child's life?" she asked calmly, still looking at the back of him.

Slowly, he turned around, saw that she was covered, then sat down in the sunflower chair. "I am not usually so . . . so lacking in vigilance. Usually I watch over several matters at one time and keep them all going at once. Usually I can handle anything that's thrown my way. In fact, I pride myself on being able to handle anything."

"You don't have to lie to me; David told me everything." When she said that the man's face turned an odd shade of lavender, and she renewed her vow to get rid of him. I don't like him, she repeated to herself.

"And what did Dr. David tell you?" the man said softly.

There was something about him that was a bit intimidating. She owed David a lot, but she wasn't going to repay anyone at the expense of her child. "He told me that you're gay and you're recovering from a broken heart and—"

"He told you that I'm gay?" Jason said quietly.

"Yes, I know it's a secret and that you don't want people to know about you, but he had to tell me. You don't think I'd let a heterosexual man stay here with me, do you?" She squinted her eyes at him. "Or do you? Is that what kind of woman you think I am?"

When he didn't reply right away, she said, "I think you'd better leave."

Jason didn't so much as move a muscle, but sat there staring at her as though he were pondering some great problem. She remembered that David had told her that his cousin had nowhere to stay, nowhere to spend Christmas. "Look, I'm sorry that this hasn't worked out. You're not an unattractive man. I'm sure you'll find . . ."

"Another lover?" he asked, eyebrows raised. "Now I must ask what kind of man you think *I* am."

At that Amy blushed and looked down at Max, who was still nursing, his eyes wide open and seeming to listen to every word that was being spoken. "I apologize," she said. "I didn't mean any slur on any group of people. Forgive me."

"Only if you forgive me."

"No," she answered. "I don't think that this arrangement will work. I don't—" Breaking off, she looked down at Max again. He was no longer sucking, but he wasn't about to let go of her. As she well knew, he thought she was one big pacifier.

"You don't trust me? You don't want to forgive me? You don't what?"

"Like you," she blurted. "I'm sorry, but you wanted to know." Sticking her finger in the side of Max's mouth, she broke his powerful suction and removed him from her breast, covering herself, all in one practiced motion. She put him on her shoulder, but he soon twisted about to see who else was in the room.

"And why don't you like me?"

At that moment she decided that her debt to David had been paid. "You have done nothing but sneer since you got here," she blurted. "Maybe we can't all afford to wear hand-tailored suits and gold watches, but we do the best we can. I think that somewhere along the way you lost your memory of what it's like to be . . . be part of the masses. When David begged me to take you in, I got the idea we could help each other, but I can see that you think you're above Billy Thompkins's widow." She said the last with a rigid jaw. She hadn't been in Abernathy for a week before she learned what people thought of Billy.

"I see," Jason said, still not moving from where he was, and he looked as though he had no intention of leaving either the chair or the house. "And what would I have to do to prove myself to you? How can I prove that I am trustworthy and can do this job?"

"I haven't a clue," she said, wrestling with Max as all twenty-two pounds of him fought to stand on her lap, but his balance wasn't good, so he wobbled about like a very strong piece of wet spaghetti.

Suddenly, Jason leaned across the room and took the baby from her, and Max let out a squeal of delight.

"Traitor," Amy said under her breath as she watched

Jason hold Max aloft, then lower him and rub his whiskery face against Max's neck. Max grabbed Jason's cheeks with his hands, and Amy well knew how he could hurt; twice Max had drawn blood with those little love holds of his.

After several minutes of tossing Max about, Jason sat the baby down on his lap, and when Max started to squirm, Jason said, "Be still," and Max obeyed. Sitting there on Jason's lap, looking utterly content, Max smiled up at his mother.

Amy hated being a single mother, hated that Max didn't have a daddy. It wasn't what she had planned. For all that Billy had lots of faults, he was a sweet man, and he would have made a good father. But fate had decreed differently, and—

"What do you want?" Amy said tiredly when she realized he was staring at her.

"A second chance. Let me ask you, Mrs. Thompkins, has he ever fallen when you have been watching him?"

Blushing, Amy turned away. She didn't know how, but Max had fallen off the bed once and off the kitchen countertop once. The second time he'd been strapped to a thick plastic booster seat and he'd landed on his back, still strapped in, looking like a turtle in his shell. "There have been a couple of incidents."

"I see. Well, this morning was my first and only 'incident.' I can assure you of that. I thought he was asleep, and since he took up all the room in the bed, I couldn't go back to sleep, so I made a few calls. It was wrong of me to assume anything, but I wasn't negligent by intent. What else did David tell you about me?"

"That you were homeless for the moment and that you came home to mend your broken heart." she said. Max, the traitor, was sitting calmly on Jason's lap, playing with his big fingers, looking for all the world as though he'd found his throne.

"Have you noticed that your son seems to like me?"

"My son eats paper. What does he know?"

For the first time the man actually smiled, just a hint of a smile, but it was there. It was a bit like seeing the figures on Mount Rushmore smile. Would his face crack?

"May I be honest with you?" he asked, leaning toward her. "I don't know diddly-squat about taking care of a baby. I've never changed a diaper in my life. But I'm willing to learn, and I do need a place to stay. Also, I think I'd like to change your opinion of me. I can be quite likable when I make an effort."

"Does this mean you can't cook either?"

"David told you I could?"

She nodded, thinking that she should demand that he leave this minute, but Max did seem to like him. Now her son was beginning to twist around and, easily, Jason held him in Max's favorite standing position. The books said that babies didn't start standing until about six months, but Max had been standing on her lap and trying to pull her arms from their sockets since he was five and a half weeks old. Maybe if Jason did watch after Max she could take a shower. A real shower. One of those where she could shampoo her hair twice, then put on conditioner and leave it. Oh, heavens! maybe she could shave her legs! And afterward maybe she could rub moisturizer into her dry skin. Making milk seemed to remove every bit of moisture from her body, and her skin felt like sandpaper.

Maybe she would fire him later. After she'd had a bath. After all, he couldn't be too bad if Dr. David had recommended him so highly. "Would you mind if I took a bath?"

"Does that mean I get my second chance?"

"Maybe," she said, but she smiled a bit. "You wouldn't let anything happen to my baby, would you?"

"I'll guard him with my life."

Amy started to say something else, but instead she scurried off to the bathroom, and an instant later the hot water was running.

CHAPTER FOUR

"DEAD," JASON SAID INTO THE PHONE, MAX SLUNG OVER his arm like a sack of potatoes. "Little brother, you are dead."

"Look, Jase, I have about twenty patients waiting to see me, so what exactly is going to cause my death this time?"

"Gay. You told her I was gay. She thinks I've just broken up with my *boyfriend.*"

"I couldn't very well tell her the truth, could I?" David said, defending himself. "If I'd told her my rich and powerful brother who owns half of New York City had agreed to help me woo her, I don't think she would have agreed."

"Well, she didn't agree," Jason snapped. "She fired me."

At that David took a deep breath. "Fired you?"

"Yeah, but I talked her out of it."

David paused, then began to laugh. "I see. She gave you a way out of all this, but you were too proud to take it, so you used your powers of persuasion to keep your job. Now you don't know what to do with the job, right? Tell me, what did you say to persuade her?"

"The kid likes me."

"What? I can't hear you. We're giving flu shots today, and there's a lot of screaming. Senior citizens' day. It almost sounded like you said that Max likes you."

"He does. The kid likes me."

"Why would that horrible child like *you?*" David half shouted into the phone. "He doesn't like anyone. Has he bitten you yet? Don't tell me he lets you hold him? He only lets Amy hold him."

"I have him right now," Jason said smugly. "And you know what, Davy? I think your Amy likes me too." At that, he hung up the phone. Let his devious little brother contemplate *that* one.

Once the phone was down, Jason looked at the bundle hanging over his arm. "Is it my imagination or do you stink to high heaven?" Max twisted around and gave Jason a toothy grin, showing two teeth in his bottom jaw. Suddenly the thought of breast-feeding an infant with teeth went through his mind, and Jason shuddered. "Brave lady is your mother. Now, hang on, and she'll be out of the shower in a minute or two."

But Amy wasn't out of the shower in a minute. Or five. Or ten. And Max began to squirm. Jason put him down on the floor, but the baby lifted his legs high in the air and began to whimper, all the while looking up at Jason with big eyes.

"I am going to kill my brother," Jason muttered in what was becoming a chant; then he began to look for changing facilities. Not that he'd know how to use them, but he had seen movies and had occasionally watched TV. Wasn't there supposed to be a tall cabinet that you put the baby on and it had shelves full of diapers and whatever else was needed? On the other hand, maybe if he thought about all this long enough, Amy would get out of the shower.

But still the shower ran, and the baby was looking up at Jason mournfully. Didn't babies cry at the drop of a hat? he thought. But this little guy was a trooper and even a bucketload wasn't making him howl. "Okay, kid, I'll do my best."

Looking about, he saw a pile of plastic-coated diapers under a table, so he figured it was now or never.

CHAPTER FIVE

AFTER WHAT HAD TO BE THE WORLD'S LONGEST SHOWER, Amy slipped into an old bathrobe that had raspberry stains on it and began to towel dry her hair as she went in search of her son. She was sure she would win the title of World's Worst Mother for leaving her son in the hands of someone she had tried to fire, but maybe Max was a better judge of people than she was, for, inexplicably, Max certainly did like this man. And considering that Max didn't like any men and only a few women, Amy was indeed intrigued.

The sight that greeted her had to be seen to be believed. Jason, wearing what had to be a handmade shirt and very formal wool trousers, had Max stretched out on the kitchen countertop and was trying his best to change his diaper. And all the while he was fiddling with the thing, Max was staring at him in intense concentration, not wriggling as he did when Amy changed him.

Putting her hand up to stifle a giggle, Amy watched until she was in danger of being discovered; then she silently ran back into the bedroom to take her time dressing.

After a luxurious thirty minutes of putting on her clothes, combing her wet hair, and even applying a little eye makeup, she went into the living room, where Jason sat on the couch, looking half asleep, while Max played quietly on the floor. Max wasn't yelling for breakfast, wasn't demanding attention. Instead, he looked like an ad for Perfect Baby.

Maybe she wouldn't fire Jason after all.

"Hungry?" she asked, startling him. "I don't have much, but you're welcome to it. I haven't been to the grocery store in a few days. It's difficult since I have no car. My mother-in-law usually takes me on Fridays, but last Friday she was busy, so . . ." She trailed off, since she knew she was talking too much.

"I'm sure that anything you have will be fine with me," he said, making her feel silly.

"Cheerios it is then," she said as she picked up Max, took him to the kitchen, then strapped him into his plastic booster seat, which she placed in the middle of the little kitchen table. She did the best she could to make the table pretty, but it wasn't easy, not with a red, blue, and yellow baby chair in the middle and Max's feet kicking at everything she set out.

"It's ready," she called, and he sauntered into the kitchen, all six feet of him. He's gay, she reminded herself. Gay. Like Rock Hudson was, remember?

As she prepared Max's warm porridge and mashed banana, she did her best to keep quiet. It was tempting to chatter away, as she was hungry for the sound of an adult voice, even if it was her own.

"David said you were looking for a job," the man said. "What are you trained for?"

"Nothing," she said cheerfully. "I have no talents, no ambition, no training. If Billy hadn't shown me what's what, I wouldn't have figured out how to get pregnant." Again she saw that tiny bit of a smile, and it made her continue. Billy always said that what he liked best about her was her ability to make him laugh.

"You think I'm kidding," she said as she held the cup of porridge up to Max's mouth. He was much too impatient to give her time to spoon-feed him, so he usually ended up drinking his morning meal. Of course a third of it dribbled down his chin and onto his clothes, but he got most of it inside him.

"Really, I'm no good at anything. I can't type, can't take shorthand. I have no idea how to even turn on a computer. I tried to be a waitress, but I got the orders so muddled I was fired after one week. I tried to sell real estate, but I told the clients that the houses weren't worth the asking price, so I was asked to leave. I worked in a department store, but the perfume caused me to break out in a rash, and I told the customers where to buy the same clothes cheaper, and the shoes, well, the shoes were the worst."

"What happened in the shoe department?" he asked as he ate a second bowl of cereal.

"I spent my whole salary on the things. That was the only job I ever quit. It cost me more than I made."

This time he nearly gave a real smile. "But Billy took you away from all of that," he said, his eyes twinkling.

Amy's face lost its happy look, and she turned away to grab a cloth to wipe the porridge from Max's face.

"Did I say something?"

"I know what everyone thinks of Billy, but he was good to me and I loved him. How could I not? He gave me Max." At that she gave an adoring look to her messy son, and in response he squealed and kicked so hard that he nearly knocked over the booster seat.

Jason stuck out a hand and steadied the thing. Frowning, he said, "Isn't he supposed to be in a high chair? Something with legs on the floor?"

"Yes!" Amy snapped. "He's supposed to be in a high chair, and he's supposed to sleep in a bed with sides that lower, and he's supposed to have a changing table and all the latest clothes. But as you know, Billy had priorities for his money and . . . and . . . Oh, damnation!" she said as she turned away to hide her sniffling.

"I always liked Billy," Jason said slowly. "He was the life of every party. And he made everyone around him happy."

Amy turned around, her eyes bright with tears. "Yes, he did, didn't he? I led a pretty sheltered childhood, and I didn't know that the cause of Billy's forgetfulness and his—" Abruptly, she halted. "Listen to me. My mother-in-law says that I'm so lonely that I'd ask the devil to dinner." Again she stopped. "I'm not complaining, mind you; Max is all I want in life; it's just that—"

"Sometimes you want an adult to talk to," he said softly, watching her.

"You're a good listener, Mr. Wilding. Is that a characteristic of being gay?"

For a second he blinked at her. "Not that I know of. So, tell me, if you need to get a job to support yourself and you have no skills, what are you going to do? How are you going to support yourself and your son?"

Amy sat down at the table. "I haven't a clue. You have any suggestions?"

"Go back to school."

"And who takes care of Max all day? How do I pay someone to take care of him? Besides, I'm much too thick to go to school."

Again he smiled. "Somehow I doubt that. Can't your mother-in-law take care of him?"

"She has a bridge club, swimming club, at least three gossip clubs, and it takes time to keep that hair of hers." At that, Amy made motions of a bouffant hairdo.

"Yes, I do seem to remember that Mildred had a real fetish about her hair."

"Religious wars have been fought with less fervor. But, anyway, you're right, and I have to get a job. I was going for an interview this afternoon."

"Doing what?" he asked, and the intensity of his eyes made her look down at the banana she was mashing with a fork.

"Cleaning houses. Now, don't look at me like that. It's good, honorable work."

"But does it pay enough for you to hire someone to look after the baby?"

"I'm not sure. I'm not very good with numbers, and I—"

"I am very good with numbers," he said seriously. "I want to see everything. I want your checkbook, your receipts, your list of expenses, whatever. I need to see your income and your outgoing money. Give it all to me and I'll sort it out."

"I'm not sure I should do that," she said slowly. "Those things are private."

"You want to call David and ask him about me? I think he'll tell you to show me any papers you have."

For a moment she studied him. It had been so long since she'd been around an adult, and it seemed like years since she'd been around a man. Billy never cared about finances. If there was money, he spent it; if not, he found a way to persuade someone to lend it to him. "There isn't much," she said slowly. "I have a checkbook, but I don't write many checks, and . . ."

"Just let me see what you have. You take care of Max, and I'll deal with the numbers."

"Do you always order people around?" she asked softly. "Do you always walk into a person's life and take it over as if they had no sense and you knew how to do everything in the world?"

He looked startled. "I guess I do. I hadn't thought about it before."

"I bet you don't have too many friends."

Again he looked startled, and for a moment he studied her as though he'd never seen her before. "Are you always so personal with people?"

"Oh, yes. It saves time in the long run. It's better to get to know people as they really are than it is to believe something that isn't true."

He lifted one thick black eyebrow. "And I guess you knew all about Billy Thompkins before you married him."

"You can laugh at me all you want, and believe me or not, but, yes, I did know. When I first met him I didn't know about the drugs and the alcohol, but I knew that he needed me. I was like water to a thirsty man, and he made me feel . . . Well, he made me feel important. Does that make sense?"

"In a way it does. Now, where are your financial records?"

It was Amy's turn to be startled at the abrupt way Jason dismissed her. What is he hiding? she wondered.

Whatever secrets he had, he didn't want anyone to know what they were.

After she gave Jason her box of receipts and her old checkbooks, she spent an hour cleaning the kitchen and pulling Max out of one thing after another. If there was a sharp edge, Max was determined to smash part of his body against it.

"Could you come in here?" Jason said from the doorway, making Amy feel like a child being called into the principal's office. In the living room, he motioned for her to sit down on the couch, Max squirming on her lap.

"Frankly, Mrs. Thompkins, I find your financial situation appalling. You have an income well below the national poverty level, and as far as I can tell you have no way to replenish your resources. I have decided to make you a, shall we say, permanent loan so you can raise this child and you can—"

"A what?"

"A permanent loan. By that I mean you'll never have to pay it back. We will start with, say, ten thousand dollars, and—"

He broke off as Amy got up, walked to the front door, opened it, and said, "Good bye, Mr. Wilding."

Jason just stood there gaping at her. He wasn't used to people turning down money from him. In fact, he received a hundred letters a day from people begging him to give them money.

"I don't want your charity," Amy said, her lips tight.

"But David gives you money; you told me he did."

"He has given my son free medical treatment, yes; but in return, I have scrubbed his house, his office, and the inside of his car. I don't take charity, not from any-one."

For a moment Jason looked bewildered, as though her words were something he'd never heard before. "I apologize," he said slowly. "I thought—"

"You thought that if I was poor, then of course I was looking for a handout. I know I live in a house that needs work." She ignored the expression on his face saying that that was an understatement. "But wherever I live and how I live is none of your concern. I truly believe that God will provide what we need."

For a moment Jason just stood there blinking at her. "Mrs. Thompkins, don't you know that nowadays peo-ple believe that you should *take* all that you can get and the rest of the world be damned?"

"And what kind of mother would I be if I taught val-ues like that to my son?"

At that Jason stepped forward and took Max from Amy as the baby was trying his best to pull her arms from her shoulders. As before, the baby went to Jason easily and quickly settled against his chest.

"I do apologize, and you have to forgive me for not realizing that you are unique in all the world."

Amy smiled. "I hardly think so. Maybe you've just

met very few people. Now, if you really want to help, you can take care of Max this afternoon while I go for the job interview."

"To clean houses," he said with a grimace.

"You find something else I'm qualified for and I'll do it."

"No," he said slowly, still looking at her as though she came from another planet. "I don't know what jobs are available in Abernathy."

"Not many, I can assure you. Now, I need to tell you all about Max, then I have to get ready to go."

"I thought you said the interview was this afternoon. You have hours yet."

"I don't have transportation, so I have to walk, and it's five miles. No! Don't look at me like that. You have, 'I'll pay for a taxi,' written all over your face. I want to make a good impression at this interview because they've said I can take Max with me if I leave him in a playpen. If I get this job, all our problems will be solved."

He didn't return her smile. "Who would you be working for?"

"Bob Farley. Do you know him?"

"I've met him," Jason said, lying. He knew Bob Farley very well, and he knew that Amy would be hired because she was young and pretty and because Farley was the biggest lecher in three counties. "I'll take care of the baby," Jason said softly. "You get dressed."

"All right, but let me tell you about his food." She then launched into a long monologue about what Max would and would not eat, and how he was to have no salt or sugar. Everything was to be steamed, not baked, and certainly not fried. Also, there was half a chicken in the refrigerator and some salad greens that could be Jason's lunch.

She went on to tell him that Max didn't really like solid food, that he would much rather nurse, so, "Don't be upset if he doesn't eat much."

Jason only vaguely listened, just enough to reassure her that everything would be fine. Thirty minutes later she was out the door and he was on the phone to his brother.

"I don't care how many patients you have waiting," Jason said to his brother. "I want to know what's going on."

"Amy's great, isn't she?"

"She is . . . different. Wait a minute." He'd put Max on the floor, and the baby had half crawled, half dragged himself to the nearest wall socket and was now pulling on the cord to a lamp. After Jason had moved the baby away from the dangerous socket and put him in the middle of the floor, he went back to the phone.

"This woman," Jason began, "lives on a tiny life insurance policy left by that husband of hers, and she has no way to make a living. Do you know where she's going for a job interview today? Bob Farley."

"Ahhhhh," David said.

"Call that old lecher and tell him that if he hires her, you'll inject him with anthrax," Jason ordered.

"I can't very well do that. Hippocratic oath and all that. If I didn't know you better, I'd say you sound a little like a jealous husband. Jason? Are you there?"

"Sorry. Max was caught under the coffee table. Wait! Now he's eating paper. Hold on a minute."

When Jason got back, David spoke in frustration. "Look, big brother, I didn't mean for you to get involved with her, just take care of the kid so I could have time with Amy. That's all you're to do. Once I convince Amy we're made for each other, I'll support her and she won't have to work. Why don't you tell her wonderful things about me?"

"If she thinks you're going to take care of her for the rest of her life, she might not marry you. She has more pride than anything else. And can you tell me why a baby can't have salt or sugar or any form of seasoning on his food?"

"The theory is that he'll grow up to crave sweets if he has them as a baby, so if you eliminate those things, he'll be healthier as an adult."

"No wonder the kid only wants to nurse and won't eat much solid food," Jason muttered, then dropped the phone to move Max away from the door, where he was swinging it and trying to hit himself in the face.

When he returned, Jason said, "Do you think she'd allow me to give her a Christmas gift?"

"What did you have in mind? Buy a business and give it to her to run?"

Since this is exactly what Jason had in mind, he didn't answer. Besides, Max was now chewing on Jason's shoe, so Jason picked the baby up and held him, and Max grabbed Jason's bottom lip, nearly pulling the skin off.

"Look, Jason, I have to go," David said. "Why don't you use your brain instead of your money and figure out another solution to this problem? Amy's not going to take your charity, no matter how you disguise it."

"I wouldn't be too sure of that," Jason said as he looked across the room to a potted plant set on a folded newspaper. "You call Farley. I'd do it, but I don't want him to know I'm here, and you say whatever you have to, but he's not to hire her. Got it?"

"Sure. How's the monster?"

Wincing, Jason removed the baby's fingers from his mouth. "Fine."

"Fine? The kid is a brat. What's that sound?"

Max had grabbed both of Jason's cheeks painfully and pulled him closer as he planted a very wet raspberry on Jason's cheek. "I'm not sure, but I think the kid just kissed me," Jason said to his brother, then hung up before David could reply.

For a moment, Jason sat down on the couch, while Max stood on his lap. Strong kid, he thought, and not bad looking. Too bad he was wearing what looked to be hand-me-downs from someone's hand-me-downs. He could believe that every kid in Abernathy had worn these overalls and faded shirt. Shouldn't a smart little fellow like Max have something better than this? So how could he arrange it?

At that moment, the newspaper caught his eye, and in the next moment he was fighting Max's hands to be able to dial his cell phone.

"Parker," he said when his secretary answered the phone. There was no greeting. She had been his private secretary-assistant for twelve years, so he didn't need to identify himself.

Within a few minutes he had told her his idea. She didn't make any complaint that it was Christmastime and he was telling her that she had to leave her home and family—if she had one, for Jason had no idea what her personal life was like—she just said, "Is there a printer's in Abernathy?"

"No. I wouldn't want the work done here anyway. Do it in Louisville."

"Any color preference?"

Jason looked down at Max, who was chewing on a wooden block that had probably been his father's. "Blue. For a manly little boy. None of those pink-and-white bunny rabbits. And add all the bells and whistles."

"I see. The whole lot."

"Everything. Also, buy me a car, something ordinary like a . . ."

"Toyota?" Parker asked.

"No, American." For all he knew Amy was against foreign cars. "A Jeep. And I want the car to be very dirty so I'll need to hire someone to clean it. And buy me some clothes."

Since all Jason's clothes were made for him, it wasn't unusual that Parker should ask if he wanted something sent.

"No. I want normal clothes. Denim. Blue jeans."

"With or without fringe?"

For a moment Jason stared at the phone. In twelve years he had never heard Parker make a joke. Was this the first one? On the other hand, did she even have a sense of humor? "No fringe. Just normal. Country clothes but not too expensive. No Holland and Holland; no Savile Row."

"I see," was Parker's toneless reply. If she had any curiosity about any of this, she didn't say so.

"Now call Charles and tell him to get down here and make this kid something good to eat."

There was a pause on the phone, which was unusual for Parker, as she usually agreed to anything he said instantly. "I was wondering where Charles would be staying, because he'll want proper equipment." Considering that Jason's private chef was a snob as well as a genius, this was an understatement.

Max was trying to pull himself to a standing position by dragging on the faded cloth on an old end table. If he pulled it off, three flower pots were going to crash onto his head. "Just do it!" Jason snapped into the phone, then shut it off and went to retrieve Max. Was this the fifth or sixth time the baby had tried to kill himself in the space of an hour?

"Okay, kid," Jason said as he untangled little hands from the cloth and picked the baby up. "Let's go see what we can do about lunch. A lunch with no sugar, no salt, no butter, no flavor at all."

At that Max again planted another wet raspberry against Jason's whiskery cheek, and Jason found the feeling not unpleasant.

CHAPTER SIX

"GET THE JOB?" JASON ASKED AS SOON AS AMY ENTERED the house.

"No," she said despondently, then reached eagerly for Max. "And I'm bursting with milk."

To Jason's embarrassment, she plopped down wearily on the worn-out old sofa, unfastened her dress, unsnapped her bra, and proceeded to feed Max, who eagerly began sucking.

"How about dinner out tonight?" he asked. "My treat."

"Ow!" Amy said, then stuck her finger in Max's mouth and made him release her breast for a moment before he latched on again. "Teeth," she said. "You know, before he was born, I was in love with the whole romance of breast-feeding. I thought it would be something sweet and lovely, and it is, but it's also . . . ."

"Painful?" he asked; then when she smiled in reply, he smiled back.

"I think I would have known that you were gay even if David hadn't told me. You're very perceptive, and for all that you look hard and unfeeling, you're really a bit of a softie, aren't you?"

"I've never been called that before," Jason said as he glanced at a faded and cracked mirror hanging to his right. Did he actually look hard and unfeeling?

"So what did Max get up to while I was gone?"

At that Jason smiled and soon found himself expending a great deal of energy into making a funny story of his afternoon with Max. "I think for Christmas I'll give him a set of knives, something he can easily hurt himself with. As it is now he has to work so hard to hit himself in the face and to try to crack his skull. I think I'll make life easier for him."

Amy laughed and said, "Knives with strings attached. Don't forget the strings, because how else can he choke?"

"Ah, yes. The strings. And I think I'll take him to visit a paper factory. I'll set him down in the middle of the place and let him eat his way out."

Amy switched Max to the other breast, and when she did so, Jason motioned for her to lift her arm so he could slide a pillow under it so she wasn't supporting the weight of Max's head. "And don't forget drawers that he can roll out then close on his fingers."

They were really laughing now, and Jason suddenly realized that for the first time in years a woman was genuinely laughing at his jokes.

"How about a pizza?" Jason said abruptly. "A huge one with everything on it. And giant Cokes and garlic bread?"

"I'm not sure I should because of my milk," Amy said hesitantly. "I'm not sure babies should have garlic-flavored milk."

"Doesn't seem to bother the Italians," Jason answered.

"That's true," Amy said, then smiled at him. "Pizza it is. But only if I can pay for my share."

Before he thought, Jason said, "You're too poor to pay for anything," then was shocked at what he'd said.

"Too true," Amy said good-naturedly. "Maybe over dinner we can figure out what to do with my future. Do you have any ideas?"

"None whatever," he said, smiling. "You could always marry some nice young doctor and never work again."

"Doctor? Oh, you mean David. He's not interested in me."

"He's mad about you," Jason answered.

"You are funny. David is in love with all the women in this town; that's why he's so popular. Besides, I'm not a gold digger and I don't want to live off any man. I want to do something, but I'm not sure what I can do.

If only I had a talent, like singing or playing the piano."

"It looks to me like you have a talent for being a mother."

Amy cocked her head to one side. "You're very sweet, you know that? Can you dial for pizzas on that phone of yours?"

"Sure," he said, smiling.

Later, as Max slept on the sofa, they lit candles and talked. He asked her about her life with Billy, and after an initial protest, she started talking, and he soon realized that she was hungry to talk.

And as she talked, he began to see the town drunk in a different light. Billy Thompkins had been a joke to the people of Abernathy since he was fourteen years old and began to drink. He wrecked cars as fast as he could get into them. His parents mortgaged their house to pay Billy's bail to get him out of jail time after time. But Amy saw something inside the man that no one else had.

Jason had ordered a giant pizza, and while Amy talked, she didn't notice that she ate three quarters of the thing. Long ago Jason had forgotten what it was like to be in a position that a pizza was a rare treat.

As soon as the last bit of cheese was gone, Amy gave a great yawn, and even though it was only nine P.M., Jason told her to go to bed. Standing, she bent to pick up Max, but Jason brushed her hands away, then scooped the baby up without waking him.

"You're a natural daddy," Amy said sleepily as she led the way into her bedroom.

Smiling at Amy's assessment, Jason put Max into the beat-up old playpen that was his bed, then quietly left the room. Oddly enough, he too felt sleepy. Usually he didn't go to bed until one or two in the morning, but something about pulling a baby away from one danger after another had exhausted him.

He went to his bedroom, pulled off his trousers, and fell into bed in his shirt and underwear and was aware of nothing until he heard a high-pitched scream from Max. Leaping out of bed, he ran into the kitchen, where he saw Max in his booster seat and Amy feeding him. They were both fully dressed yet it was still dark outside.

"What time is it?" Jason asked, rubbing his eyes.

"About six-thirty. Max slept late this morning."

"What was that scream?"

"Practice, I guess. He likes to scream. Shouldn't you get some clothes on?"

Jason glanced down at his bare legs. "Yeah, sure." Then he looked up at Amy's red face. She bared her breasts before him yet was embarrassed by his wearing more than he'd wear if he went swimming? With a smile at her turned head, he felt a little rush of pleasure that she was attracted to him.

David, he thought. David. David is in love with Amy.

"This was stuck in the front door this morning, and there's a car outside," she said, nodding toward a rolled-up newspaper on the kitchen table.

Ignoring her plea for him to get dressed, he rolled the rubber band off the newspaper and took out a note wrapped around the keys inside. It was a typed message saying that his clothes were in the back of the car and that the other matters had been taken care of. He would be contacted. "Sounds like a spy message," Jason said under his breath, then looked up to see if Amy had heard him.

But she hadn't heard anything, for her face was so full of excitement that at first he thought something was wrong with Max. But the baby was happily smearing oatmeal in his ear, so Jason looked back at Amy.

Looking like a mime, she was pointing speechlessly at the newspaper he had left spread on the table. There was a double-page ad about a huge sale in a baby store in a town about ten miles from Abernathy. The owner had put together entire nurseries, with furniture and bedding, and was selling the lot for two hundred and fifty dollars each. Amy was pointing at a photo of a bed, a rocking chair, a changing table, and a mobile that looked as though it had cowboys and horses on it. She was making a strangling sound that was a sort of, "Uh, uh, uh."

Maybe a devil got into him, but he couldn't help teasing her. "Is there any cereal in the house or has Max eaten everything?" He picked up the paper and opened it. "Looks like gold prices are down. Maybe I should buy some." He was holding the paper so the huge ad was right in front of Amy's face.

Amy finally recovered her voice. Ignoring him, she

said, "Can I afford it? Can I? What do you think? Maybe I should call David and borrow the money from him. Oh, no, we have to be there when the store opens at nine. How can I get there? Maybe David—"

At that Jason put down the paper and held the car keys in front of her nose, jingling them.

"We'll go see David," she said hurriedly. "I'll pay you back for the gas later. Look here at the bottom. I wonder if clothes are included in the outfit? 'Everything for the baby.' Oh, heavens, but Max has never had any clothes that haven't been worn by someone else. May I borrow your phone to call David?"

"I'll lend you the money," he said, wishing he'd included clothes in his orders to his secretary.

"No. I can pay David back in work, but you don't need anything."

Jason frowned at that, and he wasn't sure why. Wouldn't it be better if she did borrow from David? After all the whole idea was to get David and Amy together. And when it came to that, why hadn't David come over to visit last night?

"Go look at my car," Jason said. "Then come back in here and tell me how much you'll charge to clean it."

With a "Watch Max" tossed over her shoulder, she scurried out the front door. Ten minutes later she returned. "One hundred dollars," she said grimly. "How can you be such a pig?"

All Jason could do was give her a crooked grin. Had Parker overdone it on the car?

"And another hundred and fifty to do something with those clothes in the back. Really, Mr. Wilding, I had no idea you were such a slob."

"I, uh," he began, feeling like a little boy being bawled out by his mother.

"Now go put some clothes on, then come and eat your breakfast. I mean to be at that store when the doors open. He says he has only eight sets to give away. You know, I bet this has to do with a divorce. That's why he'd give this furniture away rather than let his wife have the money. Some people have no conscience. I wonder if there are children involved. Why are you standing there looking at me? Go and get dressed. Time is wasting."

Blinking in disbelief at the astonishing story Amy had just concocted, Jason went to his bedroom to shower and put back on his dirty, wrinkled clothes. How had Parker known to fill the car with dirty clothes that needed Amy's attention?

When he went into the kitchen to get his measly bowl of cereal, Amy was looking like the cat that stole the cream. She was up to something, but he had no idea what.

"I borrowed your phone," she said sweetly. "I hope that was all right."

"Sure," he said, then looked down at his bowl. "Couldn't wait to call David?" The words were out of his mouth before he caught them.

"Oh, no. Just a few girlfriends. But I'm afraid a couple of the calls were long distance. I'll pay you back . . . somehow."

"I have an apartment," he said, and they both laughed when Amy groaned at the thought of cleaning the place.

Amy made them leave the house at seven-thirty, and when Jason opened the car door, he was appalled. What in the world had been done to the vehicle? The inside was plastered in mud, which had seeped down into every crevice. He doubted if the windows would work because of the mud that had oozed down between the glass and the door. In order to clean the car, the door would have to be taken apart. In the back was a pile of clothes that had been given the same mud bath.

Having seen the car already, Amy was prepared and she spread an old quilt over the passenger seat, then climbed in, Max on her lap. "You don't have to tell me," she said softly, once the door was closed, "but your lover retaliated by driving your car and your clothes into a lake, didn't he?"

"Something like that," Jason muttered, thinking he was going to have a word with his secretary. When he'd said dirty, he meant, maybe, soda cans and potato chip bags.

"It's odd that the engine isn't clogged with mud, though," she said as the car started easily. "Oh, no!"

As Jason swung the car into the street, he looked at her in question.

"He filled the car full of mud, didn't he?"

"Could we not talk about my personal life?" Jason snapped. He was sick of this talk of his male lover.

For a moment Amy didn't say anything, and he regretted his outburst. "I hope they have a car seat," he said as he glanced over at her, and she smiled back.

"Do you have any cash? I don't—"

"Lots," he replied, glad the moment's discomfort was gone. "So what other jobs have you tried to get besides cleaning?" Jason asked as Amy held Max firmly on her lap. If they were spotted by the police, they'd be arrested because Max was unrestrained. And Jason refused to think what would happen to Max if they had a wreck. On impulse he reached out and gave Max's little hand a squeeze and was rewarded with a toothy grin.

Amy didn't seem to notice, as she was telling Jason about all the jobs she had applied for and even been hired to do, yet had lost for one reason or another. "Twice I've had to quit because the boss . . . Well . . ."

"Chased you around the desk?"

"Exactly. And it's just so difficult to find a job around here. I've thought I might be a good aromatherapist. What do you think?"

Jason was saved from answering that question by the sight of the store just ahead. But he was shocked at what he saw. Under the sign, Baby Heaven, there were about fifteen women with baby carriages waiting for the store to open.

"Oh, dear," Amy said. "I only called seven friends. They must have called their friends, and, oh, no, there are more cars arriving and they have to be for Baby Heaven because the other stores don't open until ten."

"You called all these people?" Jason asked.

"I was afraid they wouldn't see the ad and afraid they might miss the sale. You know, it's odd that there aren't more people here than there are. What about the other people who saw the morning paper? Maybe they know that this is just a sales gimmick and it isn't real. Maybe the owner has done this before and there isn't any merchandise. Maybe—"

Before she could launch into one of her fanciful stories, Jason got out and opened the car door for her. "Come on, let's go around the back and see if we can get in a few minutes early."

"Do you think that's fair?"

With his back to Amy, Jason rolled his eyes. "Probably not, but then this is for Max, isn't it?" he said as he took the baby from her. "Besides, it's too cold to wait out here and the store doesn't open for thirty minutes yet."

Amy gave him a dazzling smile. "You do know how to fix things, don't you?"

As Jason turned away, Max snuggled comfortably in

his arms, he couldn't help smiling, for Amy had a way of making him feel at least ten feet tall. When he pounded on the back door and it opened, he was startled to see one of his top executives from his New York office standing there wearing a gray coverall, a broom in his hand.

"You wanta see the stuff early?" the man asked, sounding as though he was not a graduate of Harvard Business School.

Annoyed, Jason could only nod. He didn't like it when his employees did things he hadn't first sanctioned. Even when Amy briefly took his arm and squeezed it, Jason was still not appeased.

Once they left the back storage area and walked into the store, Jason was even less pleased, for there were two of his vice presidents, both men wearing coveralls, both moving baby furniture around.

"You are our first customer so you can have the pick of the lot," came a feminine voice and they turned to see a striking woman standing behind them. She was, of course, Jason's secretary, only she wasn't dressed in her usual Chanel suit but in something he was sure she had bought at Kmart, and her long red hair was pulled into a bun on top of her head. And there were three yellow pencils stuck into the lump of hair. Even so, she couldn't hide the fact that she was five feet ten inches tall and as stunning as any runway model.

Parker didn't blink at Jason's or Amy's speechlessness. "What would you like?" she asked. "Blue? Pink?

Green? Yellow? Or would you like to see our one and only designer set?"

"Oooohhhh." Amy emitted a sound that came straight from her heart and out her lips, then started following Parker as though she were in a trance.

Parker kept up a running stream of chatter as she walked. "It's all closeout goods. Nothing is used, but it's all discontinued merchandise. I hope you don't mind that these are really last year's goods."

"No," Amy said in a voice unnaturally high pitched. "No, we don't mind. Do we, Mr. Wilding?"

She didn't wait for Jason's answer because before her was a sample room and even Jason had to admit that his secretary had outdone herself. He could smell wallpaper paste, so she must have worked through the night to get this done, and he must say that they'd created a fabulous room. And with his eye for merchandise, he knew that what he was seeing was the top of the top line. Parker must have bought everything in New York and brought it to Abernathy in his jet.

It was a room for a little boy, with blue-and-white striped wallpaper with a border of boats sailing a rough sea. The bed looked like a new version of a sleigh bed, but with safety bars and sides that lowered; a whole set of *Winnie-the-Pooh* characters were tucked into a corner. The linens of the bed were hand embroidered with tiny animals and plants, something that Jason knew Max would love to look at. To test his theory, he put Max in the bed, where he immediately pulled himself up, then began to grab at the mobile until he got a horse's head in his mouth.

The rest of the room was filled with furniture of equal quality. There was a rocking chair, a changing table, a car seat, a high chair, a toy box that had to have been decorated by Native Americans, and in the corner was a stack of white boxes.

"More linens and a few necessities," Parker said as she followed Jason's eyes. "There are a few pieces of clothing, but I wasn't sure of the size . . ." She trailed off.

"This costs more than I have," Amy said, and there were tears in her voice.

"Two hundred and fifty dollars for the lot," Parker said quickly.

Amy squinted her eyes at the woman. "Are these things stolen? Is this an outlet for stolen goods?"

"I would imagine that in a way, yes, they are stolen," Jason said quickly. "If these things are still in the possession of the store owner come tax time, he'll have to pay taxes on what they're worth. But if he sells them at a loss, he can write off the loss and be taxed on the amount he has received, which is a pittance. Am I right?" he asked Parker.

"Perfectly," she said, then turned back to Amy. "Perhaps you don't like this room. We have others."

"No, it's perfect," Amy said, then before she could say another word, Jason spoke up.

"We'll take it. Have it delivered today." As he said

this, he glanced at his two executives leaning on brooms and watching the scene with smug little smiles. By tomorrow everyone is all his offices would know about this. "And I think you should throw in someone to hang the wallpaper."

At that Amy gave a little whimper that said she was sure Jason was going to make the woman retract the deal.

"Certainly, sir," Parker said without a hint of a smile, then turned to Max in the bed. Now he was on his back and trying to kick the sides off, the sound reverberating through the store. "What a beautiful child," she said, then held out her arms as though she meant to pick Max up.

The baby let out a howl that shook the bed. Immediately, Amy was there, her arms out to Max. "Sorry," she muttered. "He doesn't take to strangers very well." And at that Max made a leap into Jason's arms.

Jason wasn't going to look at his two vice presidents because he knew that they would assume that Max was his. How else to explain that Jason wasn't a "stranger" to the child?

"I'll pay while you look around," Jason said as he followed Parker to a nearby counter. "The pencils are overkill," he snapped as soon as they were out of earshot of Amy.

"Yes sir," she said as she removed them from her hair.

"And what are those two doing here?"

"You had to buy the store in order to pull this off. I didn't feel that I had the authority to negotiate with that much money."

"How much could a tiny shop like this cost?"

"The man said to tell you that his name is Harry Greene and that you'd understand."

Jason's eyes rolled upward for a moment. In high school he had stolen Harry's girlfriend the day before the prom. "Did you manage to buy it for under seven figures?"

"Just barely. Sir, what do we do about the people waiting outside? The newspaper ad appeared in only your paper, but somehow . . ."

"They're friends of Amy's." For a moment he looked around Max, who was trying to grab the telephone off the desk, to see Amy running her hand lovingly over the baby furniture. "Give them the same deal. Give everything away at a loss. Make sure everything is given away for what they can afford. Split the rooms up so every woman out there gets something she needs."

When he looked back, Parker was staring at him with her mouth open. "And get those two back to New York right after they hang the wallpaper."

"Yes, sir," Parker answered softly, looking at him as though she'd never seen him before.

Jason removed Max's hands from around a curtain hanging from the top of a cradle. "And, Parker, add some toys to that lot when you deliver it. No," he contradicted himself. "Don't add anything. I'll buy the toys myself."

"Yes, sir," Parker said quietly.

"Did Charles get here?"

"He came with me. He's at your father's house, as all of us are." By her expression she looked to be on the verge of shock.

"Now close your mouth and go open the door to the other customers," he said as he peeled Max's hands off the curtain again and went back to Amy.

CHAPTER SEVEN

JASON WAS EXPERIENCING AN EMOTION HE HADN'T FELT IN a long time: jealousy.

"Isn't it wonderful?" Amy was saying in a breathless way he hadn't heard from a female since he'd left high school. "Isn't it the most beautiful room you ever saw? I never thought I could love the IRS, but since it was the cause of Max getting all these beautiful things, I could grow to love them. Don't you think so, Mr. Wilding? Don't you think the room is beautiful?"

"Yes," Jason said grumpily, while telling himself that it was better to give anonymously than to flaunt your gift. At least that's what he'd heard. But he rather wished Amy would look at him with her eyes sparkling like that.

He took a deep breath. "It is nice. The room looks great. Do you think the clothes will fit?"

"If they don't now, they will next week," she said, laughing. "See, I told you that God would provide."

Before Jason could give a cynical reply as he thought about how much these few pieces of furniture had actually cost him, since he'd had to buy the store, there was a loud, insistent knock on the door.

Instantly, Amy's face went white. "They made a mistake and they want everything back."

Jason's bad mood left him and he couldn't help putting a reassuring arm around Amy's thin shoulders. "I can assure you that everything here is yours. Maybe it's Santa Claus come early."

When she still hesitated, Jason picked up Max from the crib, where he was trying to eat the legs off a stuffed frog, then led the way to the front door, where he was greeted by the sight of a huge evergreen tree.

"Ho ho ho," came David's voice as he shoved his way inside the house. "Merry Christmas. Jase, ol' boy, you want to bring in the boxes from outside?"

"David!" came Amy's squeal of delight. "You shouldn't have."

Outside in the cold, Max sitting on his arm, Jason muttered, "Oh, David, you shouldn't have," in a falsetto voice. "I paid heaven only knows how much for a bunch of furniture and she thanks the IRS no less. But David shows up with a twenty-dollar tree and it's, 'Oh, David.' Women!"

Max laughed, raked his nails across Jason's cheek in

an attempt to pat him, then bit his other cheek in a kiss. "Why don't you do that to the divine Dr. David?" Jason said, smiling at the boy as he hoisted a big red cardboard box under his arm and took it into the house.

"You can't do this," Amy was still saying but looking at David adoringly.

"Dad and I don't want a tree. We're just a couple of old bachelors and we don't need the needles everywhere, so when a patient gave me this tree, I thought about the attic full of ornaments and thought Max would love the lights. Don't you think he will?"

"Oh, yes, I'm sure he will, but I'm not sure—"

David cut her off by going toward Jason and holding out his arms to Max. "Come here, Max, and give me a hug."

To Jason's great satisfaction, Max let out a howl that made the tree drop quite a few needles. "Doesn't seem to like you, does he?" Jason said smugly. "Come on, boy, let's go try on some of your new clothes."

"New clothes?" David asked, frowning. "What's this about?"

"Oh, David, you can't believe what has happened. This morning we went to a store where the man was selling everything cheaply so he wouldn't have to pay taxes on it and Mr. Wilding made them come and hang the wallpaper and arrange the furniture and . . . and . . . Oh, you'll just have to see it to believe it."

With a look at Jason, David followed Amy through

the old house with its peeling paint and water-stained wallpaper, to have her open a door to a dazzling nursery. It didn't take much of an eye to see the quality of everything inside. The linens, the furniture, the pretty little prints on the wall, the painted wardrobe that held a few pieces of fabulous baby clothes, were all the finest that could be bought.

"I see," David said. "And how much did you have to pay for all this?"

"Two hundred and fifty dollars, sales tax included," Amy said proudly.

David lifted a hand-embroidered sheet from the side of the crib. If he wasn't mistaken, he'd seen these in a catalog for about three hundred dollars each. "Great," David said. "By contrast my tree and old ornaments look like nothing."

"How silly," Amy said as she took his arm. "Your gift is from your heart, while this is merely from the IRS."

At that, David shot a triumphant smile at his older brother as he led Amy back into the living room.

"And I brought dinner," David said happily. "A grateful patient of mine gave me a free dinner for two at a restaurant in Carlton, but I persuaded the chef to make it a carryout for three. I hope it's still hot," he said as he looked up at his brother. "The food boxes are on the front seat of my car. Oh! and I hope you don't mind, but I signed you and Max up as guinea pigs to try a new baby food." At that he began to unload his pockets of baby food jars with hand-lettered labels, and Jason recognized his secretary's neat script.

"Rack of lamb with dried cherry and green peppercorn sauce," Amy read. "And salmon cakes with cilantro sauce. They sound a bit high fashion for a baby, and I'm not sure he should have peppercorns."

"I think the company is trying to reach the top-end market. It's just in the planning stages now, so if you'd rather not be one of their test babies, I could get Martha Jenkins to try them."

"No," Amy said, taking the jars David held out to her. "I'm sure Max will like them." Her tone said she wasn't sure at all. "Who is the manufacturer?"

"Charles and Company," David said as he winked at Jason, still standing by the door, still holding Max, still scowling. "Come on, old man, don't just stand there; let's get everything inside so we can eat, then decorate the tree."

Jason handed the baby to Amy, then followed his brother outside.

"What in the world is wrong with you?" David snapped as soon as they were away from the door.

"Nothing is wrong with me," Jason snapped back.

"You hate it here, don't you? You hate the noise and the falling-down old house, and Amy is boring compared to the women you're used to. Didn't you date some woman with a Ph.D. in anthropology? Didn't she save tigers or something?"

"It was fish. She saved whales, and she smelled like seaweed. There is nothing wrong with me. So Charles made the dinners and the baby food?"

"Is that what's bothering you? That I took credit for what you'd paid for? Look, if you want, we can tell her the truth right now. We can tell her you're a multimillionaire, or is it a billionaire by now, and that you can afford rooms full of baby furniture from what you carry in your pocket. Is that what you want to do?"

"No," Jason said slowly as David loaded his arms with boxes of Christmas ornaments. They were boxes he'd seen all through his childhood, and he knew everything that was inside them.

Suddenly David stopped and stared at his brother. "You're not falling for her are you? I mean, you and I aren't going to have to compete for a woman, are we?"

"Don't be ridiculous. Amy isn't my type at all. And she has no concept of the future. I don't know how she means to support that child on the small amount of cash she has coming in. She has no work or prospect of work. She can't do anything at all except clean things. But in spite of her situation, she has more pride than anyone I've ever met. If you told her who I was, she'd kick me out, and no doubt throw all the furniture into the street after me. She spent this afternoon scrubbing that car Parker gave me so she could pay me back the two fifty. If you knew . . ."

They were walking toward the house, and Jason was still talking.

"Knew what?" David asked softly.

"The women I date ask for five hundred just to tip the maid in the toilet. That fish woman. She was dating me only so I'd make a donation to her whales."

"So what's your problem then?" David asked. "Why are you so surly?"

"Because my little brother duped me into spending time in this one-horse town and going to baby stores and carrying old Christmas ornaments. Get the door, will you? No, the other way. You have to pull inward, then turn the knob. Is that your phone ringing or mine?"

"Mine," David said as soon as they were in the house. "Yeah," he said into the receiver. "Yes, yes, that's good. I'll be there as soon as I can get there." As he turned the phone off, he looked up at Amy, Jason, and the baby with regret. "I can't stay. Emergency."

"I'm so sorry," Amy said. "After you did all this work and now you can't stay."

"Yeah, it's a shame," Jason said as he held open the door for his younger brother. "But when work calls, you have to go."

Frowning, David made his way to the door. "Maybe we can put up the tree tomorrow. I'd really like to see the baby's expression when he first sees the lights."

"We'll make a video," Jason said quickly. "Now, I think you'd better go before somebody dies."

"Yeah, right," David said after one last look of regret tossed to Amy. "I'll see you—" He didn't finish his sentence because Jason shut the door in his face.

"You weren't very nice to him," Amy said, doing her best to frown at Jason, but he could see a hint of a smile about her lips.

"Horrible," Jason said agreeably. "But now there's more food for the two of us. And, besides, I'm much better at tree decorating than he is."

"Is that so? You have to go some to beat me. Why I've decorated trees that have made Santa weep."

"I decorated a tree so beautiful that Santa wouldn't leave my house and I had to push him out into the snow, and when he still wouldn't leave, I had to drive his sleigh and deliver all his gifts."

Amy laughed. "You win. Let's see what's in these boxes."

"Nope. We eat first. I want to try this new baby food on Max and see what he thinks. Does this fireplace work?"

"Better than the furnace," Amy replied.

"I repeat, Does this fireplace work?"

Amy giggled. "If you open the damper very wide and build the fire way back against the wall, it's okay. Otherwise it smokes a lot."

"Had experience with it, have you?"

"Let's just say that I had some pork chops in the freezer and after the first time I tried to make a fire in there, they were smoke-cured hams."

It was Jason's turn to laugh, and when he did, Max started to laugh too, banging his hands on his legs and nearly knocking his mother down.

"You think that's funny, do you?" Jason said, still laughing as he took the boy and tossed him into the air. Max was so delighted at this that he squealed until he got the hiccups, then Jason tickled him and he squealed some more.

When Jason stopped, hugging the sweaty baby close to him, Amy was looking at him in a way no woman had ever looked at him before. "You're a nice man, Mr. Wilding. A very nice man."

"Want to call me Jason?" he asked.

"No," she said as she turned away. "I'll heat dinner while you light the smoker."

For some reason her refusal to call him by his first name pleased him. He set Max on the floor, then started building the fire. It took a while because every three minutes he had to pull Max away from a life-threatening situation. But at last he had the fire going without too much smoke, he had Max interested in his Breitling watch (it would never be the same again), and Amy entered the room with an enormous tray full of food. There was also a bottle of wine and two glasses.

Jason held up one of the glasses, watching the colors in the lead crystal. Waterford. "David does know how to live, doesn't he?"

"I feel guilty eating this without him," Amy said. "After all, it was his skill as a doctor that earned the meal."

"We could always wrap it up, put it in the refrigerator, and he can have it tomorrow."

Amy looked down at the beautiful meal on the tray. There was a salad of baby lettuces and vegetables, roast lamb, potatoes . . .

She looked back up at Jason. "I don't have any plastic wrap."

"That settles it then. We'll just have to eat it ourselves."

"I guess so," Amy said seriously; then they laughed and dug in.

Max sat on Jason's lap, a huge bib around his neck, and ate everything that was offered to him. Whatever Amy had thought about his not liking solid food was disproved by the way he downed a whole jar of lamb with peppercorns; then he started in on Jason's mashed potatoes with garlic.

"But I thought babies liked bland food," Amy said in amazement.

"No one likes bland food," Jason said under his breath.

Thirty minutes later Amy had nursed Max until he fell asleep, an angelic smile on his face. "Do you think it's the food or the new room that's made him look like that?" Amy asked as she looked adoringly down at her son in his new crib.

"I think he's happy because he has a mother who loves him so much," Jason said, then smiled when Amy blushed.

"Mr. Wilding, if I didn't know better, I'd think you were flirting with me."

"I guess stranger things have happened," he said; then when she looked confused, he said, "Come on, woman, there's a tree to decorate."

In all his life, Jason knew that he'd never had as much fun decorating a Christmas tree as he had with this one. As children he and David had complained every minute they had to spend on the task. Without a woman in the home, there was no smell of cookies baking, no music playing, just their dad, who was his usual grumpy self. He put up a tree or his sister would hound him all the rest of the year, saying that she should raise the boys, not her lazy brother.

Now, as Jason strung lights that Amy had untangled, he found himself telling her about his childhood. He didn't bother explaining why he had lived with David when he was supposedly only a cousin, and she didn't ask. In return Amy told him about her childhood. She had been an only child of a single mother and when she'd asked who her father was, her mother told her it was none of her business.

Both of their stories were rather sad, and definitely lonely, but when they told them to each other, they made jokes, and Amy started a contest to see who had the grumpiest parent. Amy's mother was a fanatically clean woman and hated Christmas because of the mess. Jason's father just hated having his routine disrupted.

They began fantasizing about what a marriage between the two of them would be like, what with Jason's father playing poker and flipping cigar ash all over the room and Amy's mother with a vacuum cleaner permanently attached to her right arm.

They went on to speculate what kind of children these two would produce and decided that they themselves were actually perfect examples of what would happen if their two parents mated. Jason was so serious his face nearly cracked when he laughed, and Amy lived in a house that would make her mother's heart stop beating.

"It's beautiful," Amy said at last, standing back to look at the half-finished tree.

"I wish I had a camera with me," Jason said. "That tree deserves to be immortalized."

"I don't have a camera, but I can—" She broke off and grinned at him. "You finish with the tinsel while I make a surprise. No, don't turn around, look that way."

He heard her scurry off into the bedroom, then return and sit down in the ugly old sunflower chair. He was dying to see what she was doing, but he didn't look. Not until he'd strung the last of the tinsel did she tell him he could turn around.

When he turned he could see that she was holding out a piece of printer paper and there was a pencil and a book on her lap. He took the paper and looked at it. It was a delightful sketch of him struggling with the wires of a dozen strings of lights, the tree just behind him. The picture was whimsical, funny, and at the same time poignant, making him look as though he was putting a lot of love into the project.

Jason sat down on the sofa, the sketch in his hand. "But this is good."

Amy laughed. "You sound surprised."

"I am. I thought you said you had no talents." He was very serious.

"Not any marketable talents. No one wants to hire someone to draw funny pictures."

Jason didn't respond to her remark. "If you have more of these, get them and bring them to me."

"Yes, sir!" Amy said, standing and saluting him. She tried to sound lighthearted, but she rushed to obey his command, and in seconds, she handed him a fat, worn, brown envelope tied with a drawstring.

Jason was very aware that Amy was holding her breath while he looked at the drawings, and he didn't need to ask if she had shown them to anyone else, for he knew she hadn't. For all that she put on a brave act, life with a drunk like Billy Thompkins had to have been difficult.

"They're good," he said as he lifted the papers one by one. The drawings were mostly of Max, from birth to the present, and they were quite clever, showing all the things a baby could get into. There was one of Max with wonder on his face as he looked up at a balloon, his hands reaching for it eagerly.

"I like them," he said as he carefully put them back into the envelope. The businessman inside him wanted to talk to her about publication and royalties, but he reined himself in. Right now he thought that all he should do was give her praise.

"I like them very much and I thank you for showing them to me."

Amy gave him a smile that threatened to break her face in half. "You're the only one who's ever seen them. Except my mother and she told me to quit wasting my time."

"And what did she want you to do?"

"Become a lawyer."

At first Jason thought she was joking, but then he saw her eyes twinkling. "I can see you defending a criminal. 'Please, Your Honor, he promises that he won't do it again. He gives his word, hope to die. He'll never murder more than the twenty-two little old ladies that he has already. Pleeeeaaaaassssseeee.' "

It was such a good imitation of Amy's tone of voice that she picked up a pillow and tossed it at him, watching him do an elaborate duck as though he might get hurt by the flying object. "You are a horrible person," she said, laughing. "I would have made an excellent lawyer. I'm quite intelligent, you know."

"Yes, very, but you do tend to love the underdog."

"If I didn't, *you* wouldn't have had any place to spend Christmas," she shot back.

"That's true," he said, grinning. "And I thank you for it." As Jason said this, he looked down into her eyes and realized he wanted to kiss her. Like he wanted to continue living, he wanted to kiss her.

"I think I better go to bed," she said softly as she got up and went toward her bedroom. "Max is an early riser and there's a lot to do tomorrow." She was halfway into the room when she turned back to him. "I didn't mean to sound as though I was doing you a favor by allowing you to stay here. The truth is, you've made this Christmas wonderful for Max and me. Both of us enjoy your company very much."

All Jason could do was nod in thanks. He couldn't remember anyone ever telling him that he was enjoyed just for his company. "Good night," he said, then sat for a long time before the dying fire, thinking about where he was and what he was doing.

CHAPTER EIGHT

A SMELL WOKE JASON. IT WAS A SMELL THAT HE KNEW BUT couldn't exactly place. It was from a time long past and only vaguely remembered. Following his nose, he got out of bed, pulled on his wrinkled suit pants, and went toward the light. He found Amy in the kitchen, Max in his high chair, his face and hands covered with food, and wet clothes were everywhere. Shirts, pants, underwear, hung from the light fixture, the door jambs, the crack in the plaster over the stove. And in the middle of it all Amy stood over an ironing board using an iron that should have been in a museum.

"What time is it?" Jason asked sleepily.

"About five, I think," Amy answered. "Why?"

"How long have you been up?"

She turned the shirt she was ironing so the wrinkled

sleeve was exposed. "Most of the night. Little rascal, he does love to mix up his days and nights."

Yawning, rubbing his eyes, Jason sat down at the table beside Max's high chair and handed him a dried peach. Wordlessly, he motioned to the wet clothes hanging around the room. It had been a long time since Jason was a child and his father had spread their wet clothes about to dry, but it was a smell one never forgot. "What happened to the dryer?"

"It broke about a year ago and I haven't had the money to get it fixed. But the washer works great."

Standing, Jason put his hands in the small of his back, stretched, then walked behind Amy and unplugged the iron.

"I have to finish this. It needs to be—"

"Go to bed," Jason said quietly. "No, not a word of protest. Go to bed. Sleep."

"But Max . . . And the clothes, and . . ."

"Go," Jason ordered in a quiet voice, and for a moment he thought Amy was going to cry in gratitude. With a smile, he nodded toward the bedroom, and gratefully, she went into the room and shut the door.

"Now, old man," Jason said, "let's see if we remember how this is done." At that, Jason plugged the iron back in and picked it up.

At eight A.M., Jason's cell phone rang and he put it on his shoulder as he finished ironing a shirt.

"Did I wake you?" David asked his older brother.

"Of course," Jason said. "You know how lazy I am. No! Max, leave that alone! What do you want, little brother?"

"I want time alone with Amy. Remember? That's what this is all about. I want to take her out tonight and tomorrow. I even got tickets to the Bellringers' Ball."

Jason well knew that the Bellringers' Ball was the only social function worth attending in the entire western half of Kentucky—and it was nearly impossible to get tickets. "So who did you have to kill to get the tickets?"

"I didn't kill; I saved. I saved the life of the chairman of the committee to something or other. Anyway, he got me the tickets. Christmas Eve. I'm going to pop the question. Jason? Jason? Are you there?"

"Sorry," Jason said once he came back to the phone. "Max was pulling on a lamp cord and about to bite into it. What was it you were saying?"

"I said that tomorrow I'm going to ask Amy to marry me. Jason? Are you there? What's Max doing now?"

"He's not doing anything," Jason snapped. "He's a great kid and he doesn't do anything bad."

There was a pause from David. "I didn't mean to insinuate that he was doing something 'bad.' It's just that children Max's age do tend to get into things. It is a normal and natural process of growing up, and they will—"

"You don't need to take on that doctor tone with me," Jason grumbled.

"Boy! Are you in a bad mood this morning. Where's Amy anyway?"

"Not that it's any of your business, but she's in bed asleep and I'm taking care of Max. And doing the ironing," he added, knowing that David would nearly faint at that information.

"You're doing what?"

"The ironing. Parker dumped mud on the clothes she sent me, so Amy washed them, and now I'm ironing them. You see anything wrong with that?"

"Nothing," David said softly. "I had no idea you knew how to iron, that's all."

"So who do you think ironed your clothes when you were a kid?" Jason snapped. "Dad? Ha. He had to earn the money to buy the food, so I had to . . . never mind. What was it you wanted to tell me? Wait, I have to get Max."

"Jason, dear brother," David said minutes later, "I think I'd better talk to Amy in person. I want her to go out with me tonight and tomorrow night, and I think I should ask her myself."

"She's busy."

"Is something going on that I should know about?" David asked. "You and Amy aren't . . ."

"No, we aren't!" Jason said quickly. "The last thing I need in my life is a daffy, head-in-the-clouds female like her. The man who takes her on will have his hands full taking care of her. It's a wonder she can tie her shoes. She can't even feed herself, much less a child, and—"

"Okay, okay, I get the picture. So, what do you think?"

"Think about what?"

David gave a great sigh. "Do you think it would be all right if I took Amy out tonight and tomorrow? Can you keep the kid?"

"I can keep Max forever," Jason said with some anger. "Sure, you can take Amy out. I'm sure she'd love to go."

"I think I should ask her myself."

"I'm not going to wake her up just to talk on the phone. What time should she be ready tonight?"

"Seven."

"All right. Now give me Parker."

"She's, ah, she's not up."

Jason was so shocked at this that he left the iron on the back of a shirt until it began to scorch. "Damnation!" he said, lifting the iron. "Wake her," Jason ordered, then was surprised to have his secretary get on the line almost instantly.

After a moment to recover from his shock, Jason told Parker to get two more tickets to the Bellringers' Ball.

"You do know that that is next to impossible," she said, and again Jason paused in shock. What in the world was wrong with his secretary? The impossible never daunted her.

"Get them," he said, annoyed. In fact, what was wrong with his whole world? First, two of his executives get themselves involved in his private affairs without his permission, and now Parker was telling him that something he wanted was going to be difficult. If he'd wanted someone who couldn't do the impossible, he wouldn't be paying her the outrageous salary he did.

"I'll need my tux from my apartment in New York," he went on to say, "and Amy will need something appropriate to wear to the ball. What's that shop on Fifth?"

"Dior," came Parker's instant reply.

"Right. Dior."

"And who shall I get for your escort?" she asked.

"My—Oh, right, my date," he said, and realized that he hadn't given that a moment's thought. But then he wasn't giving any of it a thought or he'd be wondering why he was going to the ball when he was supposed to stay home with the baby. And if both he and Amy left, who would take care of Max?

"I believe there are any number of women who would be available at a moment's notice to go with you," Parker was saying in that efficient, no-nonsense way of hers.

For a moment Jason paused to think over the many available women he knew. And when he thought of them, he knew how nasty all of them would be to Amy—and how nosy. "Get yourself a dress, Parker. You'll go with me as my date."

It was her turn to be shocked, and it almost made Jason smile to hear the hesitation in her voice. "Yes, sir," she said at last.

"Oh, and get hair and makeup people over here for Amy. Think up some story so she doesn't know it's a gift from me."

"Yes, sir," Parker said softly. "Anything else?"

Jason looked down at Max happily chewing the tail of a yellow duck pull toy. From the look of the thing, his father had probably chewed on it thirty years ago, and Jason wondered if the paint was lead-free. "Everything all right there at my father's?"

"I beg your pardon?" Parker asked.

"I asked if you and Charles are comfortable at my father's house."

"Oh, yes," she said hesitantly. "I'm sorry, sir, you don't usually ask personal questions, but, yes, we are doing well. Now."

"What do you mean? Now?"

"Charles had to make a few adjustments, but he's all

right now. He should be at your house soon. And your father reminds you that you and Mrs. Thompkins and the baby are to come here for Christmas dinner. Would three P.M. be all right with you?"

Jason ignored most of what she said and got to the point. "What kind of adjustments?"

"The kitchen needed . . . augmentation."

"Parker!" he warned.

"Charles tore out the back side of your father's house and added what is actually a kitchen for a small restaurant. He had to pay the men triple time to work twenty-four hours a day to get the room done quickly. Then he bought enough equipment to furnish the room, and, well, your father is having rather lavish dinner parties each night and—"

"I don't want to hear any more. We'll be there at three on Christmas Day and don't forget the clothes."

"Certainly not, sir," Parker said as he hung up.

Ten minutes later Amy wandered into the kitchen, looking like the most grateful woman on earth—until she saw that the ironing had been done. "How will I repay you for the furniture now?" she wailed as she sat down on a rickety kitchen chair. Max was happily sitting in his new high chair, his face smeared with half a dozen various colored substances.

"I promise to get everything dirty today so you'll have more to do tomorrow," Jason said, smiling, obviously unworried about how he was to be repaid. "Now, would you mind watching Max while I take a shower? I've been in this shirt for days and I'd like to get out of it."

"Yes, of course," she murmured as she picked Max up. As soon as he'd seen his mother, he'd started to whine and wanted out of the chair.

For a moment Jason paused in the doorway. Nothing bad could happen in the next fifteen minutes, could it? he asked himself, then gave one last look at Amy and the baby and left the room.

CHAPTER NINE

"MR. WILDING," AMY SAID ENTHUSIASTICALLY THE MO-
ment he stepped back into the kitchen thirty minutes
later. "Come and meet Charles."

As soon as Jason saw his randy little chef, he knew
that he was in trouble. Charles was about five feet four,
handsome as any movie star, and utterly devastating to
women. He flirted outrageously, and Jason was sure
that more than one of his dinner guests had succumbed
to the man. But Jason never asked; he figured it was
better not to know the details of his chef's private life.
As it was, the man traveled wherever Jason went and
prepared the most delicious meals imaginable. In return
for the food, Jason overlooked certain personal foibles.

But now, seeing Charles sitting by Amy, her hand in
his, he wanted to tell his chef to get out and never
return.

"This is the man responsible for the wonderful food Max loves so much. It seems that David told a bit of a fib. It isn't really a company trying to open a line of baby food, but Charles is trying to go into business. And he lives right here in Abernathy. Isn't that amazing?"

"Yes, truly," Jason said as he took an electrical cord out of Max's mouth.

"And I've been encouraging him to open his own business. Don't you think he should?"

Charles looked up at his employer with sparkling eyes, obviously enjoying the whole masquerade.

"I hear he has a kitchen that can handle a catering company," Jason said as he glared at his chef. Only someone of Charles's caliber could get away with what the man did.

"Oh, yes," Charles said in that tone he used with women. In his kitchen he used a whole other tone, one of command that brooked no disobedience, but now he practically purred to Amy. "I have the most divine kitchen. Copper pots from France, a cook stove as big as my first apartment. You must come and see it."

"I'd love to," Amy said eagerly. "Maybe you'd give me a few cooking lessons."

"I will give you anything you want," Charles said seductively as he raised her hand to kiss the palm.

But at the exact moment that Charles's lips were to touch Amy's flesh, Jason accidently knocked over Max's high chair and the clatter made her jump away. Max was frightened by the noise, so he started to scream, and Amy grabbed him from the floor.

After a moment she had him settled, and she turned back to Jason. "So, what so you think about Charles's opening his own business? I told him you'd have good advice."

When Jason just stood there in silence, she looked nervously at Charles. "Yes, well, I think it's a good idea. Max has eaten more of your food in the last day than he has in his whole little life. If you want to do more testing, I can get some other women you can supply baby food to and they'll be your guinea pigs. And we'll all write letters of recommendation for you."

For a moment Jason smirked at this idea. Charles and baby food! The idea was laughable. Charles was such a snob that he complained about what people *wore* when they ate his food. "That woman crumbled crackers in my soup," he once said, then refused to ever again cook for her, saying that she wasn't worth his time. And later Jason found out he was right: the woman was a gold digger of extraordinary greed.

But now Jason could see that Charles was thinking about Amy's idea of going into business. Which would mean that he'd *lose* his chef!

"You don't know how difficult it is cooking for a baby," Amy was saying. "If you cook a butternut squash, you have enough for a dozen meals and who wants to eat butternut squash for a solid week?"

"I see. It is a problem. I had never tasted baby food from jars until this week. Awful, dreadful stuff. No wonder American children hate proper food and prefer living on hamburgers and hot dogs."

"Exactly. So that's why—"

She broke off because Jason suddenly stepped between them. "I think we need to get ready to go now, so you'd better leave," he said to Charles.

"But we were just getting started. I'd like to hear more about this baby food idea. Maybe I could—"

"Maybe you couldn't," Jason said as he pulled the chair back so Charles could stand. So help him, if he lost his chef to this whole fiasco of David's, he was going to—

"For you, my beautiful lady," Charles was saying, "I will deliver free dinners every night for the next two weeks. And perhaps lunch too."

"Oh, really, I haven't done anything," Amy said, but she was blushing prettily as Charles once again reached for her hand to kiss.

But Jason stepped between them and in the next moment Charles was out the door. "I could have stayed in the most expensive hotel in the world for less than what this trip is costing me," Jason muttered as he leaned against the door.

"You were awfully rude to him," Amy said, frowning. "Why?"

When Jason could think of nothing to explain his actions, he picked up Max and started toward the living room. "I think we should go shopping today," he threw over his shoulder. "Unless you have all your Christmas shopping done already."

"Oh, no, I haven't. I, uh, yes, I'll get ready in a moment," she said, then disappeared into her bedroom.

"Lesson number one, ol' man," Jason said as he lifted Max high over his head, "if you want to distract a woman, mention shopping. The worst you'll have to do is spend the day in a mall, but it's better than answering questions you don't want to answer."

CHAPTER TEN

"WAS CHARLES YOUR LOVER?" AMY ASKED AS SOON as they were in Jason's car. The vehicle was much cleaner now that she'd spent hours cleaning it, but the interior, including the upholstery, had been ruined.

"My what?" Jason asked as he swung the car into the street.

"Why do you always say that when I ask about your personal life? You can see all about my life, but I know nothing about you. What was Charles to you? You obviously know him well."

"Not as well as you think," Jason said, looking in the rearview mirror at Max as he chewed on his fingers and stared out the window. "Where did you get that coat Max is wearing?"

"Mildred," Amy said quickly, giving her mother-in-law's name. "What about Charles? Would you rather that I didn't take food from him?"

"Charles is a brilliant chef, so of course you should take his food. Can Max choke on that?"

Instantly, Amy turned around in her seat, entangling herself in the seat belt, only to see that Max wasn't chewing on anything. "I guess that means you don't want to talk about that side of your life," she said heavily as she turned back around.

Jason didn't answer but kept his eyes on the road—and his mind imagining ways to murder his little brother.

"Have you ever thought of going to a therapist?" Amy asked softly. "Being gay is nothing to be ashamed of, you know."

"Where do you think we should park?" Jason asked as he pulled into the lot of the mall. Since it was a mere two days before Christmas, there were few places. "Looks like we're going to have to hike," Jason said cheerfully, as he found a place that looked to be half a mile from the stores.

Amy was sitting still, not moving an inch, and when Jason opened the back door behind her to get Max, she still sat where she was.

"You going with us?" Jason asked, somehow pleased by her disgust with his refusal to talk about his personal life.

"Yeah, sure," she said as she climbed out of the car,

then stood back as Jason unfastened Max from the car seat and inserted him into the new stroller.

"Maybe I can change," Jason said when Max was strapped into the stroller. "Maybe I can find the right girl and she could change me." With that, he started pushing Max toward the stores.

"Right," Amy said as she hurried after them. "And tomorrow I'm going to go the other way."

"Could be," Jason said. "I guess stranger things have happened. Now, where do we begin?"

"I have no idea," Amy said, looking at the huge crowds moving from one store to another, their arms straining under the weight of the bags they carried. "Shopping isn't something I do a lot of." She was feeling as though he'd snubbed her, and she hated the way he laughed at her every time she asked him a personal question.

"I think Max needs a new coat, so where's the best shop?"

"I really have no idea," she said aloofly, turning away from him to look at the crowds. When he didn't speak, she turned back and he was looking at her with an expression of, *I don't believe a word you're saying.*

"There's a BabyGap—"

"Where would you *like* to buy Max's clothes? Money no object."

For a moment Amy hesitated; then she gave a sigh and pointed. "Down that aisle, take a left at the second intersection, four stores down on the right. But it's no use going there. The clothes cost much too much."

"Would you let me worry about the money?" he said.

For a moment she squinted at him. "Is this the way you ordered your lover around? Is this why he kicked you out?"

"My last lover threatened to commit suicide if I left, so do you want to lead or follow?"

"Why?"

"Because I don't think we can travel through these crowds side by side," he answered. He was having to speak almost into her ear to be heard over the noise.

"No, I meant why did he threaten to commit suicide?"

"Couldn't bear the thought of living without me," Jason answered, then thought, and my money. "Could we continue this later? Max is going to be hungry soon, you'll be dripping milk, and I'd like to watch a football game this afternoon."

With another sigh, Amy gave up, then turned and started making her way toward the baby store.

Jason watched her moving ahead of him and Max, and he felt better than he had in weeks, maybe in years. He wasn't sure what was making him feel so good, but something was.

It took them several minutes to make their way through the crowds to the little store at one end of an aisle off the main artery of the mall, and as soon as Jason saw the place, he admitted that Amy had taste. If she was going to fantasize about what to buy her son, then she was going to start at the top.

The walls were full of double rows of the most beautiful clothes, for boys on one side, girls on the other. Each set was a whole outfit, with shirt, trousers, hat, shoes, and jacket to match. By the time Jason made his way into the store, Amy was already looking up at the expensive little sets with stars in her eyes. As Jason entered, he saw her put out her hand to touch a little blue jacket, but she withdrew it as though she couldn't allow herself such a pleasure.

"So what do you like?" Jason asked, maneuvering Max between the stands of clothing.

"All of it," Amy said quickly. "So now that we've seen it, let's go."

Jason ignored her. "I like this one," he said, holding up a yellow-and-black set that had a matching raincoat. Little yellow boots had eyes on them, and he knew Max would like trying to get the eyes in his mouth. "What's his size?"

"Nine to twelve months," Amy said quickly. "We have to go—"

"What is it?" Jason asked, for Amy's face seemed to drain of color.

"Out. Now," she gasped, then tried to hide behind him.

Jason found he rather liked her hands on his waist and the way she hid behind him, but when he looked up, he saw nothing but another woman with a baby about Max's age entering the store.

"It's Julie Wilson," Amy hissed up at him. "Her husband owns the John Deere store and has horses."

Jason didn't see what this information had to do with anything in the known world.

"We went to prenatal classes together," Amy said; then she tightened her grip on his waist and started to pull Jason out of the store, using his big body to hide her from view of the woman.

"Aren't you forgetting something?" Jason whispered down to her, then nodded toward Max, who had managed to pull eight boxes of shoes off a shelf and was now busily eating the ties off two mismatched shoes.

"Heaven help me, I have failed motherhood," Amy gasped; then, crouching low, she made her way back to her son.

"Hello, Mrs. Wilson," the shop clerk was saying in a fawning way. "I have your order in the back. If you'll just come this way, we'll see if it fits little Abigail."

Jason recognized that tone of voice, since he'd heard it many times. It said that the clerk knew the woman and knew that she could afford anything in the shop. The snobby little clerk had not so much as asked Jason and Amy if they needed help when they entered, so he suspected that Amy was known to the girl. Abernathy was a tiny place, and even though this mall was a few miles out of the town, Jason guessed that it was known that Amy couldn't afford the clothes in this shop, therefore she was ignored.

"Let's go!" Amy said as soon as the woman had disappeared into the back.

"I have no intention of leaving," Jason said, and there was anger in his voice.

"You don't understand," Amy said, nearly in tears. "Julie married the richest boy in town, while I married—"

"The most likable boy in school," Jason said quickly, and instantly there were tears of gratitude in her eyes.

"Did she marry Tommy Wilson?"

"Yes. I told you, his father—"

"When we get home, I'm going to tell you all about Tommy Wilson and his father; then you won't be hiding from any woman who had the misfortune to marry either one of them. Now, help me here," Jason said as he began pulling one outfit after another off the shelves and slinging them over his arm.

"What in the world are you doing?" Amy gasped. "You can't—"

"I can buy everything now and return them later, right?"

"I guess so," Amy said, hesitantly; then as she began

to think about what he was saying, she picked up a little outfit with a blue teddy bear on the front of it. "I just love this one."

"Think quantity and forget about choosing."

Amy giggled, then got into the mood of pulling clothes off the racks and plonking them down onto the sales counter. There were yellow overalls with a red giraffe embroidered on the bib, a red shirt, a red-and-yellow jacket, with the most adorable red-and-yellow sandals to match. For once in her life, Amy didn't look at a price tag as she tossed things onto the counter.

When the clerk returned, Julie Wilson behind her, she stopped so suddenly that the baby carriage hit her in the heels. "Sir!" she said sternly, then opened her mouth to let Jason know that she didn't appreciate the mess they had made. But Jason held up a platinum American Express card, and the woman's frown turned into a smile.

"Did you see her face?" Amy was saying as she licked her ice cream cone. She and Jason were sitting on a bench by the fountain in the mall, Max in his carriage between them. All around them were bags and bags of clothes for Max.

"Of course, I'll have to hear the lecture from that snippy little salesgirl when I take all of it back, but it was worth it to see Julie's face. And you were marvelous." Amy was swinging her legs back and forth like a child, licking the ice cream before it melted and smiling as she watched Jason sharing his cone with Max.

"Was she really awful to you in class?"

"Worse than you can imagine," Amy said cheerfully. "She couldn't wait to tell me every rotten thing Billy had done at school. Not that she was there, but her husband was. Heavens, that must mean he's as old as you are."

At that Jason raised an eyebrow at her. "I hardly think I'm at death's door yet," he said archly.

"Got ya," Amy said, laughing. "Oh, but you were wonderful. But you shouldn't have told her that you and I were an item. You don't remember what Abernathy is like. Within two hours everyone in town will think I'm living with some great virile hunk of a man and they won't have any idea of the truth."

"And what is the truth?"

"That you've been having an affair with Charles, of course."

"I did not say—"

"And you didn't deny it, either. Hey! What are you doing?"

"I'm putting a new shirt on Max, that's what. I'm sick of this worn-out thing."

"But we have to take them back, and—" She broke off to stare at him. "You have no intention of taking these clothes back, do you?"

"None whatever."

"I wish I could understand you. Why *did* you agree to stay with Max and me in my leaky old house?"

"To give David a chance with you," Jason said simply.

"I didn't think you'd tell me the truth. Come on, Max, let's go see what the bottom half of you has done." She took the handles of the carriage and wheeled Max toward the women's restroom.

When he was alone, Jason looked around the mall. Two weeks ago he would never have believed that he would be spending his Christmas holidays like this. Usually he celebrated Christmas at some extravagantly expensive resort, and his customary gift to the woman he was with was a pair of diamond earrings. Her gift to him was something in bed. Maybe he was getting old, but sometimes he wished the women would shell out for a tie or a pair of socks.

"You are getting old, Wilding," he muttered, then got up to give his place on the bench to a woman who looked about ready to deliver twins. He picked up the bags, then walked a few stores down as he waited for Amy, and he saw in a window the perfect dress for her to wear on her date with David tonight. It was a lavender short-sleeve sweater with a matching cardigan, and a pleated skirt of dark purple with tiny tulips on it.

Jason didn't hesitate in entering the store, and immediately three attractive saleswomen ran to help him. He told them he had about five minutes, and he wanted the outfit in the window with hose, shoes, and jewelry to go with it.

The tallest of the women, a striking redhead, didn't bat an eyelash. "Underwear?"

Jason nodded curtly. "She's about that woman's size," he said, glancing at a shopper. Minutes later he'd signed the charge slip and the clothes were in the bag.

"Big one," Amy said as soon as she saw Jason, referring to Max. "Sorry we took so long. What did you buy now?"

Jason grinned at her. "I bought you something to wear tonight."

"You—Oh, I see. Gay men are good at that, aren't they? I mean, you like to choose women's clothes, don't you?"

Jason bent over her until his nose was almost touching hers. "Do you know the words 'thank you'? Or is my wanting to hear them more evidence of my sexual orientation?"

"Sorry," Amy murmured. "It's just that I—" She broke off, her eyes wide as she stared at something behind Jason. The next minute, she pushed him aside, stretched out her arms, and squealed, "Sally!" and a short, very attractive young woman came running toward Amy.

Jason stood to one side as he watched the two

women hug each other and talk over the top of one another, their words tumbling out in a cascade.

"How long—"

"When did you—"

"Why didn't you—"

"This is Max," Amy said at last, then stepped back to show her friend her son.

But the woman only glanced at the baby in the carriage, for her attention was on the gorgeous man who had his long-fingered hand on the back of the stroller. "Who is this?" she breathed, and Jason was quite pleased to be seen as a handsome man. Amy sure didn't seem to notice!

Jason couldn't help himself, but he picked up the woman's hand and kissed the back of it, then looked at her with what he'd been told were very seductive eyes. Since the woman looked as though she were going to melt and run down into her shoes, he felt good.

"This is Mr. Wilding and he's gay," Amy said in a cold voice.

"But I'm thinking of changing," Jason practically purred.

"You can practice on me," the woman said, and looked at Jason with hot eyes.

"Is Max all right?" Amy said sharply. "Mr. Wilding is Max's nanny. Gay men are good at that sort of thing, you know."

"I've been thinking of having a baby," Sally said,

never taking her eyes off Jason, "and I think I'm going to need a nanny."

"How about a maternity nurse as well?" Jason said in a low voice.

"Honey, I need a *donor.*"

"Sally, could you disentwine yourself from my nanny so we could go get something to drink? You can manage Max by yourself for a while, can't you?" she asked Jason, her lips a tight line as she glared up at him.

"I might be able to handle him," Jason said, his eyes still on Sally, as though she were the woman of his dreams. "You two go on. Max and I will take these packages to the car, then I have some, ah, personal shopping to do." He made the last sound as though he meant to buy something sexy and silky.

Before her friend could reply, Amy firmly took Sally's arm and led her to a nearby fake English pub and sat down heavily in the nearest empty booth.

"I want to know everything there is to know about him," Sally said eagerly.

"So what brings you to Abernathy over Christmas and why didn't you tell me you were going to be here?"

"I'm in a mall, not in Abernathy, and I'm here because I live six miles away," Sally said slowly. "You want to tell me what's going on? Are you having an affair with him? Or do you just look at him like he's a work of art?"

"Do you have to come on to every man you meet?"

Amy snapped as she grabbed a menu and looked at it. "Are you hungry?" When Sally didn't answer, she looked up.

"Out with it," Sally said. "I want to know everything."

"I've already told you everything. He's gay; he has no interest in me as a female, and we talk like two old hens. That's the end of it."

"I want details," Sally said as she ordered two cups of coffee from the waitress.

"No, give me a large orange juice. Milk production, you know."

Sally gave a slight shudder. "No, I don't know and don't want to know. Now, get on with it. Are you *sure* that hunk is gay?"

It didn't take Amy but a moment to get over her unusual reticence with her friend, and she was quite annoyed with herself for feeling what could almost be described as jealousy at Sally's reaction to "her" Mr. Wilding. And his to her, she thought with a grimace.

"I think his ex-lover came to the house this morning," she said, then described Jason's encounter with Charles. "There was lots of eye rolling while Charles was kissing my hand. There was definitely something going on between them. And the day before, Mr. Wilding kept glaring at two men at Baby Heaven. He paid no attention to the saleswoman, who was a knockout, but gave a hundred percent of his interest to the two men."

"Okay, so where did you find him?"

"He found me. I just opened the door and there he was. David brought him over and gave him to me."

"You mean like an early Christmas present?"

"Sort of, but don't get any ideas. He really is gay."

"He doesn't seem gay."

"And what stereotype do you have in mind for a person to appear gay?" Amy asked defensively.

"Hey! Don't jump down my throat. I was just asking, that's all. Gay or not, he's divine, and I want to know all there is to know about him."

"I don't know much, really. David insisted that his cousin needed a place to stay and to recover from a broken heart, so I let him stay."

"He could mend his broken heart in my bed any day he wanted to."

"You've been reading too many romantic novels. There is nothing between us, and there never will be. I told you: he's gay. Besides, he's very elegant, isn't he? When I first saw him, he had on a suit that probably cost more than my house."

"Amy, this cup of coffee is worth more than that rat trap of a house of yours. If you set it on fire, the fire would put itself out out of pity."

"It's not that bad."

"It's worse. Tell me more about him."

"He's odd, really. He doesn't say much, but he . . ." She looked up at her friend. "He brings me luck. Isn't that an odd thing to think about someone? But it's true; he brings luck to Max and me. Since he arrived, some lovely things have happened."

"Such as his going on one knee and telling you he can't live without you, and—"

"Stop daydreaming. First of all, Max adores him."

"Hmm . . . What else?"

"I don't know how to explain him. The truth is that I don't think I understand him myself. It's as though he's a . . ." Her head came up. "He's a bit of a turtle really. Or maybe an armadillo. He has a hard outer covering, but I think that inside he's really quite soft. I don't think he realizes it, but he adores Max just as much as my son adores him."

For a long moment, Sally leaned back in the booth and stared at her friend. "Are you in love with him?"

"Don't be ridiculous. He's a nice man and we have fun together, but he really is effeminate. He likes to shop and cook and do all the things that men don't."

"You mean, all the things that Billy didn't like, don't you? Look, Amy, I know you were the only girl in school who graduated a virgin, and I know you were saving yourself for your husband. I also know that you gave yourself to a drunken dope addict—Don't give me that look. I know Billy had his good points, but I'm a realist. You've been to bed with one man, lived with one man, and all you know is the kind of man who doesn't know how to open a refrigerator. There are other kinds of men, you know."

"Why are you always trying to make a romance out of everything? I didn't guess that the man is gay; I was told so. By David."

"Dr. David? Now, there's a hunk. You know, your Mr. Wilding reminds me of him."

"They're cousins."

"Ah, I see. So what happens next? Do you keep living with this gorgeous hunk who you can't have or do you have to return him after Christmas?"

"I have no idea."

At that Sally laughed. "Amy, you haven't changed. Only you would be living with a man and have no idea why he's there or how long he means to stay."

Amy didn't answer that, but looked down at her empty glass.

"Okay, I'll lay off. What about the other men in your life? What happened to that beautiful used car salesman?"

"Oh. Ian. He *owns* the Cadillac dealership. He's very rich, I suppose." Amy gave a sigh.

"I can see how you'd consider him tedious. Poor guy is only handsome and rich, so of what interest could he possibly be to you?"

"He's of more interest to himself than to anyone else. He seemed to think he was doing me a great favor by showing up every night. He kept calling me 'Billy Thompkins's Widow' as though he were saying that I was an untouchable."

"Welcome to small town life. Why don't you get out of here and go somewhere where no one has ever heard of Billy and his problems?"

But before Amy could reply, Sally looked as though someone had stuck a pin in her. "What time is it?"

Amy looked around to find a clock but didn't see one.

"I have to go," Sally said urgently as she gathered her things and started sliding out of the booth; then she saw Amy's face. "Don't tell me you don't know?"

When Amy shook her head, Sally gave a grimace. "Didn't you see the signs? They're all over the mall. You know Candlelight Gowns? That shop in Carlton that's about to go out of business?"

"Out of my league," Amy said, finishing her orange juice and sliding out to stand by Sally. "I could never afford to even window shop there."

"Nobody could afford that place. I don't know how they expected to sell those ritzy dresses in eastern Kentucky, but they did. Anyway, everyone knew they were about to go under, but it seems that some mysterious buyer from New York, no less, has bought the place and to launch the new shop, they're giving away a Dior dress."

When Amy said nothing, just kept walking beside

her friend, Sally said, "Hello! Dior. Doesn't that *do* anything to you?"

"No, I'm more into Pampers and Huggies. Why would anyone want a Dior dress?"

"You poor baby," Sally said. "You know, I have a theory that having a baby takes away about fifty points on a woman's IQ. I think she gets them back when the kid goes off to school, but until then she's an idiot."

Amy laughed. "You just think it's true, but I *know* it is. So what do you want with a Dior dress?"

At that, Sally rolled her eyes to let Amy know that she was hopeless. "Come on, the drawing's about to begin, and you have to enter the contest."

"Me?"

"Yes, and if you win, you have to give me the dress."

"All right," Amy said, "that's a deal."

But first Amy had to find Jason and Max, and an hour later, the three of them were standing in front of the fountain in the center of the mall and waiting for the drawing to be held. And when they drew Amy's name, somehow, she wasn't surprised. In the last few days it was as though nothing but good luck came her way.

"Sally is going to be so happy," Amy said as the crowd turned around to look to see if the winner was in the audience.

"Why?" Jason asked, smiling down at her, Max in his arms.

"Because I promised her that if I won, I'd give her the dress."

Jason grabbed her arm as she turned away. "You did what?"

"I have no need for a dress like that. Where would I wear it?"

"Oh. I forgot to tell you. David got tickets to the Bellringers' Ball for tomorrow and he wants you to go with him."

For a moment Amy just blinked at him, as though she didn't understand what he was saying. Then she grinned and said, "I hope Sally doesn't mind having a dress that's been worn once," and the next moment she went up to the podium to accept her prize. She wasn't surprised when she found out that the dress was in her size and that the prize included a free hair and makeup makeover by Mr. Alexander from New York on the night of her choice. When she told them she wanted it tomorrow night, she wasn't shocked to hear that Mr. Alexander was going to be in the Kentucky area tomorrow.

When she said all this to Jason, he said, "That's because Mr. Alexander is probably Joe from the local beauty shop. He went to New York once, so he now bills himself as being from there."

"Still . . ." Amy said, "a great many odd things have happened to me since . . ." She looked up at him.

"Since David started courting you?"

"David? Courting me? Are you out of your mind?"

"I think you're missing something if you can't see what everyone else can. Dr. David is in love with you and wants—"

"Oh, you are ridiculous. Look, it's nearly time for lunch and I have to feed Max, so we better go home."

Jason didn't answer her, but put his hand on the small of her back and half pushed her into a very nice Italian restaurant. They were first served bread with a dish of oil from a bottle filled with garlic cloves. The oil was much too spicy for either of the adults, but Max sucked the oil off three pieces of bread.

After lunch they went to three toy stores, and amid Amy's protests that grew weaker by the minute, Jason bought Max sackfuls of toys. In the car on the way home, she wailed, "How am I going to repay you? You *must* return all those clothes and you have to take back those toys. There is nothing you own that's dirty enough for me to make the kind of money that I'd need to repay—"

"David's going to pick you up in an hour, so you'd better hustle to get ready."

"Hustle?" Amy asked, sounding as though she'd never heard the word before.

"Mmmm," was all Jason said as he swung the car into the driveway. "You have to nurse Max before you go or you'll be in pain all night, and—"

"Would you mind!" she said, annoyed. "I think I know my own milking needs better than you do."

She had meant to put him in his place, but instead, she'd made herself sound like a cow. When he didn't say anything, she looked at him sideways and said, "Maybe I should apply for a job at the local dairy," and they both burst into laughter.

But as she got out of the car, she said, "I can't go. I have nothing decent to wear out with a doctor," and Jason thrust a heavy dark green bag into her hands. Amy opened it only enough to see that something gorgeous was inside. "How did you know that I love lavender?" she asked softly.

"Intuition. Now go and feed Max and get out of here."

"Mr. Wilding, you are my fairy godmother," she said, smiling up at him; then she put her hand over mouth at the use of the word *fairy*. "Oh, I didn't mean . . ."

"Go!" he ordered. "Now."

Grabbing Max from him, she ran into the house, and all three of them were smiling.

CHAPTER ELEVEN

AS SOON AS AMY LEFT WITH DAVID, JASON PICKED UP HIS telephone and called his father's house. When his father answered, he was startled at the noise in the background. "What's going on?" Jason half shouted into the phone.

"If it isn't my newly turned gay son," Bertram Wilding said. "So how's the gay scene?"

Jason looked toward heaven and again vowed to kill his brother. "Could you cut the jokes, Dad, and put my secretary on the line?"

"Cherry?"

"What? I can't hear you. No, I don't want a cherry pie; I want Parker."

"Cherry Parker, old man."

"Ah. Right. I knew that." And he did, he told himself. Vaguely, he remembered thinking that Cherry was an odd name for an icy woman like Parker. "Would you put her on?"

"Sure thing. I think she's in the kitchen with Charlie."

At that, he put the phone down, and Jason could hear his steps on the wooden floor. "Cherry?" Jason whispered. "Charlie?"

"Yes, sir," Parker said when she picked up the phone, and for the life of him, Jason couldn't imagine a more inappropriate name for her than "Cherry." "What can I do you for?" When Jason was silent, she said, "Sorry. I've spent too much time in Kentucky."

"Yes, well," Jason murmured, not knowing what to say in reply. "I need you to do something for me."

"I assumed as much. I didn't think it was a social call."

For a moment Jason held the phone away from his face and looked at it. When this was over and he got back to New York, he was going to pummel his staff back into shape.

"I'm going to dictate a list of toys that I want you to buy; then I want you to wrap them up in white tissue paper and tie them with red or green ribbon. You are to put labels on the gifts saying they're from Santa Claus. Got that?"

"Rather easily," Parker said.

Again, Jason grimaced. His secretary was really being too insolent. "And I want you to deliver them into the house on Christmas Eve. Put them under the tree."

"I see. And how do I get into the house?"

"I'll leave a key under the back doormat."

"Ah, the pleasures and safety of small town life. How I miss it."

"Parker, when I want your personal comments, I'll ask for them."

"Yes, sir," she said, but she didn't sound contrite in the least. "Is there anything else?"

For a moment Jason felt a bit guilty for his outburst. It was just that too many things in his orderly world were coming apart. "Do you have your dress for tomorrow night?" he asked in an attempt to be less dictatorial.

"You bought me an Oscar de la Renta, quite expensive."

"Good," he said; then, not knowing what else to say, and hearing laughter in the background, he hung up without a farewell.

In the next moment, he made another call and issued an invitation.

"Well, well, well," Mildred Thompkins said when Jason opened the door, Max on his arm. "So you're the angel Amy keeps going on and on about. Don't just stand there; let me in; it's cold out here."

"You're not going to tell her, are you?" Jason asked, sounding like a little boy begging her not to tell his mother.

"Tell Amy that her gay guardian angel is really one of the richest men in the world?"

"Not quite. And, before you ask, I'm *not* a billionaire."

"Come here, darlin'," she said to her grandson, and the baby went to her. "So you want to tell me what's going on here? Why are you masquerading as some gay man when I happen to know that you pursued every female in Abernathy all during high school, and how many homes do you have around the world?"

"I can see you haven't changed," Jason said, smiling and looking with fascination at the lacquered mass of hair on Mildred's head. The strands wove in and out in an intricate pattern that wouldn't have moved in a hurricane. "Still nosy as ever."

"I'm interested in Amy," Mildred said simply. "I want what's best for her."

"Since Billy isn't here to give it to her?" Jason asked.

"That was a low blow and you know it. My son may have had his faults, but he did one good thing in his life: he married Amy and produced this child." She gave Max a hug and a kiss, pulled his hands away from her glasses, then said, "No, that's not true. He did another good thing. On the night he died Billy was drunk, very very drunk, and he was driving about sixty on the twisty old River Road. But he was sober enough—and kind enough—that he turned his car into a tree rather than hit a busload of kids coming back from a ball game."

"I always liked Billy," Jason said softly.

"I know you did, and you were always good to him. And that's why I came by to see how you and Amy were getting along. Amy is the best. She sees the good in people. Don't get me wrong. She's not one of these idiots who thinks that everyone who doesn't have a tail and horns is a good person. It's just that Amy can see good in a person when others can't. And her belief in them makes them try harder. Maybe if Billy hadn't died, she'd have made something good out of him. But then . . . Oh, well, it's better not to speak ill of the dead. Billy left behind a beautiful wife and Max."

Her head came up. "So now, you want to tell me what's going on and why you're living with my daughter-in-law in this falling-down old heap?"

Jason ignored her question. "You want to baby-sit tomorrow? I have to go somewhere."

She narrowed her eyes at him. "You know, a lot of odd things have been happening lately, like someone buying Baby Heaven and Candlelight Gowns and—"

"What? Someone bought a dress shop?"

"Yeah. That shop in Carlton that put on the drawing today for that Dior gown. Now, we may be pretty country in Kentucky, but we do know that a place like Candlelight Gowns doesn't carry a one-off Dior gown. Do you know what that dress cost?"

"I imagine I'll be told," Jason said heavily. "Tell me, did you hear the name of the buyer for this dress shop?"

Mildred smiled at him as she shook a rattle for Max.

"Only that he was from New York. Did you know that the owner of the shop was an old football rival of yours? I seem to remember one game where you were to pass him the ball, but you didn't. Instead, you ran with it, and made the touchdown that won the game. What was that boy's name?"

"Lester Higgins," Jason said heavily.

"That's it. He married a girl whose father owned that shop, and Lester tried for years to make a go of it but couldn't." She was watching Jason's face and her smile was broadening. "So now maybe he finally found someone to take that shop off his hands. Someone who can afford it."

"Don't look at me. I used to be rich, but then I came to visit Abernathy and my resources have plummeted."

"Can't make a profit on a dress shop in Kentucky even when you give away twenty-thousand-dollar gowns as a sales gimmick?"

Suddenly, Jason grinned at her. "You are still the nosiest gossip in four counties. You want to baby-sit tomorrow?"

"So you can go to the Bellringers' Ball? I hear that that jet of yours is paying so much to Jessie Green to use his landing strip that he's thinking of retiring."

Jason groaned. "All right, you win. You get your gossip, but I get someone to take care of Max tomorrow. Deal?"

"Sure. You call and order pizza while I get the bottle

of bourbon from the car. It's no use looking to see if Amy has any in the house. She'd probably be afraid that Max would drink it."

"You haven't changed, Mildred. Not one bit."

"Neither have you," she said, smiling. "And you were always my favorite."

"Along with all the other boys in town," he said, smiling as he picked up the phone.

"And you should see him play with Max!" Amy was saying. "He'll spend twenty minutes encouraging Max to crawl; he has endless patience. And everything good seems to happen when he's around. I win things, find great bargains, and did I tell you that he does the ironing and lets me sleep?"

"Twice," David said, looking down at his salad.

"Oh, sorry. It's just that I've never lived with anyone so unselfish. Not that I'm really living with him, but, you know . . ." She trailed off, moved her fork around in her lettuce, and wondered what Mr. Wilding and Max were having for dinner.

"Amy, would you rather go home?" David asked, leaning across the table to her.

"No, of course not. I'm having a wonderful time. It's great to get out of the house."

"You certainly look nice. That color suits you."

"Mr. Wilding bought this for me," she said before she thought. "All right, that's it. I promise not to mention his name again. Tell me, did you save any lives today?"

"Half a dozen at least. Would you like to go dancing after this?"

"Can't," she said, stuffing her mouth full, trying to make up for lost time, since David was nearly finished and she had been talking too much to eat. "Milk," she muttered.

"What did you say?"

Amy took a drink of her lemonade. "Milk. I have to feed Max. I told him that I should work in a dairy, since I can't get a job anywhere else."

"You told Max that?"

"No, uh, I told . . ."

"Jason. I see." For a moment David was silent; then he looked up at Amy. "Did he tell you about the ball tomorrow night?"

"Yes, but not until after I'd won a dress by Dior."

"You won a dress? And by Dior, no less. You have to tell me about this."

Amy couldn't help herself as she rattled off about the whole day, starting with Jason's ironing, then seeing Julie Wilson in the mall and how Jason bought Max all those clothes. "Of course he has to take them back," she said, her mouth full of steak, "and he will, but he hasn't done it yet. We just have to talk about it."

"What about the dress?"

"Oh, yes, the dress." Amy told him what Sally had

said about the store in Carlton going out of business, then having been bought by a new owner, so they were giving away a dress. "And I won it. And a makeover, so tomorrow I should look presentable."

"You always look presentable," David said, but Amy didn't seem to notice the compliment.

"In my case I'm glad the dress is strapless, as it makes for easy access." She had meant that as a joke, but when she looked up at David's intense stare, she turned red. "Sorry. I'm forgetting where I am. I make breast-feeding jokes all the time and I shouldn't. They're taste-less." Heaven help her, but she couldn't stop herself. "Well, maybe not tasteless to Max. Especially after I eat something hot and spicy." She gave David a weak smile. "Sorry."

"Do you and Jason share jokes?" David asked softly.

"Yes. He's a good audience, and he laughs at my jokes no matter how tasteless they are."

"But not to Jason."

"I beg your pardon."

"You just said that your jokes weren't tasteless to Max, and I said they weren't tasteless to Jason either."

Amy looked at him blankly, still not understanding. "Yes, of course. This is good; what is it?"

"Beef."

"Ah, yes. Did I tell you about Charles?"

"This is another man?"

"No, silly, he's the one who makes the baby food you

gave me. He's a beautiful man, and you should have told me the truth."

"Yes, I should have. Why don't you tell me the truth?"

"You'd be bored."

"No, honest," he said. "I'm beginning to find this whole story fascinating. I'm meeting new people I've never met before. There's the very funny and unselfish Jason. And there's Max the Huggable. And now there's Charles the Beautiful. Who else is in your life?"

Amy jammed a piece of meat the size of a golf ball in her mouth, then made motions that she couldn't talk until she'd chewed it.

"Amy!" came a masculine voice from beside them. "Don't you look divine? Are we still on for New Year's Eve?"

Amy waved her hands and pointed toward her full mouth as she looked up at Ian Newsome.

"I think Amy is going to be busy on New Year's Eve," David said firmly, glaring up at the man.

"Is that so? Did you get my Christmas gift, Amy?" Ian asked, smiling down at her.

Amy, still chewing, shook her head no.

"Oh? Then I'll have to bring it over myself on Christmas morning. Or maybe I should say that I'll *drive* it over." He turned to David. "How's that little clinic of yours doin', Doc? Still beggin' people to donate to it? And are you still livin' in that tiny house over on River Road?" Before David could reply, he turned back to Amy, winked, waved, and was gone.

"I really hate that bastard, don't you?"

Amy found that she hadn't yet finished chewing the huge piece of steak.

"You want some dessert?"

"Milk," Amy mumbled. "Max."

"Yeah, sure," David said, then signaled for the waitress to bring the check. "Might as well leave. What a night!"

Amy wouldn't allow David to walk her to the front door. She felt guilty that she didn't, since, after all, he had paid for such a nice dinner for her and he was taking her to the ball tomorrow, but still, she just wanted to be inside. "I'm home," she called out softly, and when there was no answer, she had a moment of panic. Had Mr. Wilding gone? Had he taken Max?

But in the next second Jason appeared, Max in his arms, tears on the baby's face. "Gimme, gimme," Amy said, stretching out her arms. "I'm bursting." In seconds, she was on the couch and Max was happily sucking.

"Have a good time?" Jason asked, standing over her.

"Oh, sure. Great. Is there any of that casserole left from lunch?"

"I think so," he said, smiling down at her pleading look for a moment; then he went into the kitchen and filled a plate full of cold salad and cold meat. "You need one of those quick ovens," he said as he handed her the plate.

Amy took the plate with one hand, but she had no lap to set it on. While looking about, Jason took the plate from her, cut off a bite, and fed it to her on a fork. "A microwave," she said when her mouth was empty. "But Charles's food is good cold or hot. Did you have dinner?"

"Yes, and I thought you did too, so why are you hungry?" He fed her a piece of potato in a dill sauce.

"You know," she said, waving her hand; then she turned sharply. "What's that?"

"The coffee table," he said, scooping up cold beef cooked with red wine. "Or it's supposed to be, I guess. Maybe we could find a furniture store that's going out of business." He was referring to the big electrical spool that she had in the middle of the room.

"No, *that*," Amy said, mouth still full.

"The glass? It's a glass. Haven't you seen one before?"

She ignored his attempt at humor. "What is on the glass?"

Jason turned, stared at the single glass sitting on the table; then, with his back to Amy, he smiled. He was sober when he looked back at her. "Lipstick," he said. "Red lipstick."

"It's not mine." She was looking at him as hard as she could as he put more food into her mouth.

"Don't look at me. It's not mine either."

"I know that all gays aren't cross-dressers," she said. "So whose lipstick is that?"

"Ahhhhh."

"Jason!"

"What happened to 'Mr. Wilding'?"

As she switched Max to the other side, she still glared at him. "Did you have a guest?"

"I did, actually. Nice of you to ask."

"I don't think you should have," she said tightly. "You never know what a person has in mind when a baby is involved. I am very concerned about Max's safety."

"Me too, but then this was a woman I've known for a while." He fed her the last bite on the plate.

"I think you should have asked my permission before you invited a woman into this house. Into my house, that is."

"I'll do that next time. You want something to drink? I have some beer. Max would probably like it."

"So who was she?"

"Who was she who?"

"The woman who left red lipstick on that glass, that's who."

"Just a friend. What about a Coke? Or a Seven-Up?"

Amy glared at him. "You're not answering me."

"And you're not answering me. What do you want to drink?"

"Nothing," she said, inexplicably feeling very angry. Max had fallen asleep before he'd finished nursing, and she knew she should wake him, but she didn't have the heart to do it. Instead, she just wanted to go to bed.

What business was it of hers if he had visitors, male or female? "I'm very tired," she said, picking up Max and turning toward her bedroom. "I'll see you in the morning."

"Good night," he said cheerfully, then went to his own bedroom.

Hours later Jason awoke to the sound of glass breaking and immediately swung his long legs off the bed. He had fallen asleep in his clothes, the light still on as he went over a market report for a company he was trying to buy.

In the kitchen he found Amy, a broken glass on the floor, and she was trying to pick up the pieces with her bare hands while walking about in her bare feet.

"Get back from that," he said, annoyed. "You're going to cut yourself." When she looked up at him with pain-filled eyes, he knew that something was wrong. Striding across the glass in his bedroom slippers, he swept Amy into his arms and carried her to a chair by the kitchen table. "Now, tell me what's wrong."

"Just a headache. It's nothing," she managed to whisper, but even that slight sound made a look of pain cross her face, and she shifted uncomfortably on the seat.

"Nothing?" he said. "How about if I drive you to the emergency room of the hospital and let a doctor have a look at you?"

"I have some pills," she said, then gestured vaguely toward her bedroom. "They're in—"

She broke off because Jason had left the room, but in seconds he was back with his cell phone to his ear. "I don't care what time it is or whether you ever get any sleep," he said into the receiver. "I'm not a doctor, but I can see when someone is in serious pain. What do I do with her?"

"Right," Jason said into the phone. "And how long has she had these? Uh huh. Uh huh. I see. I'll call you if I need you again."

Jason put down the phone and looked at Amy. "David said hot compresses and massage. And he's given you pills that you were to take at the first sign of pain. Why didn't you take them?"

"I was busy," she said, looking up at him with mournful eyes. "I'm sorry to keep you up, but my head hurts so much."

Jason went to the sink, turned on the tap, let it run to get hot, then soaked a tea towel in the hot water. "Here, now," he said, handing it to her. "Wrap this around your forehead and tell me where the pills are."

But when Amy started to speak, she had to close her eyes against the pain, so Jason bent, swept her into his arms and carried her into the bedroom. In her bathroom medicine cabinet he found a bottle of pills that were labeled "For migraine," so he brought two of them and a glass of water to Amy.

He meant to leave her then, but she was curled into a ball and he knew that tension and lack of sleep had as much to do with the headache as anything else. David said on the phone that new mothers often got head-aches and what they needed more than pills was TLC.

When Jason sat down on the bed beside Amy, she started to protest, but he didn't listen to her. Instead, he leaned back against the headboard and pulled her up so she was leaning against his chest. The washcloth had grown cold, and her hair around her forehead was damp, either from the compress or from sweat, he didn't know which.

Gently, he put his long, strong fingers to the back of her neck and began to massage. At the first groan from Amy, that was all the encouragement he needed. Slowly, he stroked her neck and up to her head, and as the minutes ticked by, he could feel her neck and head relaxing. "Trust me," he said when she didn't want to seem to relax completely.

But his deep strokes made her forget any awkwardness of their being in bed together, and seemed to make her forget everything else in the world. His hands moved down her back, running along her spine, then outward over her ribs, then back up her arms. There was a lot of tension in her upper arms, and he managed to release it.

After about thirty minutes she was limp in his arms, fully supported by him, as trusting of him as Max was.

In another ten minutes Jason realized that she was asleep, so he gently put her down on the pillow and eased his long legs from under her body. When he was standing by the bed, he pulled the cover over her; then, on impulse, he kissed her cheek and tucked her in as though she were three years old.

Smiling, he turned away to leave the room.

"Thank you," he heard Amy whisper as he started back to his own bedroom, and Jason smiled in answer.

CHAPTER TWELVE

WHEN JASON FIRST HEARD THE SOUNDS IN THE KITCHEN and knew they weren't the sounds of Amy and Max, he frowned. Already it had become part of his life to hear Max's high-pitched squeal and Amy's laughter at the morning antics of her son. But then, on second thought, maybe it was just Amy in the kitchen.

With a wicked grin on his face, he got out of bed wearing only the bottom of his pajamas and sauntered into the kitchen. Then, to his pure disgust, he found it was Charles in there, puttering around with the knobs on the stove.

"Expecting someone else?" he asked, one eyebrow raised as he looked Jason up and down, noting his bare chest.

Jason returned to his bedroom to pull on jeans and a

shirt before he spoke to his chef. "What are you doing here at this hour?" Jason growled as he sat down at the table and ran his hand over his unshaven face. "And how did you get in here?"

"I'm trying to work this powerless range, and you told Cherry that there was a key under the mat, remember? And, besides, it's after nine in the morning. And what were you doing last night to make you sleep so late?" Charles asked with a lascivious little smirk.

"I remember telling Parker where the key was, not you," Jason said pointedly, ignoring Charles's insinuations.

Charles was unperturbed. "She's not really your type, is she?"

"Parker?" Jason asked, his voice filled with horror.

"No, her." Charles nodded toward Amy's bedroom door.

"You could be fired, you know," Jason said, glaring at the little man.

Silently, Charles turned to a porcelain bowl on the counter behind him, lifted the lid and held it under Jason's nose. It was crepes with hot strawberry sauce, Jason's favorite.

In reply, Jason just grunted and looked toward the overhead cabinet that held the dishes. Within seconds he was eating double forkfuls. How was Charles able to always find the best produce no matter where he was?

Jason was willing to bet that these lusciously ripe strawberries didn't come from the local supermarket. On the other hand, based on what the last few days had cost him, he thought it best not to ask where the strawberries had come from.

"I really am thinking of starting a baby food business," Charles said seriously. "Maybe you can advise me in what I should do to get started in my own business."

It was on the tip of Jason's tongue to tell him to forget it, because to help Charles meant that he'd lose him as his personal chef. Instead, Jason acted as though his mouth were too full to talk. Some part of his conscience said, "Coward!" but the strawberry crepes won over his higher moral values.

"Of course I guess everything depends on Max," Charles was saying. "Do all babies have such educated palettes?"

Here Jason was on safe ground. "Max is unique in all the world, one of a kind. Speaking of which . . ." He trailed off as he listened silently for a moment, then rose and went to Amy's bedroom door, opened it, and tiptoed inside. Minutes later he came out with a sleepy-looking Max and a clean diaper.

"I didn't hear anything," Charles said. "You must have great ears."

"When you get to be a—" Jason didn't say "father,"

as he meant to, but stopped himself. "Get to be a man of experience," he finished, "you learn to listen for things."

But Charles wasn't listening to a word his employer said, because his wide-eyed interest was on the fact that Jason had thrown a dish towel down on the kitchen table and was changing the baby as though he'd done it all his life. All Charles could think was that this was a man who had everything done for him. His clothes were chosen and purchased for him by his valet, his car was driven for him, meals cooked for him, and anything that was left over, his secretary did for him.

Charles recovered himself enough to smile at the baby. "And how do you like strawberries, young gentleman?" Max's reply was a toothy grin, but Charles's reward was when Max grabbed the crepes with both hands and sucked and chewed until there was nothing but sauce on his hands. And on his arms, face, hair, and even up his nose.

"How utterly gratifying," Charles said, standing back and watching Jason clean Max with a warm cloth. "He is without prejudice. Without preconceived ideas. His culinary gusto is the purest form of praise."

"Or criticism," Jason said, annoyed that Charles was still hinting that he wanted to start his own business.

"Afraid of losing me?" Charles asked, one eyebrow arched, knowing exactly what was in his employer's mind.

Jason was saved from answering by a pounding on the front door. As he went to open it, Max draped over his arm, Amy came out of the bedroom, a ratty old robe over her nightgown and blinking sleepily. "What's going on?" she asked.

When Jason opened the door, he was shoved aside by a thin blond man who was followed by two other thin young men and one woman who were carrying huge boxes, plastic cloths slung over their arms. All four of them wore nothing but black, lots of black, layers of it. And all of them had hair bleached to an unnatural white blondness that stuck out at all angles from their heads.

"*You* must be the one," the first man, who was carrying nothing, said as he pointed at Amy. He had three gold earrings in his left ear and a heavy gold bracelet on the wrist he was extending. "Oh, dearie, I can see why I was told to come early. That *must* be your natural color of hair. What was God thinking when He did that to you? And, dear, where did you get that robe? Is it kitsch or have you had it since the Nixon administration? All right, boys, you can see what we have to do. Set up here and there, and over there."

He turned, looked Jason up and down, and said, "And who are you, darling?"

"No one," Jason said emphatically, then tossed a look at Amy. "Max and I are going *out.*"

Amy gave him a look that begged him to take her with him, but Jason had no pity. Heartlessly, he grabbed jackets for him and Max, then was out the front door before it closed. When he'd told Parker to have someone do a makeover, he'd meant maybe hair rollers for half an hour and a little eye shadow. Amy possessed natural beauty; she didn't need the help of an army of beauticians to prepare for a party.

For all that Jason pretended to leave the house because of the arrival of the makeover people, the truth was that he was glad to have Max to himself for a while. It was amazing how important the adoration of a child could make you feel, he thought. And it was even more amazing the lengths that a person would go to to entertain a child.

Jason knew that he had a whole morning before Max would have to nurse again, so he had the baby to himself for hours. The carriage was in the back of the car, so he drove to the tiny downtown of Abernathy and parked. Since Max was still in his pajamas, the first thing he had to do was buy him something to wear.

"Haven't I seen you somewhere before?" the man who owned the Abernathy Emporium said, squinting at Jason. Since the man had served Jason, David, and their father hundreds of times while the boys were growing up, he should remember him.

"Mmmmm," was all Jason said as he put the baby overalls and T-shirt down on the counter along with a snowsuit for a two-year-old. It would be too big for Max now, but it was the best-looking one they had, and Max did have his pride.

"I'm sure I know you," the man was saying. "I never forget a face. Did you come with them city people this mornin' to do up Amy's face?"

"I need diapers for a twenty-pound kid," Jason said, starting to take out his credit card, then paying instead with cash. He didn't want the man to read his name on the card. Maybe it hadn't been such a good idea to come to Abernathy; he should have gone to the mall.

"It'll come to me," the man said. "I know it will."

Jason didn't say anything, but put his hand through the handles of the plastic bags, then wheeled Max out of the store. That was a close one, he thought as he pushed Max back toward the car. But the encounter had taken him back in time to when he lived in Abernathy, and now he could see the place with the eyes of an adult, an adult who had traveled all over the world.

The town was dying, he thought, looking at peeling paint and faded signs. The little grocery store where his father had shopped twice a week and where Jason had stolen candy once had a broken pane of glass in front. He had stolen only once in his life. His father had found out and had taken Jason back to the store.

Attempting to teach Jason not to steal again, his father had arranged for him to sweep the store's wooden floors and wait on customers for two weeks.

It was during those two weeks that Jason got his first taste of business and had loved it. He found that the more enthusiastic he was, the more he believed in a product, the more he could sell. At the end of the two weeks both he and the store owner regretted having to part company.

The Abernathy dime store windows looked as though they hadn't been washed in years. The Laundromat was disgusting.

Dying, he thought. The malls and the larger cities had killed poor little Abernathy.

By the time Jason reached his car, he was feeling quite bad about the place, as he did have a few good memories there, in spite of what he told David. Thinking of whom, he wondered why his brother would want to go through med school, then move back to this funeral-waiting-to-happen of a town.

Jason got into the car, turned on the ignition, waited awhile until the car was warm, then got into the back with Max and proceeded to dress him in his new clothes. "Well, *you* won't have to live here," he said to Max, then halted for a moment as he thought about what he was saying.

There would be David to consider, of course, but

Jason figured he could talk his brother 'round. David couldn't possibly love Amy more than he, Jason, did. And no man on earth loved Max more than he did. So of course they'd spend their lives together.

"Want to go live with me in New York?" Jason asked the silent baby as he chewed on the laces of his new shoes. "I'll buy you a big house out in the country, and you can have your own pony. Would you like that?"

Jason finished dressing the baby, put him in his car seat, then headed for the clean, homogenized mall. Since it was Christmas Eve, there were few shoppers, so he and Max could stroll at their leisure and look in all the windows. But Jason saw nothing as he thought about what he wanted to do.

It wasn't difficult to see what the last few days had meant to him. Max and Amy were now as much a part of his life as breathing, and he wanted them with him always. He'd buy a huge country house within commuting distance from New York and Amy and Max could live there. Amy would never have to worry about cooking or cleaning again, as Jason would make sure that they were taken care of.

And they would be there when he got home, just waiting for him. And their presence would make life easier, he thought. He'd return from long, hard days at the office and there would be Amy with oatmeal on her chin and Max in her arms.

On impulse, he stopped in an art store and bought Amy a huge box of art supplies: watercolors, chalk, pencils, and six dozen sketchbooks of the finest quality paper they had.

"Either somebody likes to draw or you're tryin' to get a girl into bed with you," the clerk, who looked to be all of seventeen, said as he rang up the sale.

"Just give me the slip to sign," Jason snapped.

"Aren't you in the Christmas spirit?" the young man said, undaunted by Jason's scowl.

After he left the art store, he passed a jewelry store, and as though a hand pulled him inside, he entered. "Do you have engagement rings?" he asked, then was horrified to hear his voice crack. He cleared his throat. "I mean—"

"That's all right," the man said, smiling. "It happens all the time. Now, if you'll just step over here."

Jason glanced down at the tray of diamond solitaires in front of him with contempt, then back up at the man. "You have a vault in this store?"

"Oh, I see, you're interested in our security system," the man said nervously, and from the way his hand was hidden under the counter, he looked as though he were about to push a button and summon the police.

"I want to see some of the rings you have in the vault."

"I see."

Jason could tell that the stupid little man didn't see at all. "I want to buy something much nicer than any of these. I want to buy something expensive. Understand?"

It took the man a moment to stop blinking, but when he did, he grinned in a way that Jason found quite annoying, but the next moment he scurried into the back, and twenty minutes later Jason left the store with a tiny box in his trouser's pocket.

Jason took Max back home at noon to allow him to nurse. Neither male recognized Amy at first, as her head was covered with pieces of aluminum foil. Max looked as though he were about to cry as he always did with strangers, but Amy's arms felt familiar, so he settled down.

"How adorable," one of the thin young men said with sarcasm, his lip curled in distaste as Amy nursed Max, every inch of her flesh hidden from view.

"Don't hit him, Mr. Wilding," Amy said without looking up.

At that, the young man looked at Jason with such interest that he went into the kitchen, but Charles was still there, and now he was cooking lunch for the whole lot of them. Finally, Jason went into his room and called Parker.

As was becoming a habit with her, she took a long time to get to the phone. He told her he wanted her to call a realtor in the surrounding areas around New

York and fax him details of estates for sale. "Something suitable for a baby," he said. "And, Parker, I hope I don't have to tell you to mention this to no one, especially my little brother."

"No, you don't have to tell me that," she said, and Jason wasn't sure, but he thought he heard anger in her voice. And, oddly, she hung up before he did.

Jason took Max out to lunch. They shared a huge steak, butternut squash, and tiny green beans with almonds—and Jason had them grind the almonds so he could share them with Max. When that wasn't enough, they had crème brûlée, with burnt sugar on top and raspberries on the bottom.

After the meal, Max slept in his stroller while Jason bought more gifts for everyone. He bought things for David, for his father, for Amy (a new bathrobe and four cotton nightgowns that buttoned from neck to hem), and, on impulse, something for Parker. He got her a pen-and-pencil set. When he saw a cookware store, he bought Charles something the clerk assured him was unique: tiny ice cream molds in the shape of various fruits. For Max he bought a set of hand puppets and a bubble gun that ran on batteries and produced huge, glorious soap bubbles.

Feeling quite proud of himself, Jason headed home with a car full of gaudily wrapped packages.

When he entered the house, a tired, fussy Max in his

arms, Amy stood there in all her glory, the product of many hours of work—and Jason didn't like what he saw. She looked beautiful in the long ivory column of satin that was the dress. It was rather plain, strapless, tight about Amy's prodigious bosom, then opening to a pleat in front and flowing to the floor.

She was gorgeous, true, but she looked too much like all the women he had dated for so many years. This was a woman who didn't need any man; she could have them all if she wanted them. And she was a woman who knew she was beautiful. She had to know it if she looked like that.

Looking at Jason's face, Amy laughed. "You don't like it, do you?"

"Sure. It's fine. You're a knockout," he said without expression.

"Meow," said one of the thin men. "Jealous, are we?"

Jason gave the man a quelling look, but the thin hairdresser just turned away, laughing.

"It doesn't matter," Amy said, but her voice said that it did matter and that she was hurt by Jason's lack of enthusiasm. "David's the one who counts, since I'm going with him."

"Ooooh, the kitten has claws," the thin man said.

"Lance!" snapped the head hairdresser. "Shut up. Let the lovebirds alone."

At that Amy laughed, but Jason put Max on the

floor, then went to plop down heavily on the old sofa in the living room. Everyone else was in the kitchen, either eating or cleaning up and putting supplies away. Amy followed her son and Jason into the living room.

"Why don't you like it?" she asked, standing before him.

Jason had a newspaper in front of his face and didn't put it down. "I don't know where you got that idea. I told you that you look great. What else do you want?"

"For you to look at me and say that. Why are you angry with me?" There were almost tears in her voice.

Jason put the newspaper down (it was three weeks old anyway) and looked up at her. "You look great, really, you do. It's just that I think you look better the way you are naturally." He thought that would appease her, but it didn't, and he watched her frown, then turn away to look at Max as he sat on the floor chewing on a small cardboard box.

"He'll bite off a piece and choke on it," Amy said, letting Jason know that he wasn't being a very good nanny. Lifting her heavy satin skirt, she strode out of the room, leaving Jason to wonder what he had done wrong.

"Women," Jason said to Max, who looked up and gave him a grin that showed all four of his teeth.

Thirty minutes later David arrived with a flat velvet box, a dozen white roses, and Jason's limo. "I knew what the dress looked like," David was saying, "but then everyone everywhere knew what the dress looked like, and, well, Dad and I thought pearls might look nice with it. They aren't real, but they look good."

With that, he opened the box and revealed a six-strand choker with a clasp of carved jade surrounded by diamonds. And Jason knew very well that the pearls and the diamonds were quite real. And, he had no doubt what David had paid for them.

"I've never seen anything so beautiful," Amy gasped.

"They're nothing compared to you," David answered, and Jason had to repress a groan.

But maybe he didn't do well at repressing it, because Amy said, "Don't mind him. He's been like that since he got back. I think he believes I should wear a straw hat and calico."

"It's his image of Abernathy," David answered, speaking about Jason as though he weren't standing there and glaring at the two of them.

"And we should be attending a hayride, not a ball," Amy said, laughing.

David held out his arm as though they were square-dancing and Amy took it. "Now claim your partner and do the Strutter's Walk," he said, sounding like a square dance caller.

"Yee haw!" Amy kicked the back of her skirt out of the way as she followed David around the room.

"All right, that's enough," Jason said, grimacing at

the two of them. "You've had your fun, now get out of here."

"We should go, David," Amy said. "I'll probably fall asleep by nine o'clock."

"Not while *I'm* with you, you won't," David said mischievously as he leered down the front of her gown.

"The only thing you're going to get there is dinner."

"I'm a hungry man," David answered, making Amy giggle.

"I think that 'man' is the key word here," Jason said ominously. "You need to remember that Amy is a mother and that she needs—"

"You are not my father," Amy snapped, "and I don't need to be told—"

"I'm ready, how about you?" David said loudly. "And the limo is waiting. Shall we go?"

Once they were in the car and Amy was staring out the window, David said, "What was that all about?"

"What was what about?"

David gave her a look that told her she knew exactly what he was talking about.

"I don't know. Mr. Wilding and I have gotten along beautifully, but ever since the hairdressers arrived this morning, he's been insufferable. He stomped around like a bear and made the whole staff, who were so nice to me, run and hide in the kitchen. Charles says the most devastating things about him, and—"

"Like what? What does Charles say?"

"That Mr. Wilding once walked past a cow and immediately turned it into frozen steaks. But he also says that Mr. Wilding can boil a kettle of water by looking at it. And, oh, other things. I don't understand why Mr. Wilding's been so nice these last days, but today he's so awful. If the people who came today are gay, shouldn't Mr. Wilding be nice to them since he's gay too?"

"It doesn't always work that way," David said, but he could hardly speak because of the effort it took not to laugh. "Ah, what else did Charles have to say?"

Amy looked at David, blinking for a moment. "Oh, you mean, like that Mr. Wilding doesn't sweat, doesn't excrete anything, if you know what I mean." She turned away for a moment to hide her red face. "That Charles really does have a wicked tongue."

David was about to burst with laughter. "And what about women? Surely Charles must have said something about Jason's women."

"You mean his men, don't you?"

"Yeah, sure. Whatever. What did Charles say?"

"Marble goddesses. Charles said that if a woman, ah, burped around him, Mr. Wilding would die of apoplexy. But, David, that's not true. Last night Mr. Wilding helped me get rid of a migraine. He stayed with me for a very long time, rubbing my temples until I fell asleep."

"He did what? I think you should tell me everything."

When Amy finished, David was looking at her in astonishment. "I've never heard of Jason doing anything like that. He's . . ."

"He's a very unusual man, is what he is," Amy said, "and I can't figure him out at all. I just trust Max's judgment and Max adores him. And I think Mr. Wilding adores Max too."

CHAPTER THIRTEEN

"YOU REALLY ARE THE MOST WICKED MAN," AMY SAID, laughing. They were in Jason's damaged car, driving back to the old, drafty place they called home. "I can't believe you managed to get a date *and* tickets to an event like that on such short notice. And *what* a date! Although I can't say that she seemed to like you very much."

"Parker? I mean Miss Parker? She likes me fine. And I got a date because I'm a damned good-looking guy, in case you haven't noticed."

"Mmm. Well, you're passable, when you aren't scowling, that is. So tell me *everything*."

"My hair is natural, my teeth are all mine—"

"No, idiot," she said, laughing more. "Tell me about Miss Parker. Whatever did you say to make her laugh like that?"

"Laugh? I don't remember her laughing," Jason said seriously.

"She is a bit solemn, isn't she? But you danced with her and she laughed. I heard her. I *saw* her and it was a real belly laugh."

He gave a one-sided grin. "Jealous, are you?"

"So help me, if you don't tell me, I'll . . ."

"You'll what?"

"Tell Charles to stop sending food over and I'll cook for you."

"You are a cruel woman. Okay, I'll tell you, but all I did was ask her if she was one of those women who falls in love with her boss." When Amy looked at him in puzzlement, he continued. "You know how some women pine away for their handsome, rich, powerful boss, so they never marry, never have a family of their own?"

"I've seen that in movies but never in real life," Amy said. "But I don't understand. Who is the owner of Baby Heaven?"

"Some guy I know."

"Ahhh, I see."

"See what?"

"That you're not going to tell me. Is her boss gorgeous?"

"Makes that Gibson guy look like a troll."

"Somehow, I doubt that. But, anyway, Miss Parker found the idea of being in love with her boss hilarious?"

Jason frowned. "Actually, she did."

"So why does that bother you?"

"Who said it bothers me?"

Amy threw up her hands in helplessness. "I can't imagine why I thought it bothered you. But then maybe it was just because when she laughed and walked off the dance floor, you stood there for a full two minutes glaring at her back. I was afraid her hair was going to catch on fire."

"And well it should!" Jason snapped. "Her boss has been good to her, paid her well for years."

"Oh."

"What is that supposed to mean?"

"Nothing. Just that money is no substitute for personal feeling."

"Maybe he didn't want personal feeling; maybe he just wanted a competent assistant!"

"What are you getting so angry about? How long did she work for him?"

"Several years. And what do you mean, '*did*' work for him? She still does as far as I know."

"Well, it won't be for long."

"And what does that mean?" he asked as he swung into the driveway and parked beside Mildred's Oldsmobile. He knew he was being irrational and short-tempered, but he couldn't help it. The evening hadn't gone as he'd hoped. Now that the ball was over, he didn't know what he'd been hoping for, but maybe he'd wanted, even expected, Amy to . . . What? he asked himself. Declare undying love for him?

Over the course of the evening he'd tried to keep his attention on Parker, and the others at the party, but he'd only had eyes for Amy. But she had seemed oblivious. But David had noticed.

"What were you and David arguing about?" Amy asked as he helped her out of the car, taking care that her satin dress didn't touch the gravel of the drive. She'd looked divine tonight. Pearls and white satin suited her. He gave a little smile at her back as he thought of the engagement ring burning a hole in his pocket. Maybe tonight he'd give it to her.

Inside the house, Mildred was holding a fretful Max, and when the baby saw Amy, he leaped into her arms, and for a while the two of them held on to each other as though they'd been separated for years.

"So how did it go?" Mildred whispered as she and Jason stood by the front door.

"All right," Jason answered. "Nothing special." He wasn't going to tell the town gossip anything.

"If nothing unusual happened, how come *you're* bringing Amy home when she left with your brother?"

"Sssh," Jason warned. "Amy thinks David and I are cousins."

Mildred turned her head sideways to look up at him. The weight of her hair moved to one side, and for a moment Jason thought she must have astonishingly strong neck muscles to hold something like that up.

"Have you thought about what Amy's going to say when she's told that you've played her for a fool?"

"It's not quite like that," Jason said stiffly.

"Oh? You don't think buying a baby store, then telling her all that furniture cost two hundred and fifty dollars isn't assuming she's an idiot?"

"She believed it, and that's all that counts."

Amy had taken Max into his bedroom, so he and Mildred were alone in the room. "Look, I'm planning to tell her tomorrow."

Mildred gave a low whistle. "Merry Christmas, Amy."

"Don't you think you should go home?"

"I think *you* should go home," Mildred retorted. "I think Amy should be given a fair chance at a man and not be involved in this sick game you and David are playing."

"Sick?" he asked, one eyebrow raised. "Isn't that a bit strong?"

"So, Jason, how are the men in your life?"

At that, he opened the front door. "Thanks for taking care of Max."

Mildred gave such a great sigh that Jason almost thought he saw the curtains by the door move, but the older woman's hair stayed perfectly in place. "Don't say I didn't warn you."

"I consider myself warned." The second he closed the door, Amy stuck her head around the bedroom door.

"Clear?" she whispered.

"Yes," Jason answered, grinning. "You can come out now."

She was wearing her old bathrobe, and Jason thought of the new one wrapped and placed under the tree. "How's Max?"

"Asleep and snoring. He was exhausted, poor baby."

"I know how he feels," Jason said.

"Oh," Amy said flatly. "You want to go to bed?"

He couldn't help teasing her as he yawned. "Yeah. I'm bushed." He pulled the tie to his tux open and gave a greater yawn.

"Me too," she said, but she didn't sound tired.

"On the other hand," Jason said slowly, "we could build a fire—if we can get the damper open—make some popcorn and you can tell me what you enjoyed most about the evening."

"You fire. Me pop," she said before she hurried off to the kitchen.

In record time a blazing—if smoky—fire was going and Amy and Jason were in front of it, a huge tub of buttered popcorn and glasses of ice water between them.

"So what were you and David fighting about?" Amy asked.

Jason groaned. "Not that again. What did you think of that blonde's dress?"

"I think she'll be a good mother."

Jason looked at her in consternation.

"With a set like that she'll be able to produce a *lot* of milk," Amy said, deadpan, making Jason smile.

"All plastic."

"And how would you know?" she asked.

"I danced with her, remember?"

Laughing, Amy said, "So what made David leave early so that you ended up taking me home? And don't you *dare* tell me it was an emergency at the hospital."

"Difference of opinion," Jason said tightly.

For a moment Amy stared at the fire. "All night, I felt as though all of you knew something that I didn't," she said quietly.

"It's Christmas and we all have secrets."

"Right. Stupid little Amy can't be told."

"What are you talking about?"

"Oh, nothing. What were you and my mother-in-law whispering about?"

"Are you going paranoid on me?" Jason asked, trying to distract her. "Did you have a good time?"

"Yes," she said hesitantly.

"But?" he asked as he ate a mouthful of popcorn.

"Something was missing tonight."

"And what could have been missing? You were the most beautiful woman there."

"You're sweet. No, it was something else. It was . . .

Well, for one thing, there was the woman in the rest room."

"What woman? She say something catty to you?"

"No, actually, she talked about you."

Jason took a while before speaking. "Does she know me?"

"Would it be a crime if she did?"

"Depends on what she knows. What did she say?"

"That you'd break my heart."

"Ah," Jason said flatly. When he said no more, Amy looked at him in the firelight.

"Do you often break women's hearts?" she added softly.

"Every day of the week. Twice on Sunday."

Amy didn't laugh. "What's going on?"

"What do you mean, 'what's going on'?"

Suddenly, Amy put her face in her hands and began to cry. "Stop it! Just stop it! I *know* something is going on, but no one will let me in on the joke. Sometimes I think *I* am the joke."

"The woman in the rest room upset you, didn't she?"

At that, Amy got off the floor and started toward the bedroom. "I'm going to bed," she said, and her voice was without emotion.

Jason caught her before she reached the door, his hand closing about her arm. "Why are you angry with me?"

"Because you're part of it. Tonight . . . Oh, you'd never understand."

"Try me."

"It was all so beautiful. I know it's a cliché, but I felt like Cinderella. Poor little Amy Thompkins with her leaky house at a real live ball. Everyone looked so beautiful. And the jewels! If they'd lit one candle in the middle of the room, the sparkle of the diamonds would have illuminated the whole place. It was all like a dream, a fantasy."

Gently, Jason led her back to the living room to sit on the sofa. "But what was wrong?"

"I felt a sense of . . ." Looking up at him, there were tears in her eyes. "I felt a sense of doom. That's it. I feel that something awful is about to happen and I have no way to stop it. Everything has been so wonderful lately and my mother warned me to be suspicious of good things. She said we were put on this earth to suffer and if something good happened, it was the work of the devil."

"That isn't always right," Jason said softly, then he lifted her hand and kissed her fingers one by one.

"What are you doing?" she asked suspiciously.

"Making love to you."

Angrily, she jerked her hands from his and tried to get up, but he blocked her way.

"Would you mind?!" she said, her voice full of steel.

"Yes, actually I do mind." Again he lifted her hand and began to kiss the back of it.

"I changed Max's dirty diaper with that hand and didn't wash," she said to the top of his head.

"You know how much I love the kid," he said, but didn't stop kissing. In spite of herself, Amy smiled; then she put both hands on his shoulders and pushed. When he was upright she glared into his eyes. "You're gay, remember?"

"Actually, I'm not. David lied." Jason went back to kissing her hand; Amy pushed him away, and her expression said it all.

"All right," he said, leaning back against the old sofa. "David wanted me to stay with you and baby-sit Max so he could take you out. He's in love with you."

When Amy said nothing, he turned to look at her. She had the oddest expression on her face. "Go on," she said.

"David didn't want any hanky-panky between us, so he told you I was gay."

"I see. Is that it?"

"More or less," he answered, then bent down to get his glass of ice water and drank deeply.

"So you two have been fighting over me?" she asked softly.

Jason swallowed. "Well, actually . . . Well, yes, we have. I was just supposed to keep Ian Newsome away, but I . . ."

"You what?"

"I fell in love with you and Max," he said, but he

stared at the fire, not at her. He'd never before told a woman he loved her. He had a feeling that most of the women he'd known in New York would have responded by getting a calculator and figuring their cut of his wealth. When Amy said nothing, he turned to look at her. Her oval face was pale and she was staring straight ahead.

"What else have you lied to me about?" she asked softly.

"Nothing of any consequence," he said quickly, his breath held. If she said she loved him now, when she had no idea of his wealth, he'd know forever after that she loved him for himself. Suddenly he knew his whole life could change in this moment and if he'd ever tried to sell anything, he'd better sell himself now.

"I love you, Amy. I love you and Max, and I want you to marry me. That's what David's so angry about. He wanted you for himself, so he conned me into staying with you, but Max . . . Max was a blessing from the beginning. He liked me, and you know how I adore him, and I want—"

"Oh, shut up and kiss me," Amy said, and when Jason turned and saw that one side of her mouth was turned up into a smile, he felt as though he'd been freed from slavery.

Quickly, he swooped Amy into his arms and carried her into her bedroom. He didn't need to be told that she'd want to be where she could hear her son. Our son, Jason thought. His wife; his son; his family.

"I love you, Amy," he said as he nuzzled her ear. "I love the way you make me feel. I love how you need me."

There was something about what he was saying that bothered Amy, but she couldn't pinpoint what it was, for at the moment she couldn't think much of anything. He was kissing her neck, sliding the gown from her shoulders.

It had been so very, very long since she'd been touched by a man. And she'd die before she said anything to further sully her late husband's memory, but, at the end, Billy was drunk most nights. But Jason was sober and clean and, oh, so beautiful. His long-fingered hands were moving over her body in a way she'd only dreamed of. Inch by inch he removed her robe, then her old gown, kissing as he removed her clothes. His warm hands ran up the sides of her breasts. How long it had been since her breasts had been anything but utilitarian!

"That's nice," she said, closing her eyes, letting sensation overtake her. His hands moved between her thighs, kissing and caressing.

"I like this," she said dreamily. "Does it have a name?"

"Foreplay," he said, smiling into her eyes. "Like it?"

"Oh, yes. May I have some more please?"

"I'll give you all I have," he said as he kissed her breasts.

When he entered her, Amy gasped, because, for the first time ever, she was ready for lovemaking.

"Oh, my goodness but that is nice," she said, and the way she said it made Jason laugh as he rolled onto his back and pulled her on top of him.

"Now *you* do the work."

Obviously this was a novel experience to Amy, and Jason was pleased by her expression. "A virgin mother," he murmured, his hands on her hips, guiding her.

"Don't ever stop," Amy murmured as her hips moved up and down. When she exploded against him, she collapsed, limp and sated.

"Yes," was all she could say, and feeling as secure as Max must feel in her arms, she snuggled onto his chest and let him hold her. Jason pulled the sheet over both of them, and they fell asleep in each other's arms.

A loud thud awoke Amy, and she sat bolt upright, immediately afraid that Max had fallen, but when she checked on him she saw that her son was fast asleep in his new crib. His knees were tucked up under him, his well-padded rear end stuck into the air, his head was turned toward her, drool running down the side of his mouth.

Walking into the nursery, she went to her baby, gently blotted his mouth, tucked the quilt about him, then returned to her room to fetch her nightgown. It was flung over the end of the bed, and she was careful not to wake Jason as she put it on. But she needn't have worried, for both her men were in what she called "coma sleep"—you could perform major surgery and they'd not know it.

Smiling, Amy bent and kissed Jason's forehead, then put on her old robe and went into the living room. For a moment she was disoriented, as the Christmas lights were on and the pile of gifts was as tall as the sofa.

"Santa Claus," she read as she looked at tag after tag on the white packages.

"David," she whispered, then felt a bit guilty at the way she'd treated him at the ball. She went into the kitchen to fix herself a cup of tea. She was wide awake, and now, in the middle of the night, when Max was asleep, was the only time she had to think. As the water boiled and she got out a cup and a tea bag, she thought about the ball. She was sure that every other woman in the world would have loved the ball, but Amy had been bored by it. Sure, it was lovely and everyone had looked splendid, but all she'd wanted to do was go home to Jason and Max. There she was wearing a Dior gown and pearls—fake but who could tell?—and all she really wanted was to be home in her old bathrobe with her son and her gay boarder.

Everyone at the ball knew everyone else, and of course everyone knew Dr. David, so Amy had had time to sit alone at a table with a nonalcoholic drink and think—and remember. In all her life she didn't think she'd had a happier, more secure feeling than she'd had in the last few days. Every minute had been an adventure. Since David had entered her house with his gorgeous gay cousin, Amy's life had been turned upside down. Mr. Wilding—or Jason, as she called him to herself—seemed to have a magic wand he could wave to fix anything. It wouldn't surprise her to wake up one morning and find that the roof over the dining room had been repaired.

And, now, tonight, she thought with a sigh. Tonight he'd said he loved her, told her he wasn't gay, said . . . Oh, she couldn't remember all she'd heard or felt tonight. All she knew was that this ball had changed her life.

When the kettle boiled, she poured hot water over the tea bag, liberally added milk, then went into the living room to sit and look at the Christmas tree. Now she could smile when she remembered how she'd felt tonight when she'd looked up to see Jason walk in with that gorgeous redhead on his arm. At that moment if someone had handed Amy a shotgun, she could have blown a hole through Miss Cherry Parker's tiny never-had-a-baby waistline. Better yet, Amy thought, she'd have liked to fire a cannon and hit both of them.

When Jason and that woman sat down at the table with Amy and David, she wasn't in the least surprised.

What had surprised Amy was the instant animosity that came from mild-mannered David. Immediately, the two men had said things to each other under their breath, things Amy couldn't hear.

Taking a deep breath, Amy had leaned toward the tall, divinely beautiful Miss Parker and said, "What will happen to Baby Heaven now?"

The woman was closer to Jason, so maybe she could hear what the two men were saying. And maybe the fact that she could hear and Amy couldn't was why Amy decided to engage her in conversation.

"Baby Heaven?" the woman said, reluctantly pulling away from where Jason and David were engaged in furious conversation.

"Where you work," Amy said loudly. "That *is* where I saw you, isn't it?"

"Oh, yes, of course."

The two men stopped arguing for a moment, and Miss Parker turned to Amy. "What was it you asked me?"

Amy cleared her throat. "What will happen to Baby Heaven now that all the merchandise is sold? Will you have a job?"

"Oh, yes." The woman kept looking at the two men to see if they were going to start arguing again.

"So you *will* have a job," Amy said loudly, demanding the woman take her attention away from the men.

"Job? Oh, yes. The owner has many businesses. Baby Heaven is just one of them." She looked back at the men, who'd started again.

"I see," Amy said even louder. "Where will you work? Abernathy or somewhere else?"

"New York," the woman said over her shoulder, her eyes and ears on the men.

"Ah, so you're slumming. I thought so. You have the look of a big city about you. Ever seen a tractor, Miss Parker?"

The woman turned and gave her full attention to Amy. "Mrs. Thompkins, I grew up on a farm in Iowa. I was driving a harvester at twelve years old because I was nearly six feet tall even then and I could reach the pedals. By the time I was sixteen I was cooking daily for twenty-three ravenous farmhands. So tell me, Mrs. Thompkins, how many calves have *you* delivered?"

Amy gave the woman a weak smile and excused herself to go to the rest room. So much for her attempt at being catty. "Better stick to what I do best," she said to herself, then wished with all her might that she knew what that was.

It was in the rest room that she had the strangest encounter. A woman with long dark hair, expertly pulled back into a chignon, wearing a slinky red satin dress, was putting on lipstick to match her dress. When she saw Amy, she nearly jumped, and for a moment Amy thought she was supposed to know the woman. It's the dress, she told herself. Not too many Diors in Kentucky, but when Amy left the stall, the woman was still there and she made no pretense that she was doing anything except waiting for Amy. And, for some reason, Amy wanted to bolt. She had her hand on the door before the woman spoke.

"So, you're with Jason Wilding."

Amy took a breath and straightened her spine before turning back to the woman. "Not really. I'm with Dr. David, his cousin. Miss Parker is with Jason." And Amy had no doubt that Miss Parker could handle anything this woman was about to dish out.

"Oh? That's not what I saw and heard," the woman said. "From what I could hear David and Jason were fighting over *you.*"

"What did they say?" Amy said before she thought to control her tongue.

"Are both those men in love with you?" the woman asked as she looked Amy up and down.

At that Amy relaxed, smiled, and decided to wash her hands. "Oh, yes," she said. "They want to fight a duel over me. Pistols at dawn. Or maybe they'll use swords."

The woman turned back to the mirror. "More like scalpels and cell phones."

Amy laughed and decided the woman wasn't predatory, as she'd first thought. "How about fax machines versus color copiers?"

"Or your Internet dialer against mine," the woman

said, smiling at Amy in the mirror; then she paused for a moment. "That's some dress you're wearing. Buy it around here?"

"Hardly. I won it in a contest. It's a Dior from a shop in New York."

"Ah, I see. A contest."

Again Amy wanted to leave, but somehow, she couldn't. "Do you know Mr. Wilding?" she asked tentatively.

"Dr. David?"

Amy had a feeling the woman was teasing her. "Jason."

"Ah, *that* Mr. Wilding. I've met him. How do you know him?"

"He's living with me," Amy said brightly, then smiled smugly at the woman's look of shock. But she soon recovered.

"Living with him? Not married to him?"

Amy laughed. "You don't know him very well, do you?" She'd love to tell the woman Jason was gay, but, on the other hand, let her think Amy had reeled in a hunk like Jason. The woman didn't answer Amy's question.

"I think I should ask how well *you* know him. And what's he doing at a dud of a thing like this?"

That snobby question made Amy's lips tighten. "Jason Wilding is here because he *likes* it here, because this state makes him happy."

At that, the woman put away her lipstick and looked at Amy in amusement. "I don't know what's going on, but a man like Jason Wilding doesn't attend some cheap affair in Nowhere, Kentucky, because it makes him *happy.* Jason Wilding only does things because they earn him more money. He's the only man on this planet who actually does have a heart of gold."

"I don't know what you're talking about," Amy said, confused. "Jason, Mr. Wilding, is staying with us, my son and me, that is, because he has nowhere else to stay and no one to spend Christmas with."

At that the woman laughed. "My sister used to be just where you are now. She too felt sorry for Jason Wilding and she took him in, and he repaid her by— Oh. I can see you're not going to believe anything I say, so maybe I'll just send you something."

"No, thank you," Amy said as she put her nose in the air. But the woman wasn't listening as she withdrew a tiny cell phone from her evening bag and began to dial.

Amy didn't wait to hear half of the conversation but rushed back to the table with the intention of telling either Jason or David about the woman, but when she got there, the table was empty.

"What did I expect?" she said aloud. "That they'd all be worried about why I'd taken so long?"

"*I* was worried and I don't even know you," said a handsome man standing about six inches away from her. "What a beautiful . . . necklace," he said, but he wasn't looking at Amy's pearl necklace; he was looking down her cleavage. "Are they real?"

"As real as mother's milk," she said, smiling up at him, and he laughed.

"Would you like to dance? Or would your escort die from the absence of your company?"

"Yes, her escort would die," came Jason's voice over the top of her head, and to Amy's delight she looked from one handsome, scowling face to another.

"On the count of three, draw your cell phones and *dial!*" she said.

The man looked at her in puzzlement, but Jason clamped down on her upper arm and pulled her to the dance floor.

"Where in the world were you? Is Max all right?"

"Shouldn't I ask you that, since I left him with you?"

"Mildred has him," Jason said tightly. "Who was that man and what was he saying to you?"

"That I have a nice set of pearls," she said, glancing down at her cleavage.

"Have you been drinking?"

"No, I've had two encounters with female piranhas though, so maybe I should have a drink. But then, I survived both attacks and I still have my skin."

"Amy . . ." Jason said in a warning voice. "What is going on?"

"Other than the fact that my date seems to have

dumped me? And my gay nanny has turned my child
over to someone else so he can attend a ball with a
woman so gorgeous she puts tulips to shame? And a
woman in the rest room—"

"Tulips? Why tulips?"

"I like them," Amy said, sighing. Why couldn't he
stay to the point? "Why are you here?"

"Just looking out for things." He was holding her in
his arms, and she had to admit that it felt wonderful.

"How did you get tickets to this event?" she murmured as her head touched his shoulder and stayed
there.

"Long story," he murmured back, his cheek against
the top of her head, but he didn't elaborate.

After that they danced together to one old song after
another. No rock and roll that would separate partners
was played at the Bellringers' Ball. When they at last
returned to the table, they found a note from David
saying he'd taken Miss Parker home and would Jason
please escort Amy? It was a tense note and Amy felt
guilty at ignoring her date, but then Jason's big hand
closed around hers and he said, "Let's go home, shall
we?" and the way he said "home" almost made Amy
cry.

So now she was sitting on the sofa, staring at the
Christmas tree lights, and wondering whether it was
Jason or David who'd played Santa and put all the
white wrapped gifts under the tree.

It was cool in the room, so she snuggled her feet under her, her hands wrapped around the still-warm mug. Her tenant wasn't gay, and they'd made love, and this morning was her son's first Christmas. Standing, she took a deep breath, stretched, and thought she might just go back to bed and wake Jason up and . . . Well . . .

Smiling, she started back to the bedroom, but paused because she saw a fat brown envelope on the floor by the front door. The heavy oak door had an old-fashioned brass mail slot in it, and someone had pushed the thick envelope halfway through it. Must be the thump I heard, Amy thought, then wondered who would drop a package through a door slot at two o'clock in the morning on Christmas Day.

Idly, she picked up the envelope, yawned, started to put it on the table with the broken leg that stood by the door, but curiosity got the better of her. "Probably just a particularly aggressive advertiser," she murmured as she opened the top of the envelope.

When she first pulled the papers from the envelope, she didn't know what she was seeing. They seemed to be photocopies of newspaper articles. "Entrepreneur Closes New Deal," "Wilding Buys Everything!" were some of the headlines.

"Wilding?" she said aloud, then thought of David. But what had David done to engender articles written about him? Had he saved so very many lives? By the fourth page she'd flipped, the name "Jason" began to jump out at her.

Taking the package to the kitchen, she put the kettle back on to make herself another cup of tea to sip while she read. But the kettle boiled dry, and Amy turned off the stove while she continued reading.

It was four A.M. when she finished, and she wasn't surprised when she looked up to see Jason standing in the doorway wearing only the trousers to his tux.

"Come back to bed," he said seductively, but Amy didn't move. "What's wrong?" he asked, but he didn't seem too concerned.

"You're very rich, aren't you?" she asked softly.

Jason had been heading toward the teakettle, but he paused to look at the articles spread out on the table. They were all faxes, so someone had called and had this information faxed to Abernathy.

"Yes," he said as he picked up the kettle, then filled it and put it back on the stove. When he turned back to Amy, she was wearing an expression he'd never seen before.

"Look Amy, about last night—"

She interrupted him. "Last night wasn't important. Sex isn't important, but the lies that led up to the sex are *very* important."

"I never meant to lie," he said softly. "It started out quite innocent but . . ."

"Go on," she said. "I'd like to hear this. I was told

you were gay and that turned out to be a lie, but I forgave that. Of course, I admit that it was in my own selfish interests to forgive that. I was also told that you desperately needed a home over Christmas, and that seems to have been a lie too. According to what I've just read, that last one was a very *big* lie. And you certainly do date some smashing-looking women."

"Amy—" He reached out to touch her, but she lifted her palms to let him know he was to stay away.

Jason turned off the kettle, then sat down across from her. "Okay, so I lied. But when I told you I loved you, that wasn't a lie." He took a deep breath.

"Now I guess I'm to fall into your arms and we live happily ever after."

"That would be the ending I have in mind," he said with a one-sided smile.

Amy, however, didn't smile. "Who is Miss Parker?"

"My secretary."

"Oh, I see. And I guess she arranged the two-hundred-and-fifty-dollar nursery set."

"Yes," Jason said, his eyes burning into her.

But Amy kept looking at the articles. "And the contest for the dress? Was it arranged by her for you?"

"Yes."

"My, my, but you've been busy. Santa Claus should work as hard as you."

"Look, Amy, it started as something I was doing to help my brother, and—"

Her head came up. "Brother? David? Ah, yes, of course. How stupid of me. Did you two have a couple of great laughs at the impoverished widow and her half-orphaned child?"

"No. Amy, believe me, it hasn't been like that. I think you should listen to my explanation."

She leaned back in the chair, her arms folded across her chest. "Okay, so tell me."

Jason had earned a lot of money in his life because he just didn't care about the outcome of the deal. If he won, good, if he lost that was okay too. It was the game that he enjoyed. But now he very much cared about the outcome of this "meeting."

"My brother, David, believed he was in love with you. I say believed because last night I set him straight on that one. Anyway, he said Max was such a tyrant that—"

"Max? A tyrant?"

"Well, I mean, I didn't know how old Max was until after I accepted David's bet so—"

"Bet? You made a *wager* over me?" Her voice was rising. "You mean like a man betting the plantation on the turn of a card?"

"No, not at all," he said, but his eyes didn't meet hers. "Please, Amy, let me explain."

She waved her hand then leaned back against the chair.

"David wanted me to be Max's nanny, so to speak,

so he could have some time alone with you. He bet me that I couldn't handle the job. That's all it was. And he told you I was gay so you'd let me stay here. It was that simple."

"I see. And where does the nursery furniture and the dress come into this farce?"

"You needed the things, so I, uh, I arranged for them. . . ." He trailed off at the look in her eyes.

"I see," she said again, but her facial muscles were rigid and her eyes cold.

"No, Amy, I don't think you do see. I have fallen in love with you."

"Sure you have. It says in here that you give quite a bit to charity. How gratifying it must have been to make a donation directly to the poor."

"That isn't the way it was. Well, maybe it was that way in the beginning, but it changed. I've come to love both you and Max."

"And what do you plan to do with us now?"

Jason looked bewildered. "I want to marry you."

"Of course. What was I thinking? You didn't by any chance buy me a great big diamond ring, did you?"

Based on her tone of voice, Jason started to lie but decided against it. "Yes," he said simply. "A huge diamond."

"That makes sense. That fits. I guess you've planned our futures too, haven't you?"

Jason didn't answer, just looked at her across a table covered with reprints of everything that had ever been published about him. His mind was racing as he tried to figure out who had sent these to her, but he had a suspicion. At the ball he'd seen the sister of a woman he used to date. After going out for a few weeks they had parted ways amicably. Then she had approached him several months later and wanted to begin things again. When he'd turned her down, as gently as he could, she'd flown into a rage and sworn she'd get even with him. So now, Jason wondered if the sister he'd seen last night across the room, her eyes staring at him coldly, had had these pages faxed here and had made sure Amy received them.

When Jason didn't reply to Amy's question, she continued. "Let me guess. You plan to buy Max and me a huge house within commuting distance of New York City and you plan to visit us on weekends. Maybe you'd helicopter in, right? And you'd open accounts for us everywhere so I could buy Dior any time I wanted. And Max could have all the finest toys and clothes. Nothing but the best for *your* family, right?"

For the life of him Jason could see nothing wrong with the picture she was painting.

Slowly Amy began to smile. "Sounds good to me," she said at last. "How about some tea to celebrate?"

"Yes. Please. I'd like that."

Slowly, Amy got up from the table, with her back to him, filled the kettle, and opened a few tins as she looked for the tea bags.

But Jason was so relieved he didn't pay any attention to what she was doing. "How about a summer home in Vermont?" he was saying. "We'll get some place with stone walls and acres of . . . of fruit trees."

"Sounds great," Amy said, her voice flat. But she knew he wasn't listening to her. He was in his own little daydream of a happy, idyllic life in which he had a loving wife and child to come home to. Whenever he could find the time, that is.

"Here you are," she said, smiling.

Jason tried to take her hand and kiss it, but she pulled away to sit down at the opposite side of the table.

"Did you see the movie *Pretty Woman*?"

"Can't say as I did." He was smiling at her sweetly.

"It's about a businessman, a billionaire, who falls in love with a prostitute."

"Amy, if you're implying that I think of you as a—"

"No, let me finish. The movie was a great success, and everyone I know loved it, but—"

"You didn't."

"No, I did, but I was worried about what happened later. What would happen five years down the road when they had an argument and he threw it in her face that she'd turned a trick or two? And what about his education versus hers? His money against her lack of it?"

"Go on," Jason said cautiously. "What's your point?"

"Drink your tea before it gets cold. You and I are like the couple in that movie. You've done everything, proven everything to yourself."

"I hardly think—"

"No, it's true. You have."

"Amy, you're a lovely woman, and—"

"And women don't need to prove anything, is that right?"

"I didn't mean that."

"Look," she said, leaning toward him. "If I left here with you, you'd swallow me up like the Richard Gere character would have swallowed the young woman played by Julia Roberts."

"What?" Jason asked, rubbing his hand over his eyes. Now that the crisis had passed, he found that he was quite sleepy. Why did women always want to discuss things in the middle of the night? "Could we talk about this in the morning?"

Amy didn't seem to hear him. "Why do you think I've refused to take charity?" she asked. "Everyone knows me as the drunk's widow, but I needed to prove that I was worth more than that. I don't want Max known as the drunk's kid." She leaned toward him. "And I most certainly don't want him known as the billionaire's kid."

"I'm not a billionaire." Jason could barely keep his eyes open. The clock over the stove said five A.M. "Amy, sweetheart," he said. "Let's discuss this in the morning." Rising, he took her hand and led her back to the bedroom, where he removed her robe then held the covers back from the bed. When she was under the covers, he slipped in beside her and snuggled her in his arms. "Tomorrow we'll go over all of this, I promise. I'll explain everything, and we can talk about all the movies you want. But right now I—" He broke off to give a jaw cracking yawn. "Now I . . . love you . . ." He was asleep.

Beside him, Amy took a deep breath. "I love you too," she whispered. "At least I think I do, but right now I have an obligation that is more important than my love for a man. I'm Max's mother, and I have to think of him first before my own needs."

But there was no reply from Jason.

When Amy saw that he was asleep, she angrily threw back the covers and stood, glaring down at him. "It takes more than a private helicopter to be a father," she said quietly, then turned on her heel and went to the hall closet, where she pulled out an old duffel bag; then, without realizing what she was doing, she began to throw clothes into it. "To be a father, Jason Wilding, you need to be a teacher as well as a money provider," she said under her breath. "And what would *you* teach him? To *buy* whatever he wants? To lie his way into a woman's heart? Would you teach him that he can do any devious, underhanded, sly thing he wants to a woman, then all he has to do is say 'I love you,' and those three words erase all the lies?" She leaned very close to his sleeping face. "Jason Wilding, I don't *like* you. I don't like the way you use your money to trick people, to connive behind their backs. You have treated me, Max, and, actually, this whole town with contempt."

The only reply she received was that he rolled to his other side and kept on sleeping.

Drawing back, she looked down at him, and suddenly, she was calm and she knew what she had to do. "Max and I aren't for sale. Unless the currency used is good deeds," she said as she almost smiled. "I'm going to leave now, but please don't look for me, because even if you find me, you still won't be able to buy me."

With that she turned away and went into her son's room.

CHAPTER FOURTEEN

ONE YEAR LATER

"Mr. Evans to see you, sir," Mrs. Hucknall said to Jason's back.

Jason didn't bother to turn around, but gave a nod as he continued staring out the floor-to-ceiling windows. Manhattan lay thirty stories below, the people and cars looking like toys. He didn't know why he still bothered hiring the private detectives. Twelve months ago his whole life revolved around the reports of the first one he'd hired. The reports were called in daily, and Jason took the calls wherever he was. But when the detective could find no trace of Mrs. Amy Thompkins and her baby son, Jason had fired the man and hired someone else.

In the last year he'd hired and fired more detectives than he could count. He'd tried everyone from sleazy guys whose ads promised to catch any cheating hus-

band to men retired from Scotland Yard. But no one
could find the single woman and her little boy.

"You have nothing to go on," he'd been told again
and again—and it was true. First of all, there were no
photos of Amy past the age of twelve. Mildred, her
mother-in-law, had taken pictures of her grandson, but
Amy wasn't in them. The people in Amy's hometown
said that the house Amy had grown up in burned down
the week after Amy's mother's death, so maybe all the
pictures of her had been destroyed then. Maddeningly,
Amy seemed to have been absent every time photos
were taken for the high school yearbook.

The detectives said that all she had to do was go
to some two-bit lawyer in some one-horse town and
change her name. The lawyer would run the announce-
ment in some local rag sheet and, "Not even God would
read it," one detective said. And with a new name, Amy
could be anywhere. America was full of single women
with kids and no fathers.

One by one, Jason fired each man; the truth was too
painful to hear. So now he'd spent a whole year paying
people to look for one woman and one child and they'd
come up with nothing.

Jason heard the current detective enter the room, but
he didn't bother to turn around. It wasn't until the man
cleared his throat that Jason whirled about. "What are
you doing here?" he snapped, for David stood there.

"Wait!" David said as Jason was about to press the

button that called his secretary into the office. "Please, five minutes; that's all I ask."

Jason moved his finger off the buzzer, but by his stance, he wasn't softening. "Five minutes, no more. Say it, then get out."

Instead of opening his mouth to speak, David thrust his hands in his trousers' pockets and walked about the room. "I always hate your offices," he said conversationally. "They're always so cold, all that glass and these pictures! Who chooses them for you?" When he looked back at his brother, Jason was scowling.

"Four minutes," Jason said.

"Want to see pictures of my wedding?"

Jason didn't answer, just glared at his brother. A year before on that horrible morning when Jason woke up to find Amy and Max gone, he and David had had a fight in which they'd nearly killed each other. David blamed Jason for everything, saying he drove Amy and Max out into the snow, with no means of support, no friends or family, no help of any kind.

And Jason blamed his brother for having started it all in the first place. But in spite of the argument, Jason had a search party looking for Amy within an hour of waking up. But by then the trail was already cold. A woman traveling alone with a baby was too common a sight and an unremarkable one; no one had noticed either of them.

It was after the disappearance that the real rift between the brothers came, because Parker took David's side. Jason's loyal secretary, a woman who had been Jason's right arm for years, was suddenly his enemy. For the first time since he'd known her, she'd stood against her employer and told him what she thought of him.

"No wonder she left you," Parker had said, quietly at first, but her voice came from deep within her and carried more volume than the loudest siren. "You have no heart, Jason Wilding. You look at people as goods to be bought and sold. You think that because you pay me a high salary, you can treat me as though I'm not human. You thought because you bought Amy's baby a roomful of furniture that she would fall down at your feet in everlasting gratitude. But the only thing men like you foster is greed. You made me want more and more money from you until I was beginning to despise myself.

"But I need my self-respect back, so I'm leaving your employment."

Nothing in the world could have stunned Jason more than Parker's defection. When he turned away, he expected never to hear from her again, but that was far from what actually happened, for three months later he received an invitation to the wedding of Dr. David Wilding and Miss Cherry Parker.

To Jason, still trying his best to find Amy and Max, the marriage seemed the ultimate betrayal. Now, he could hardly bear the sight of his brother. If David hadn't called him and made up that lie that their father was dying . . . If David hadn't thought he was in love with a widow with a baby . . . If Jason hadn't fallen for David's hard-luck story . . .

"What do you want?" Jason demanded, glaring at his brother.

"Family, that's all. Getting married, settling down, changes a man. I want you to come to Christmas dinner. Cherry's a fine cook."

"She has a nice kitchen to do it in," Jason said, remembering the bill he'd received for the addition of a fabulous kitchen to his father's house. And that was another thing: his chef had left him to try to start his own business in gourmet baby food. Jason had tried to be pleased when he heard that Charles wasn't doing very well, but instead he felt bad for his former cook. Charles's cocky arrogance didn't go over too well with bankers, and he'd had no luck in finding the funds to back his business.

"Is that still bothering you?" David snapped. "Damnation, but I'll pay you back for the bloody kitchen. I don't know how, but I'll do it."

Suddenly, David sat down on a chair across from Jason, who was standing rigid behind his desk. "What do you want from all of us? What do you want from *life?* Do you think that if you find Amy, she's going to come back to you and live inside your golden cage? She didn't want to be a prisoner, no matter how beautiful the surroundings. Can't you understand that? Can't you forgive her? Forgive *me?*"

Jason didn't move, but stood still as he stared at his brother. How could he explain that for a few short days he had been happy? Plain, old-fashioned *happy.* During his time with Amy and Max, it had given him pleasure to buy things for other people, to do things, to listen, to laugh. Amy had a way about her—

He had to cut himself off from thinking about her or he'd go crazy. There wasn't a day that went by that he didn't think about how old Max was now. He was walking by now, maybe even talking.

Or maybe he wasn't. For all he knew, Amy and Max were dead. There were some awful people out there in the world and—

"I can see that you won't give up," David said as he stood. "But then, that's what makes you strong. And makes you weak. Look, it's Christmas Eve and I need to fly home. I want you to come with me, and—"

"I have plans," Jason said, glaring at his brother. Tonight his apartment would be full of people, for tonight was the anniversary of the last time he'd seen Amy and Max. Tonight he was going to drink champagne until he was drunk, and tomorrow he was not going to wake up alone.

"All right, I tried," David said as he started for the door. "If you need us you know where we are."

He started to say more, but at the stony look on his brother's face, he shrugged, then walked to the door. But he paused with his hand on the knob. "I know you're still grieving for Amy and Max, but there are other people in this world. There are even other children." When Jason made no reply, David sighed and left the office.

Jason buzzed his secretary. "Call Harry Winston's and have them send me a selection of engagement rings."

"Engagement?" Mrs. Hucknall said.

"Yes!" he snapped, then punched the button to cut her off.

CHAPTER FIFTEEN

"OH, JASON, DARLING," DAWNE PURRED AS SHE RUBBED her perfectly toned body against his. "The party is perfect." Somehow, she made the word sound like "Purrrrr-fect." "I have never seen so many famous people in one room before."

Jason sat on the chair in silence as he sipped what had to be his fifth glass of champagne and looked at all the people. They were indeed famous and rich, he thought, as well as beautiful. The women had that glossy sheen that came from many hours spent in beauty salons the world over. Their skin and hair glowed with health and cosmetics that cost more than the resources of several small countries combined.

"What's wrong with you?" Dawne asked, a slight frown marring her perfect forehead, although Jason knew that it hadn't been perfect when she was born. It had been "lifted," as most of her had been lifted and augmented. She looked about twenty-seven, but Jason chuckled as he realized that it wouldn't surprise him to find out that Dawne was seventy-five years old.

"Why are you looking at me like that?" she asked. She was perched on the arm of his chair, her long, lean, well-muscled thigh within reaching distance.

"I was wondering how old you are."

Dawne almost choked on her drink, and he could see spots of anger growing on her perfectly made-up cheeks. "You're in a mood tonight, aren't you?" she said, her lips tight. "Why don't you get up and talk to your guests?"

Suddenly her face brightened, as though she wouldn't allow herself to get angry with him. "I know what would cheer you up. How about if I give you your Christmas gift now?"

"I have enough ties," he said.

"No, silly, it's not a tie; it's . . . ." Leaning over so her breasts were against his shoulder, she whispered her plans for seduction.

Drawing back, Jason gave her a small smile. "Don't you think I should stay out here with my guests?"

At that, he could see a look of hurt in her eyes. She got up and walked away, leaving him alone.

When she was gone, Jason didn't know whether to be glad or to feel even more alone than he usually did. Damn his brother, he thought yet again. He'd been doing fine until David showed up with his talk of marriage and a family. That visit, combined with its being Christmas Eve and the anniversary of Amy's disappearance, was about to unhinge him.

Jason had anticipated that tonight would be difficult, so he'd hired a well-known interior designer to put on a party in his apartment that would take his mind off his troubles. And Jason had to admit that the designer had done a bang-up job, as the party was exquisite. The decorations were magnificent, with crystals sparkling in candlelight in the designer's theme of silver and white.

The food was wonderful, each mouthful a delight. Or at least that's what Jason had been told; personally, he hadn't touched anything but the champagne.

So if everything in his life was wonderful, why was he so miserable? Sure he'd lost a woman he thought he loved, but didn't other people break up every day? And did they go into a decline that a year later still haunted them?

Jason knew that if he had any sense, he'd do what he had been advised by everyone from the detectives to his own brother and forget about finding one woman and a little boy. As one of the detectives had said, "If I had your money, I wouldn't be worried about any woman; I'd buy myself all of them." Jason had fired the man on the spot and had tried to clear the words from his head.

But now, looking at the glittering people in the glittering apartment, he remembered them. "Buy myself all of them," the man had said. And wasn't that what Amy had said, more or less? That Jason was trying to *buy* himself a family?

He signaled the waiter to refill his glass, then kept on staring at his guests. In the last year Jason had done everything he could to forget that last night with Amy. Twelve whole months of refusing to think about it, to remember it. Twelve long months of hanging on to his anger. If she'd just listened to him . . . If she had thought about his side of things . . . If she'd just been willing to wait until the morning to talk . . .

Jason drained the glass, then held it up for another refill. But tonight, in spite of the fact that he was in very different surroundings and the giant tree in the corner bore no resemblance to the one he and Amy had decorated, it was as though he were back with her.

Images came before him until he could hardly see the roomful of people. He remembered Amy laughing, Amy teasing, Amy's excitement at being able to buy her child some furniture.

The waiter started to fill Jason's glass again, but he waved him away; then Jason put his hand over his eyes for a moment. For the first time since Amy left he thought, Why didn't I listen?

His head came up, and he looked about him. No one was looking at him. No, they were all too busy looking at each other and enjoying Jason's food and drink to give a thought to their host, who was quietly sitting in a corner and going mad.

I am going mad, he thought. For one whole year he hadn't had a moment's peace. He'd tried to carry on a life, but he hadn't been able to. He'd dated women, beautiful women, and today he'd even thought that he'd ask this latest one, Dawne, to marry him. Maybe marriage was what he needed to make him forget. Maybe if he had a child of his own . . .

Breaking off, his breath caught in his throat. What was it David had said? There are "other children." In Jason's mind there was only one child: Max.

But he'd lost that child because he had—

Again Jason rubbed his hand over his eyes. Maybe it was all the alcohol he'd consumed; maybe it was the anniversary, but tonight he couldn't work up his usual anger at himself, at David, at the town of Abernathy, at his father, at anyone.

"She left because of me," Jason said to himself.

"Jase, come and join us," said a man to his right.

Jason recognized him as the CEO of one of the largest corporations in the world. He'd come to the party because he was afraid he was about to be fired, so he was trying to get a job with Jason. In truth, every person in the room was there because he wanted something from Jason.

Shaking his head, Jason turned away from the man.

Amy left because Jason had wanted to put her in a house and leave her there. He'd wanted to take away her freedom, her free will, all while causing himself no inconvenience whatever.

It was a hard truth to look at, Jason thought, very, very hard. And if he'd succeeded in persuading Amy to marry him, where would he be tonight?

He'd be here, he thought, just as he was right now, because he would have continued to think that CEOs were important people.

And where would Amy be? he wondered, and he knew the answer. He would have bullied her into attending also. He would have told her that, as his wife, she had an obligation to attend his business parties and help him earn money.

Money, he thought as he looked about at the people in the room. The sparkle of the jewelry on them was enough to blind a person. "You'd swallow me up," Amy had said. He hadn't understood a word she'd said that night, but now he did. He could see her in this glass-and-chrome room, with its designer tree and the well-designed people, and he could almost feel her misery.

"Other children," David had said. "Other children."

Maybe he couldn't have Max or Amy, but maybe he could do something in life rather than make money.

"Other children," he said aloud.

Instantly, Dawne was at his side, and Jason looked at

her as though he'd never seen her before. Reaching into his pocket, he withdrew the ring with the huge sapphire and handed it to her.

"Oh, Jason, darling, I accept. Gladly." Ostentatiously, making sure everyone in the room saw, she reached up to put her arms around his neck, but Jason gently took her wrists and put them down at her sides.

"I'm sorry I've been a bastard. I think you already know that I'm no good for you," he said.

"But, I want you to have this ring. Wear it in good health." He looked away, then looked back at her. "Unfortunately I have to cut this evening short; I've just remembered somewhere I have to be." With that he turned away from her and went into the hallway. Robert, his butler, was right behind him.

"Going out, sir?"

"Yes," Jason answered as the man held up his coat and Jason slipped his arms inside.

"And when shall I say that you'll return?"

Jason looked back at the party. "I don't think I will return. See that everyone is taken care of."

"Very good, sir." Robert then handed Jason his cell phone, something that Jason was never, ever without. Jason took the instrument, then looked at it as though he'd never seen it before.

In the next second he dropped the thing into the trash bin; then he started for the door.

"Sir!" Robert said, for the first time losing his composure. "What if there is an emergency? What if you're needed? Where can you be reached?"

Jason paused for a moment. "I need to talk to somebody who knows what it feels like to lose a child. You know that little church over on Sixty-eighth Street? Try me there."

As his butler's jaw dropped, Jason left the apartment.

CHAPTER SIXTEEN

※〜※〜※〜※

ONE YEAR LATER

The President of the United States of
America would be pleased to attend the
grand reopening of the town of Abernathy,
Kentucky. He has asked me to convey his
particular interest in the *Arabian Nights*
mural in the public library as the tales are
favorites of his.

JASON READ THE LETTER AGAIN AND WAS ABOUT TO GIVE
a whoop of joy and triumph—until he looked at the
second paragraph, in which the president's secretary
asked that the dates of the reopening ceremony be
confirmed. "But that's . . ." He broke off in horror
as he looked at his watch to check today's date, then
glared at the calendar on his desk to reconfirm his sus-
picions.

"Doreen!!!" he bellowed at the top of his lungs, and

after about three minutes his secretary came wandering into his office.

"Yeah?" she said, looking at him with big, bored eyes.

Jason had long ago learned that nothing, not any intimidation on earth, could overset Doreen's complacency. Calm down, he told himself. But then he had another look at the presidential seal on the letter and tranquillity be damned.

Silently, he handed her the letter.

"That's good, isn't it? I told you I'd get him here. We got connections, me and Cherry."

Jason put his head in his hands for a moment and tried to count to ten. He made it to eight, which was a new record for him. "Doreen," he said with controlled, exaggerated calm. "Look at the dates. How far from now is the date when the president is due to arrive?"

"You need a new calendar?" Doreen asked in puzzlement. " 'Cause if you do, I can get you one from the store."

Since Doreen had been spending six thousand dollars a month on office supplies, Jason had had to cut off her charge accounts, and he did *not* want to reopen them. "No, I can read one of the ten calendars that are on my desk. Doreen, why is the president coming in a mere six weeks when the opening is planned for six *months* from now? And why does he think the library murals are about the *Arabian Nights* when the painter has been commissioned to do nursery rhymes?"

"Nursery rhymes?" Doreen blinked at him.

Jason took a deep breath intended to calm himself, but instead thought of ways to murder his brother. David had, once again, conned his "wiser," older brother into something that was driving Jason insane. Doreen was Cherry Parker's sister, and David had begged and pleaded for Jason to hire her to help him supervise the rebuilding of Abernathy. At the time, Jason had readily agreed because he missed Parker and he'd never found anyone half as efficient as she was.

But Doreen was as inept at business as Parker was adept. Doreen was as inefficient, as disorganized, and as scatterbrained as Parker was perfect. Within three hours of her employment, Jason had wanted to fire her, but Parker was pregnant and she'd started crying, something that had completely disconcerted Jason, since he'd had no idea that Parker could cry.

"Can't you just keep her for a few days?" David had pleaded. "This pregnancy isn't easy for Cherry, and Doreen is her only sibling, and it would mean so much to both of us. After all, you're so good at this that you could do it without a secretary."

Jason had been flattered and, ultimately, persuaded.

That was eight months ago. Parker was still pregnant, still crying at the least thing, and Jason was still trying to work with Doreen as his secretary. If she wasn't misunderstanding everything he said, she was buying things, such as six cases of red paper clips and twelve dozen Rolodexes. "In case we run out," she'd given as an explanation. To make matters worse, she'd also made it a personal mission to help him get over Amy.

"Nursery rhymes," Jason said tiredly. "You know, 'Humpty-Dumpty,' 'Little Miss Muffet,' that sort of thing. We hired a man to paint them, and he's to start on Monday. It's going to take him three *months* to paint the whole library, but the president is coming in six *weeks* to see them. Except that the president expects to see *Arabian Nights*, not nursery rhymes."

Doreen stared blankly at him. Maybe he should call David again and see if his wife had given birth yet, for the minute Parker delivered, Doreen was out of here.

"What about the knights?" she asked at last.

"Nights? As in *Arabian Nights*? Or are you asking whether the painter will work nights?" With Doreen, one never knew.

"No, silly, knights, like in *Robin Hood.*"

Jason wanted to scream. "There are no knights in *Robin Hood.*" Heaven help him, but he was beginning to understand her!

"Oh," Doreen said, blinking. She was beautiful in a blank sort of way, with enormous eyes that she rimmed in black, which made them seem even larger, and she had about fifty pounds of crinkly blonde hair. The men of Abernathy nearly swooned when they saw her.

"Doreen," Jason said, this time with more urgency. "Where did the president of the United States get the idea that we were doing *Arabian Nights* murals?"

"From that man who discovered the world and rode with the Robin Hood knights," she said.

Unfortunately for him, Jason sometimes almost enjoyed trying to piece together the logic of Doreen's thinking. Now what she'd said rambled about in his head: man who discovered the world, Robin Hood, and knights. It was the name Columbus that gave him a clue. "The Knights of Columbus," he whispered, and when Doreen rolled her eyes as though she was frustrated at his slowness, he knew he was right.

The Knights of Columbus were one of the sponsors of the remodeling of the old Abernathy Library, and for some reason, Doreen had chosen them to fixate on. How she got from Knights of Columbus to *Arabian Nights* intrigued him—as Doreen's brain often did.

"What made you think the library murals were going to be about the *Arabian Nights*?" he asked softly.

Doreen gave a sigh. "Mr. Gables really likes Princess Caroline, and since she's there, of course that's what she would like."

It took Jason a moment to follow her reasoning—if

it could be called reasoning. Mr. Gables owned the local pet store, which was next door to the building where the Knights of Columbus met, and Princess Caroline lived in Monaco, which sounded like Morocco, which is part of the Arab world.

"I see," Jason said slowly. "And Mr. Gables's interest in the princess made you think the library was to be painted with *Arabian Nights* stories instead of fairy tales."

"They'd look better than Humpty-Dumpty, and, besides, the president won't come to see Little Bo-peep."

With a glance at the letter, Jason had to admit that she had a point in that. "You see, Doreen," he said patiently, "the problem is that a man is flying in from Seattle to paint the murals and he'll be here tomorrow. The man has spent the last year working on the drawings for the murals, and—"

"Oh, is that what you're worried about? I can fix that," she said, then left the room.

"Here," she said when she returned a moment later. "This came two weeks ago."

At first Jason wanted to bawl her out for leaving a letter lying around for two weeks before showing it to him, but he decided to save his energy and read the letter. It seemed that the mural painter had broken his right arm and would be out of commission for at least four months.

"You aren't going to yell again, are you?" Doreen asked. "I mean, it's just a broken arm. He'll get well."

"Doreen," Jason said as he stood, glad that there was a desk between them or he might be tempted to wrap his hands about her neck and squeeze. "In six weeks the president of the United States is coming here to see a town that is months away from completion, and he wants to see murals in a library that have yet to be painted because I have no painter." At the end, his voice was rising until he was nearly shouting.

"Don't you shout at me," she said calmly. "It's not my job to hire painters." At that she turned and walked out of the room.

Jason sat down so hard the chair nearly collapsed. "Why did I give up business?" he muttered, and, once again, when he looked back on his former life, he remembered it as efficient and organized. When he'd moved everything back to Abernathy, he'd tried to take his key staff with him, but for the most part they'd laughed at him. His butler had laughed heartily. "Leave New York for Kentucky?" the man had said, highly amused. "No, thank you."

And that had been the attitude of everyone else who'd worked for him. So he'd returned to his hometown virtually alone. Or at least that's how it had felt at the time.

Jason looked at the baby pictures of Max that covered the upper right-hand side of his desk. Two years, he thought, and he'd not heard a word about either of them. It was as though the earth had opened its jaws and swallowed them whole. All he had were these photos that he'd begged from Mildred, Amy's mother-in-law, and had framed in sterling silver. Nothing but the best for his Max.

At least he still thought of the child as his. And again in this he was alone, for no one had any sympathy for him when it came to his pining away for Amy and a baby he'd known for only a few days.

"Get over it!" his father had said. "My wife died. She had no choice in leaving me, but that girl you wanted *left* you and she hasn't called since. You should take a hint and get it through your thick skull that she didn't want you and your money, so she hightailed it out of here."

"My money has nothing to do with this," Jason had said quietly.

"Yeah? Then why are you spending a fortune paying a bunch of snoops to try and find her? If she wasn't for sale when she was here, what makes you think you can buy her when she's not?"

Jason had no reply to his father's words, but then his father was the only person on earth who could reduce Jason to a naughty nine-year-old boy.

David was even less sympathetic than their father and his cure for his big brother had been to introduce him to other women. "Kentucky courtship" is what David called it, and Jason had no idea what his brother meant until the food started arriving. Single women, divorced women, women contemplating a divorce, showed up on Jason's doorstep with jars and dishes of food.

"Just thought you might like to taste my bread-and-butter pickles," they'd purr. "I won a blue ribbon at the state fair last year."

Within three weeks of his arrival, Jason had a kitchen full of every kind of pickle, jam, and chutney known to mankind. His refrigerator was always full of cakes and coleslaw.

"Do they think I'm a man or a hog to be fattened for the kill?" Jason asked one night in a bar as he looked at his brother over a glass of beer.

"A little of both. It is Kentucky, you know. Look, big brother, you ought to take one of them out. You ought to get back into life and stop mooning over what you can't have."

"Yeah, I guess so, but . . . You don't think they'll try to pickle me and enter me in the fair, do you?"

David laughed. "Maybe. Just in case, you should try Doris Millet first. Her specialty is mulberry gin."

Jason gave a bit of a smile. "Okay. I'll try. But . . ."

"I know," David said softly. "You miss Amy and Max. But you need to get on with living. There are lots of women out there. Look at me. I was mad about Amy, but then I met Cherry, and—" He broke off because it was still a sore spot with Jason that he'd lost his magnificent secretary and was now stuck with Doreen.

So Jason had dated one female after another, and without exception, they all fell in love with his money.

"What do you expect?" his sister-in-law had snapped. "You're rich, handsome, heterosexual, and eligible. Of course they want to marry you."

Jason liked Cherry much better as a secretary than he did as a pregnant relative. He didn't need to be reminded that his greatest asset was his bank account.

"What you've done is sanctify her," Cherry said in what had become her usual tone of exasperation. She wasn't handling pregnancy well, as her body was so swollen even her nose was fat. And the doctor had put her on bed rest. "Amy Thompkins is a very nice person but not out of the ordinary. There are lots of Amys out there; you just have to find them."

"But *she* didn't want to marry me," Jason said with a sigh.

Cherry threw up her hands in exasperation. "Are you only interested in women who don't want to marry you? If that's your logic, then you should be madly in love with *me.*"

"Ah," Jason said with a smile. "I can guarantee you that that's not the case."

Cherry threw a pillow at him. "Go get me something

to drink. And put some ice in it. Lots of ice; then come back here and find the remote control. Oh, Lord, is this child never going to be born?"

Jason practically ran out of the room to obey her.

So now he'd been back in Abernathy for nearly a year, and it seemed to him that he'd been out to dinner with every female in the state of Kentucky, several from Tennessee, and a couple from Mississippi. But none of them interested him. He still thought of Amy, still thought of Max, at least twice an hour. Where were they? What did Max look like now?

"Amy probably has six men fighting over her," Mildred Thompkins had said just last month. "She has that endearing quality that makes men want to do things for her. I mean, look at you. You gave up everything to help her."

"I didn't give up anything, I . . ." In the eyes of a great many people his efforts to save his hometown were great and noble, but to his relatives and almost-relatives in Abernathy, Kentucky, he was simply "moonin' over a girl."

Whatever the truth was, it wasn't an attractive picture, and many times he'd vowed to remove Max's photos from his desk and do his best to get serious about one of the many females he'd dated. As his brother had pointed out, he wasn't getting any younger and if he did want a family, he should get busy with it.

But now he had other problems. In a very short time, the president of the United States was coming to Abernathy to see some *Arabian Nights* murals, and Jason didn't so much as have a painter. Out of habit, he picked up the phone and started to tell Doreen to get Mildred on the line, but he knew where that would lead. Doreen would want to know which Mildred he wanted, as though he didn't call Max's grandmother three times a week.

Jason dialed the number that he knew by heart, and when she answered, he didn't bother identifying himself. "You know some local who can paint *Arabian Nights* murals in the library and do it real fast?"

"Oh? You're asking me? You're asking someone from little old Abernathy? What happened to your fancy big city painter?"

Jason gave a sigh. The rest of the world acted like he was a saint, but the people of his hometown thought that he was doing what he should have done a long time ago, and they thought he should be doing more of it. "You know that the man was considered the best in this country and one of the top painters in the world. I wanted the best for this town, and—" He paused to calm himself. "Look, I don't need an argument this morning."

"So what's Doreen done this time?"

"Invited the president six months early and changed the murals from nursery rhymes to *Arabian Nights*."

Mildred gave a whistle. "Is this her best yet?"

"No. She'll never top the one where she had the food delivered on the day after the three hundred guests arrived. Or when she sent the new furniture to South America. Or when she—"

"Cherry deliver yet?"

"No," Jason said, his jaw clenched. "The kid is eleven days late now, but David says maybe the dates are wrong, and—"

"What's this about the murals?" she asked, cutting him off.

Quickly, he told her the problem. In the past year in Abernathy, Mildred had been invaluable to him. She knew everyone and everything. No one in the town could so much as bat an eyelash without Mildred knowing about it. "Don't put those two men on the same committee," she'd say. "Their wives are sleeping together and the men hate each other."

"Their wives . . . ?" Jason had said. "In Kentucky?"

She just raised her eyebrows. "Don't get uppity with me, city slicker."

"But *wives?*" Jason felt that he was losing his innocence.

"You think that because we speak slowly that we're some sort of living Pat Boone movie? But then, even ol' Pat's changed his image, hasn't he?"

So now when Jason had a problem, he knew to call Mildred. "Do you know someone or not?"

"Maybe," Mildred said finally. "Maybe I do, but I don't know if this person will be . . . available."

"I'll pay double," Jason said quickly.

"Jason, honey, when will you learn that money can't solve every problem in the world?"

"Then what does he want? Prestige? The president will view his work. And considering how often Abernathy changes things, two hundred years from now, the murals will still be there. Whatever he wants, I'll pay it."

"I'll try," Mildred said softly. "I'll give it my best shot and let you know as soon as I know."

After Mildred hung up the phone, she stood still for several minutes, thinking. Despite her retort about money, she knew in her heart that the Jason who had come home to Abernathy a year ago was not the same man he was today. He had returned to his hometown with the thought that he was going to play Santa Claus and everyone in town was going to fall down and kiss his feet in gratitude. But instead he had encountered one problem after another, and as a result, he had become *involved*. He'd started out wanting to remain aloof, distant, apart from the townspeople, but he hadn't been allowed to, and she believed if the truth were told that now he wouldn't have it any other way.

Now, still staring at the phone, she smiled in memory of all the women in Abernathy who had done their best to win his hand in marriage. Or just plain, old-fashioned, win him in bed. But as far as Mildred knew Jason hadn't touched a hometown girl. What he did on his frequent trips back to New York, she had no idea, but he had been nothing but a gentleman to the women of Abernathy.

Much to their fury, Mildred thought with amusement. There wasn't a sewing circle, book club, or church meeting in three counties that didn't discuss what was going to be the outcome of Mr. Jason Wilding's moving back to Abernathy, Kentucky.

But, Mildred thought, with a smile that was growing bigger by the minute, Jason still had the photos of Max on his desk and he still talked about Amy as though he'd seen her just last week.

Mildred put her hand on the phone. Wasn't it a coincidence that Jason desperately needed a mural painter and she just happened to know someone who could paint murals?

"Humph!" she said, picking up the phone. About as much a coincidence as it was that she'd easily conned Doreen into giving her the mural painter's address in Seattle; then Mildred had written him a note saying he was no longer needed. Then Mildred had sent a letter to Jason saying the painter had broken his arm. That Doreen had taken weeks to give the letter to Jason just added to Mildred's beautifully planned scheme.

She dialed a number that was burned into her memory, then held her breath before the phone was answered, her mind full of doubt. What if she didn't need a job right now? What if she refused? What if she was still angry at Jason and David and everyone else in Abernathy for playing a trick on her? What if she had a boyfriend?

When the phone was answered, Mildred took a deep breath, then said, "Amy?"

CHAPTER SEVENTEEN

AMY LEANED BACK AGAINST THE HIGH SEAT OF THE PLANE, pulled her cashmere coat tighter about her, and closed her eyes for a moment. Max had finally dozed off, and it was a rare time of quiet for her.

But in spite of the quiet, or at least the roar of the plane, she couldn't sleep. Inside she was excited and nervous and jumpy. She was going to see Jason again.

Closing her eyes, she thought back to that horrible night when she'd "escaped." How noble she'd been that night! How full of telling a man that she didn't need him or his money. How full of romance she'd been, basing her life on the way she thought a movie should have ended—or would have if it had been real life.

Amy pulled the blanket back over Max, since he'd squirmed about in the airline baby cot and uncovered himself. She and Max were flying business class, so she didn't have to hold a heavy, struggling two-year-old on her lap for the whole flight.

Settling back, Amy closed her eyes again and tried to sleep, but she still saw Jason's face. Reaching down, she pulled the thick portfolio from inside her carry-on bag, opened it, and looked at the articles again. Over the past two years she'd collected everything that had been written about Jason Wilding.

He'd sold most of his businesses and become what *Forbes* magazine called America's Youngest Philanthropist. And most of his philanthropy dealt with the town of Abernathy, Kentucky.

Amy again read an article about how Jason Wilding had transformed the small, poor, run-down, dying town of Abernathy into something healthy and prosperous. The first thing he'd done was to invest heavily in the struggling baby food company, Charles and Co.

With amusement, the article told how Wilding had handed four million dollars to a tiny advertising company in Abernathy and told them to promote the new baby food on a national level. Until Jason Wilding appeared, the company had done nothing more than draw ads for local businesses for the local newspaper. But to the surprise and no doubt delight of everyone, the article said, the tiny advertising company did a good job. "Who will ever forget the TV ad of the baby with the 'yucky' face?" the article said. "Or the one with the society hostess emptying jars of Charles and Co. baby food on crackers to serve as canapés?"

The advertising campaign was a great success that year, and Charles and Co. was named as one of the fastest growing companies in the country. "And now they're going international, both in sales and in content. Who would have thought of serving beef Stroganoff to a baby?"

And all the food was made and bottled in Abernathy, Kentucky, giving thousands of jobs to a town that had once had a fifty-two percent unemployment rate. "And the few who did have jobs had them outside the town," the article said. "But Jason Wilding changed that."

There were other articles that dealt less with facts than with the philosophy of why Wilding had done what he had. "What's in it for him?" was the question that everyone wanted answered. Why would a man give up so much to gain so little? It was even rumored that Jason Wilding didn't own so much as a single share in Charles and Co. baby food, but no one believed that.

Amy put the articles down and closed her eyes. How would she react when she saw him again? Had the last two years changed him? There had been next to nothing written about his personal life, so all she knew was that he dated a lot, but still wasn't married.

"Sleep," she whispered out loud, as though she

could command her mind to be still, but when it didn't work, she took out her sketch pad and began to draw. It was cold on the plane, and she'd read that the airlines kept their cabins that way to keep the passengers quiet and in their seats. Warm the cabins and the travelers would wake up and start talking and walking about. "Rather like we're lizards," Amy had thought at the time.

Mildred had told her that Jason wanted something from the *Arabian Nights,* so Amy had spent quite a bit of time looking at previous illustrations to get some ideas of what to do. Since all the stories seemed to be either about sex or extreme violence, she wondered how she was going to illustrate them for a public library.

"You can do it," Mildred had said. "And you can stand to see Jason again. He's still in love with you and Max."

"Sure he is," Amy said. "That's why he's dated nearly every woman in Abernathy, at least that's what one article said. And he didn't spend a lot of time trying to find me, did he?"

"Amy, he—" Mildred began, but Amy cut her off.

"Look, there was nothing between us back then except that he thought I was a charity case. He had such a good time playing Santa Claus to me that he decided to do it with an entire town. Have they erected a statue to him yet?"

"Amy, it's not like that. He doesn't have an easy time here. You should meet Doreen."

"Ah. Right. Remember, I only plan to be in Abernathy for six weeks. I may not be able to meet all the women he's involved with in that time."

"All right," Mildred said. "Have it your way. All I ask is that you come back here with my grandson and let me see him. Please, I beg you. You can't be so cruel as to deny a grandmother—"

"All right!" Amy acquiesced. "I'll do it. Does he know that it's me who's coming?"

"No. He has no idea that anyone knows where you are. Not that *I've* known for very long. So, tell me, did my grandson ever learn to crawl?"

"No. He went from sitting to running. Mildred, could you please let up on the guilt?"

"No. I think I'm rather good at it, don't you?"

In spite of herself, Amy smiled. "The best," she said softly. "You're the best."

So now Amy was on the plane, Max sleeping beside her. She was going back to Abernathy and she was going to see the man who had haunted her every thought for two years. But for all her thoughts, all that she'd read and been told by Mildred, she knew that she had done the right thing in leaving Jason two years before. Maybe he hadn't changed, maybe he was still trying to buy his way into whatever he wanted, but she had certainly changed. She was no longer the innocent little Amy who was waiting for a man to come along and take care of her. Now, when she looked back on it, she thought maybe that was what she was doing when she met Jason.

But, somehow, on that early Christmas morning, she had found the courage to walk away. Now, two years later, she still marveled at the courage she'd had that night, a courage born out of fear, because she foresaw a future without freedom. She had seen a future in which she and Max and any other children she'd have would be swallowed up in the machine that was Jason Wilding.

So she'd left Abernathy on a bus and gone to New York, where she called a girl she'd gone to high school with. They'd kept in touch over the years, and she was delighted when Amy showed up. And it was this friend who'd helped Amy get into a publishing house to show her drawings to an editor, and when Amy got a job illustrating children's books, her friend helped her get an apartment and a baby-sitter for Max. Of course the pearls that David had given Amy had helped. She'd been astonished when she realized that they were real, and the money she received from the sale of them had furnished the apartment and paid four months' rent.

She'd done well, she thought as she looked down at her sketch pad. She wasn't wealthy, wasn't famous, but she was self-supporting. And Max was happy. He went to a play group three days a week, and every minute that Amy wasn't working, she spent with him.

As for men, Amy hadn't found much time for them. Between work and Max, there weren't enough hours in the day. Quite often on the weekends she and Max went out with her editor and the editor's husband, Alec, and their daughter, and Alec tossed Max around in that particularly male way and that seemed to be enough for the boy. Someday soon, Amy thought, she was going to start thinking about men again, but not yet.

Hurriedly, she began to sketch some of her ideas for the murals, and she wasn't surprised to see that every man in the pictures looked like Jason.

When the plane landed, Amy's heart was in her throat. Gently, she woke Max, who started to complain because he hadn't finished his nap, but when he saw that they were in a new place, curiosity overrode the grumpies. Once in the terminal it was difficult to hold Max, as he was determined to ride on the luggage carousel.

As promised, Mildred had a car and driver waiting for her, and his instructions were to take Amy and Max directly to her house.

But Amy had her own ideas. "We'll get out here," she said to the driver as he turned onto the main street of Abernathy. "Please tell my mother-in-law that we'll be there in an hour or so." She wanted to see the changes that she'd read about. Holding Max's hand, she walked slowly down the street and looked at each shop.

She thought she had an idea of what Jason would have done to the town, but she was wrong. She thought he'd make it into a tiny New York, with Versace boutiques and a zillion art galleries. But he hadn't. Instead, he'd merely repaired and painted what was there. And he'd removed the modernization from many of the stores. In a way, walking through town was like a step back in time—except that it wasn't quaint. It wasn't like a stage set or one of those re-creation towns they had in amusement parks.

No, Abernathy looked like what it had become: a healthy, prosperous farm town, with people bustling about and businesses doing well. Amy walked slowly, Max twisting and turning to look at everything, as he liked to see new people and new things.

Suddenly Max halted in front of a shop window, and Amy nearly tripped as he pulled her up short. In the window was a display of pinwheels, and a fan was blowing them about, round and round. Amy's first thought was that they were only pinwheels, nothing special, but she realized that to a child used to complicated, noisy toys, they were wonderful.

"Come on then," she said, and Max's face lit up with a grin.

Minutes later they emerged from the store with Max holding a shiny blue pinwheel in one hand and a candy wrapper in the other. His mouth was distorted around a huge chocolate-coated piece of dried fruit, and Amy was smiling. Home, she thought, was where the store owner gave away a free piece of candy to a bright-eyed child.

At the end of the street was the Abernathy Library. The front door was open, and there were several pickup trucks outside and workmen moving in and out of the door.

Amy took a deep breath. She was going to see Jason soon; she could feel it. Even though she'd spent little time with him, it was as though all of the town was now filled with him. Everywhere she looked reminded her of him. This is where we bought Max a pair of shoes, she thought. And this is where Jason made me laugh. And this is where—

"Shall we go in?" she asked Max, looking down at him as he sucked on his candy. "This is where Mommie is going to work."

Max gave her a nod, then looked at his pinwheel as a breeze made it twirl around.

Taking another deep breath, Amy walked up the stairs, Max beside her. At first it was too dark in the room to see anything, but as her eyes adjusted, she saw that the workmen were nearly finished. They were removing scaffolding and leaving behind clean white plaster walls ready for her murals. She could see that she was to paint across the front of the checkout desk, then up the side of the wall, over and down again. There was a great blank wall in the reading area, and she assumed that this was where the main mural was to go.

As she was looking at the walls, thinking how what she'd planned to paint would fit, out of the back came a man, a pretty blonde woman following him. As soon as she realized it was Jason, Amy stepped back into the shadows and stayed quiet. He was looking at a set of plans, the woman seeming to be content to stand beside him silently.

Now Amy stood where he couldn't see her and watched him. He looked a bit older; the creases that ran down the side of his mouth seemed to be deeper. Or maybe it was just a trick of the light. His hair was the same though: a great thick gray mane of it that grazed the back of his collar.

Damn! He was more handsome than she remembered. Damn, damn, and double damn!

When the curvy blonde leaned over him, Amy wanted to snatch the woman bald. "But I have no right," she whispered to herself, causing Max to look up at her in question. Smoothing back her son's hair, she smiled down at him, and he turned away to stare at the man standing a few yards in front of them.

Amy tried to give herself a pep talk. She was here to

do a job and nothing more. A job that she needed very much. A job that . . .

Okay, she told herself. Get over it. Get over Jason. Remind yourself of what a trick he played on you. Remember every photo you've ever seen of him with a gorgeous woman draped across his arm.

She took a deep breath, tightened her grip on Max's hand, and stepped forward. Before he turned to see her, she said, "Jason, what a pleasure to see you again."

As he turned around, she held out her hand to shake. "You haven't changed at all," she said, nodding toward Doreen, who stood close beside him. "Still the ladies' man, I see." She gave a wink at Doreen as though they were bosom buddies in on some secret.

Amy was afraid to stop talking for fear that she might collapse. Jason's eyes on hers were almost more than she could bear. She wanted to throw her arms around him, and—

"Where have you been?" he demanded, sounding as though she'd gone to the grocery and hadn't come back for five hours.

"Oh, here and there. And where have you been? As if I needed to ask." She knew she was making a fool of herself, but the blonde was everything she wasn't and it bothered her. Of course it couldn't be jealousy. But Amy did wish she had a boyfriend whose name she could drop.

"It looks as though you've done all right," he said,

nodding toward her cashmere coat with the paisley scarf about the neck. Under it she wore a cashmere sweater, trousers of fine wool, and boots of the softest kid leather. Gold glowed warmly from her ears, neck, wrists, and belt buckle.

"Oh, quite well. But as . . ." Frantically, she looked about, then saw a bag of Arnold potato chips. "As Arnie says, I take well to nice things."

Jason was scowling and, inside, Amy was smiling. Her heart was racing at her lie, but then she looked at Doreen and couldn't seem to prevent herself from continuing. "Max, come here and say hello to an old friend of mine. And yours."

She picked up Max, who was staring at Jason with intense eyes as though he was trying to place him. Jason wanted to take the boy in his arms, but instead his pride took over. What had he expected? That Amy would someday come back into his life, sobbing, telling him that she needed him, that the world was a cold, cruel place and that she must have his arms to protect her? Is that what he'd hoped for? Instead, it was just as everyone had said; she'd gone on with her life while Jason had stood still and waited.

So now was he to tell her that she meant everything to him? That while she was having a mad affair with some guy named "Arnie," he had thought of her every minute of every day? Like hell he would!

Suddenly, just as he was formulating an appropriate response to Amy's introduction, Doreen flung her arm around his waist and grabbed him in a shockingly intimate way.

"Oh, honey, isn't Max just the cutest little thing?" Doreen gushed, ignoring Jason's murderously bewildered glare. "I just can't wait until we have one of our very own."

"Honey?" Amy said, and Jason was amazed to see that she looked a tiny bit shocked.

Again, the overly helpful Doreen jumped in. "Oh, that. Well, Jason doesn't like it when I call him 'honey' in public, but I keep telling him that it's okay—engaged people call each other silly names all the time."

"Engaged?" Amy barely whispered the word.

Jason started to remove Doreen's arm from his waist, but she caught his fingers in hers, then leaned against him as though they were Siamese twins joined at the hip.

"Oh, yes," Doreen purred. "We're to be married in just six weeks' time, and we have sooooo many things yet to buy for the house. In fact, we haven't even bought the house yet."

Jason had to stop himself from staring at Doreen in flabbergasted awe. He supposed Doreen thought she was helping his cause by concocting this story, but this time she'd truly gone too far. How in heaven was he going to explain his way out of this? And would Amy even believe him?

"I'm sure that Jason can afford any house you want," Amy said softly.

"Oh, yes, and I know just the house I want, but he won't agree. Don't you think that's mean of him?" She poked Jason in the arm and ignored his furious gaze.

"Dreadfully," Amy said, her voice low.

"But then I guess your Arnie would buy you the best house in town," Doreen said.

Amy straightened her spine. "Of course he would." She flipped the wool challis scarf about her coat collar. "The biggest and best. All I'd have to do is hint and it would be mine. And I'm sure Jason will do the same for you."

"Well, when I do get him to agree, *you* must help me pick out all the furniture."

"Me?" Amy asked dumbly.

"You are the artist, aren't you?"

For a moment both Jason and Amy stared at her.

"I am, actually, but how did you know?" Amy asked.

"You look like an artist. Everything on you matches. Now me, I have trouble matching black and white. Isn't that so, sweetheart? But Jasey loves me just the way I am, don't you, honey bunch?"

Jason tried again to move out of Doreen's grip, but

she was holding on tighter than a set of lug nuts to a wheel rim. It did occur to him to hit her over the head with a lunch box that was sitting nearby, but he decided it would be best to explain to Amy once they were alone.

"You, ah, you're to paint the murals?" Jason asked while his hand slipped behind his back so he could try to peel Doreen away from his side.

"Yes," Amy said solemnly, no longer effervescent. "Mildred said there was a mix-up about dates and what was to be painted, so she asked me if I could help out. I brought some sketches that maybe you'd—" She broke off because Jason had given a muffled grunt as though something had hurt him. "Are you all right?"

"Sure," he said, his free hand rubbing his side as though he were in pain. "I'd like to see your sketches. Maybe we could get together tonight and—"

"Now, honey, you promised me that tonight we'd pick out china and silver. We're getting Noritake and real silver," she said to Amy. "Jason, darling, is so very generous, aren't you, my dearest? At least about everything except a house, that is."

"Perhaps there are limits to every man's generosity," he said pointedly, glaring down at Doreen with murder in his eyes.

"Gee, I bet Arnie is generous, isn't he? I mean, look at that coat you're wearing. He is generous, isn't he?"

"Yes, of course," Amy answered, looking into Jason's

eyes for a moment and wishing that she'd never made up this man Arnie, wishing she'd told him the truth. Wishing . . .

"When would you like to see the sketches?" Amy asked. "I think you should approve them before I start painting. And I'm going to need some assistants, people who can do fill work."

"Sure, anything you need," Jason said as he at last managed to get Doreen's hands and arms off his body.

But the moment he was free, Doreen stepped between the two of them. "That's just what he says to me all the time. Anything you need, Doreen. Anything at any time. So it's odd that he won't buy me a house, don't you think? Maybe you could persuade him."

"Maybe," Amy said, then looked at her watch. "Oh, my, but I have to go. My mother-in-law will—"

"Oh, then you're married," Doreen said.

"Widowed."

"That's too bad. I am sorry. When did Arnie die?"

"He didn't. He . . . I really must go. Jason, it was good to see you again. I'll be staying at Mildred's, so if you need to talk to me about . . . about work, you know the number." With that she grabbed Max's hand and practically ran from the building.

Outside the car and driver that Mildred had sent to meet her at the airport were waiting for her.

"I hope you don't mind, miss," the driver said as she

and Max got in, "but Mrs. Thompkins sent me back to get you and the boy to take you home to her."

"No, no," Amy said hurriedly. "I don't mind. Just go fast!"

Before I start crying, she could have added.

But she managed to hold back her tears until she got to Mildred's, where she found that her mother-in-law had engaged a professional nanny to help with Max. Within minutes Max had decided he liked the woman, and they went into the kitchen to have cocoa.

"Everything," Mildred said. "I want to know everything that's wrong with you."

"I've ruined my life, that's all," Amy said, sobbing into the pile of tissues Mildred handed her.

"It won't be the first time."

"What?" Amy looked up with red eyes.

"Amy, dear, you married a man who was an alcoholic and on drugs, which, may God rest his soul and even if he was my only child, was a disastrous thing to do. Then a rich, handsome man fell madly in love with you and you ran off with just the clothes on your back. And a baby to support. So I'd say that you'd already ruined your life several times."

Amy started to cry harder.

"So what have you done this time?"

"I told Jason I was in love with another man because she was so pretty and they were standing so close and it was like I left yesterday and I think I'm still in love with him, but nothing has changed. He's still the same man I ran away from. He still buys and sells whole towns, and all those women of his are so beautiful and—"

"Wait a minute. Slow down. You act as though I know anything about why you left and where you've been with my grandson for these last two years. And if that makes you feel guilty, it was meant to. Now, slow down and tell me why you agreed to return if you didn't think you were still in love with Jason."

"My editor wants me to get this job so we can use a quote from the president on my next book."

"How did you get started in the book business?"

Amy dried her eyes a bit. "I got a job in New York illustrating children's books. I've done quite well actually and there have been some really successful illustrators who—"

Mildred waved her hand. "You can tell me all that later. So what happened with Jason this morning?"

"He's engaged to be married."

"He's what?"

"He's going to get married. But what did I expect? That he'd been pining away for *me* all these years? In all these two years I've had only two dates, and I only went on those because they were for lunch, so I could take Max. But Max didn't like either man. In fact, with one of the men, Max—well, it was really very funny, although the man didn't think so. Max and I met him in

Central Park and—" She stopped because Mildred was giving her a look. "Okay, I'll try to stick to the point."

"Yes, and right now the point is Jason. Just who is he engaged to?"

"Her name is Doreen and you even tried to warn me about her."

Mildred's jaw dropped so far down her chin almost hit her knees.

Amy didn't seem to notice. "She's beautiful: tall, blonde, curvy. I can see why he's fallen for her. Why are you laughing? Is my misery funny to you?"

"I'm sorry. But, Doreen! You have to tell me everything. Every word that was spoken, every gesture, everything."

"I don't think I want to if you're going to laugh at me. In fact, I think maybe Max and I should stay somewhere else."

"Jason is not engaged to Doreen. She is his secretary and she's the sweetest thing but, unfortunately, the worst secretary in the world."

"You don't have to be efficient for someone to love you. I've always been—"

"Jason told Doreen to order duck à l'orange for a dinner for backers for the new municipal pool. Doreen thought he wanted orange ducks, so she had the pool filled with two hundred pounds of orange Jell-O, then had a farmer unload four hundred chickens in the building because she couldn't find a duck farm."

Amy stared at Mildred. "You made that up."

"When Jason was furious, she thought it was because she'd ordered chickens instead of ducks."

Mildred paused a moment to let that sink in. "Doreen files everything by what color the paper feels like. Not what color anything is, just what color it feels like. The problem comes when she tries to retrieve anything because she only knows what it feels like when she's touching it."

"I see," Amy said, her tears drying. "And if she can't find the paper, how can she feel it so she can find it?"

"Exactly. Doreen ordered all new signs for every business in town. They all came back with Abernathy spelled Abernutty."

Amy laughed.

"Doreen collects red paper clips. Ask her about them. She can talk for hours about her collection. She has red paper clips from every office supply store within a hundred and fifty miles, and she will tell you that the amazing fact is that they *all come from the same company.*"

Amy started to laugh in earnest. "And Jason wants to *marry* her?"

"Jason wants to kill her. He calls me every few days and tells me the latest method he's come up with to kill her. He can be quite ingenious. I liked the one where he crushed her under a mountain of red paper clips, but I said it might give her too much pleasure."

"If she's so inept, why did he hire her? Or keep her? Why was he hugging her?"

"Doreen may be horrible at her job, but it wasn't exactly her idea to be a secretary in the first place," Mildred said with an arched brow. "You see, she's Jason's former secretary's sister, you know, the formidable Parker."

"Yes, of course. Parker did everything for him. She helped him do all those things to me."

"Yes, yes, Jason was vile. He bought your kid clothes, arranged for you to have a fabulous night out, made Christmas a dream come true, and—Okay, I'll stop. Anyway, Parker married David and—"

"David? Dr. David? Jason's brother?"

"The very one. Parker was staying at David's house while Jason was with you, and they got to know each other, and, well . . . Anyway, Jason could never replace Parker, so when she begged him to hire her sister, Jason jumped at the chance. He wanted to fire Doreen the first day because she sold his car for a dollar—no, that's another story—but he found out that day that Parker was pregnant and David said it would make his wife miscarry if he fired her sister."

"My husband died while I was pregnant, but I didn't miscarry," Amy said.

"Ssssh. Let's not tell our little secrets, all right? I'm sure David just wanted peace, so once again he conned his big brother." Mildred paused to chuckle. "Jason constantly says that he wants to go back to New York, where the people are less conniving, underhanded, and devious than they are here in Abernathy.

"Anyway, Jason agreed to keep Doreen on until Parker had her baby, and at last count that baby was nearly two weeks late. However, my guess is that once the baby is born, David will figure out another reason his brother should keep Doreen on. But if he doesn't fire her soon, I really do think Jason will murder her."

"Or marry her," Amy said heavily.

"I want you to tell me about that," Mildred said seriously. "What exactly did Doreen say?"

"Something about houses and silver . . . I don't know. I was pretty miserable and Max likes him."

"How do you know?"

"Because she said so. She told me that they were picking out china patterns and—"

"No, I mean, how do you know about Max liking Jason?"

"Because he was more interested in Jason than he was in pulling books off the shelves or seeing what was in the paint cans. And he stood by me and didn't climb on anything. But then Max always did like him."

Mildred listened to all of this without saying a word; then she narrowed her eyes at Amy. "My grandson needs a father. And you need a husband. I've had all I can take of you living in secret somewhere else and my not being able to see my only grandson whenever I want and—"

"Please, Mildred. I feel bad enough as it is."

"You don't feel bad enough that you can make up to me for missing two years of my grandson's life," Mildred snapped.

At that, Amy stood. "I think I should go."

"Yes," Mildred said quietly. "You should go. You should run away, just as you did when Jason wanted you to be his wife." Her voice lowered. "And just as you did when you married Billy."

"I did no such thing!" Amy protested, but she sat down again. "Billy was always good to me. He—"

"He gave you a reason to hide. He gave you a reason to stay away from everything in life. You could have a baby and stay in that old house, and no one expected any more from the wife of the town drunk, did they? Did you think that I didn't know what was going on? I loved Billy with all my heart, but I knew what he was like and I saw what was going on. And after Billy died, you were afraid of stepping outside of that house.

"So tell me, Amy, what did you do when you ran away from Jason? Hide some more? Did you stay in an apartment somewhere and draw your little pictures and only go out with your son?"

"Yes," Amy said softly as tears began to form in her

eyes again. Great big drops were spilling over and running down her cheeks, but she made no move to wipe them away.

"Okay, Amy, I'm going to tell you some hard truths. You've hurt Jason Wilding to the point where I don't know if he'll ever recover. He's had a difficult life, and he's learned not to give his love easily. But he offered his love to you and Max, and you spit in his eye and walked away from him. You really, really hurt him."

Amy took a deep breath. "So how do I get him back? I was horrible this morning. I lied and said dreadful things. Should I go to him and tell him the truth?"

"You mean tell him that you've learned your lesson and that you want him so much that you ache inside?"

"Yes, oh, yes. I didn't know how much I wanted him until I saw him again."

"Honey, if you go to a man and tell him you were wrong, you'll spend the rest of your life apologizing to him."

"What? But you just said that I'd hurt him. Shouldn't I tell him that I'm sorry I hurt him?"

"You do and you'll regret it."

Amy stuck her finger in her ear and wiggled it as she tried to open the passage. "Forgive me, but I seem to have gone deaf. Would you go over this again?"

"Look, if you want a man, you have to make him come to you. You know you're sorry you ran out, but you can't let him know it. You see, to a man, conquest is everything. He has to win you."

"But he did already. He went to a lot of effort for Max and me before, but I had some weird idea that I wanted—"

Mildred cut her off. "Who cares about the past?"

"But you just said that I run away and hide and—"

"You do. Now, listen, I've just come up with a plan. That's 'Plan' with a capital *P*. By the time we get through with Jason Wilding, he won't know what hit him."

"I think I'm jet-lagged, because I'm not hearing things properly. I thought your sympathy was with him. I thought he was the wronged person."

"True, but what has right got to do with it? Look, you can't win a man with apologies and truth. No, you win them with lies and tricks and subterfuge. And sexy underwear helps."

Amy could only blink at this woman with her fantastic hairdo. Mildred Thompkins didn't look like the type of woman to use subterfuge on a man. No, she looked more as though she were the type to rope and brand a man. "Underwear?" Amy managed to say.

"Did you ever get that body of yours in shape?"

"I, ah . . ."

"Thought so. Well, I'll get my hairdresser Lars to do something with you. In front of Jason, of course. And maybe we'll even get Doreen her house. Why not? Jason can afford it, and Doreen will probably marry some gorgeous man who knocks her around, so she'll need a house. And you're going to need a lot of help with those murals of yours. And—Why are you looking at me like that?"

"I don't think I've ever seen you like this before."

"Honey, you ain't seen nothing yet. Now, let's go see my grandson."

CHAPTER EIGHTEEN

WHEN AMY AWOKE TWO MORNINGS LATER, SHE KNEW exactly where she was. She was in what had once been her own bedroom in the Salma house. Quietly, she threw back the comforter and padded into the next room to check on Max. He was sound asleep, on his stomach, looking as though he hadn't moved all night.

Poor little thing, she thought, he'll probably sleep another couple of hours.

After tucking the cover about him and smoothing his hair back, she went into the kitchen. But this kitchen bore no resemblance to the old kitchen she'd once tried to cook in. There were no more rusty, broken appliances, no more cracked and peeling linoleum.

Amy wasn't surprised to see freshly brewed coffee in an automatic maker and muffins, still hot, on the counter. "With love, Charles," the card beside the pot read. On a hunch, she opened the refrigerator door and wasn't surprised to see that it was fully stocked. There was a breakfast meal of crepes and strawberries for Max, a red bow tied around the top of the little basket. That Charles somehow knew that Amy and Max were now staying in the house where Max had spent his first seven months didn't surprise her. No one kept a secret in Abernathy.

With coffee, two muffins, and a warm hard-boiled egg in her hand, she went into the living room, and smiled when she saw a fire in the fireplace—a fire that didn't smoke. It would be heavenly to sit and drink and eat and to be able to think in peace about how she got here in a mere twenty-four hours.

It had all started because Max wouldn't stay with Mildred and the new nanny, she thought with a smile. But then, didn't everything start with Max?

Yesterday, as Amy had entered the library, she could feel the heat of Max's body as he lay against her, his head down on her shoulder as he did when he was hurt or, as now, exhausted. Nine-thirty, she'd thought. She'd wanted to have two drawings transferred onto the walls by now, but instead she was just arriving at the library.

Jason had greeted her with a face full of fury.

"How do you expect us to get this done in just six weeks?" he said angrily. "Are you unaware of the time pressure we're under? The opening of the library is six weeks away. The president of the United States is coming. Maybe that doesn't mean much to you, but it means a lot to the people of Abernathy."

"Be quiet, will you?" Amy said, not in the least intimidated by him. "And stop looking at me like that. I've had all I can take of bad-tempered men this morning."

"Men?" Jason said, his face darkening. "I guess your . . . your . . ."

She knew that he was trying to say "fiancé," but the word wouldn't pass his rigid lips. Maybe it would eventually be fun to play the little game that Mildred had concocted, but not now. Now she was too tired.

It was as though Jason suddenly read Amy's mind. "Max," he said softly. "You mean Max."

"Yes, of course I mean Max. He was awake most of the night. I think that being in a new place frightened him, and after a few hours he didn't like being pawned off on the nanny Mildred hired. Max has never liked staying with strangers. He's very selective about the people he likes."

Jason gave her a raised-eyebrow look that said, *That's how we got into all this in the first place,* but he didn't say anything. Instead, with an ease that was as though he'd been doing it every day for years, Jason took the tall, heavy, sleeping toddler from Amy and settled him on his shoulder, where Max lay bonelessly. "He's exhausted," Jason said, frowning.

"He's exhausted? What about me?"

"As long as I've known you, you've never had any sleep," Jason said quietly, his lips playing with a smile.

"True," she said, smiling back.

"Come on," Jason said as he walked toward double doors at the end of the room. When he opened one, Amy drew in her breath.

"Beautiful, huh?" Jason said over his shoulder, his voice quiet so he didn't wake Max. "This was the room the Abernathys built so if they wanted to go to the library, they didn't have to sit with the hoi polloi."

The room was indeed nice, but not because there was anything unusual in it, no carved moldings, no imported tile work. What made the room so beautiful was the proportion of it, with windows all along one side of the room, looking out over the little garden at the back of the library. Going to the windows, Amy looked out and realized that the garden was walled off from the larger play area behind the main part of the building.

"Oh, my," she said. "Is that a private garden?"

"Of course. You don't think the Abernathys were going to play with the town's kids, do you?"

"They sound lonely," she said, then turned back to Jason and held up her arms to take Max. "Here, let me have him. He gets heavy."

Jason didn't bother to answer her, but carefully put Max down on a couple of cushions that were piled on the floor, then pulled a Humpty-Dumpty quilt over him.

"Looks like you're prepared for children's naps," she said, turning her head away so she didn't have to watch him with her son. Sometimes Max stared at men as though they were creatures from another planet, and it made Amy feel bad to think of his growing up without a father.

"Yes," Jason said as he held the door open, waiting for her to leave before him. He didn't shut the door but left it open so they could hear Max if he awoke. "I'm making that into a children's reading room," he said. "We'll have storytellers and as many children's books as the room will hold." He didn't ask, but his eyes were begging her to say that she liked the idea.

"The children of Abernathy are very lucky," she said.

"Mmmmm, well," he said, embarrassed but pleased, she could tell.

"So where do I begin?"

"What?" he asked, staring into her eyes.

"The murals? Remember? The ones that can't wait."

"Oh, yes," Jason said. "The murals. I don't know. What do you think?"

"I need an overhead projector and some assistants and—"

"There's just me."

"I beg your pardon," Amy said.

"Me. I'm your assistant."

"Look, I'm sure you're good at completely renovating a whole town, but I don't think that you can paint camels. Besides, you must have lots to do. After all, you are getting ready for your wedding, aren't you?"

"Wedding? Oh, yeah, that. Look, Amy, I really have to explain."

Part of her wanted to keep her mouth shut and listen, but part of her was scared to death to hear what he had to say. She liked to tell people that she'd been happy when she was married but the truth was that the whole idea of marriage, maybe even the idea of a relationship, scared her to death.

"Could it wait?" she asked nervously. "I mean, whatever you have to tell me, could it wait? I really need to . . . to call Arnie. He'll be worried about me."

"Sure," Jason said as he turned his back to her. "Use the phone in the office."

"It's a long distance call."

"I think I can afford it," Jason said as he went back into the room where Max was sleeping.

"It's awful between Jason and me," Amy said to Mildred over the phone. "Really awful. And I don't know how long I can keep this farce going."

She paused to listen. "No, he hasn't asked me to marry him. He's going to marry Doreen, remember? Stop laughing at me! This is serious.

"No, Max is fine. He's sleeping in the Abernathy Room. Jason is going to make that into a reading room for children.

"No! I am *not* going soft on you. It's just that *I* have never been good at being devious, underhanded, and deceitful." Pause. "Well, if the shoe fits . . . Wait. You'll never guess who just walked in. That's right, but how did you know? You sent her? And *you* bought her *that* dress? Mildred! What kind of friend are you? Hello? Hello?"

Frowning because Mildred had hung up on her, Amy put the phone down and found that her anger at her mother-in-law had put some starch in her spine. Also the sight of Doreen in a teeny, tiny blue dress that looked to be made of angora, a dress that she'd just found out her mother-in-law had bought for the woman, had sent more anger through her. Whose side *was* Mildred on?

"Doreen, don't you look lovely?" Amy said as she left the office, then gritted her teeth as she saw the blonde wiggle up to Jason. But when Amy saw Jason watching her and not Doreen, Amy gave a big smile. "So when do we start looking for a house for you two, and buying furniture?"

"I think that we need to get these murals done first," Jason said sternly. "Every second counts."

"We have to eat dinner," Amy said brightly. "So why not have take-out in the car on the way to a furniture store? Or, better yet, how about antiques?"

"Used furniture?" Doreen said, sounding disappointed in Amy. "I want new things."

"True antiques go up in value should you ever need

to sell them," Amy said, her eyes boring into Doreen's. "Not that you ever would want to sell, but if you buy new furniture, six weeks later you won't be able to get what you paid for them. Antiques increase in value. You can sell them and make a profit."

With great solemnity, Doreen nodded. "Antiques," she said softly, then nodded again.

And in that moment Amy and Doreen formed a bond. Amy wasn't sure how Doreen knew or for that matter how she herself knew what was going on, but both women knew everything. There was a look exchanged between them that said, You help me and I'll help you. Doreen couldn't be so dumb as not to know that within a very few days she was going to lose her job for gross incompetence, so why not get what she could while she had the opportunity?

"Oh, Jason has *no* idea how long these wedding plans take. He won't even take time to look at all the goodies I've registered for over at the mall." Doreen frowned and shook her head disappointedly.

"I bet you've chosen Waterford and sterling, haven't you?"

Doreen's smile broadened. "I knew you were a good person. Isn't she, Jason, darling?"

"Look," Jason said, peeling Doreen's hands off his arm. "I think we should get something straight here and now. I am not—"

"Oh, my goodness, look at the time," Amy said.

"Hadn't we better get to work? And, Jason, I would like it very much if you helped me paint. I can use the time to tell you all about Arnie."

Jason's face darkened. "Give me a list of what and who you'll need and I'll see that you get everything." With that he turned and walked out of the library.

For a moment Amy and Doreen stared at each other; then Doreen took a breath. "Tonight?" she asked. "You'll go shopping with me tonight?"

Amy nodded, and Doreen broke into a grin.

And that, Amy thought now as she sipped her coffee and ate her muffin, had been the beginning of one of the most extraordinary days of her life. Looking back at that long day now, she couldn't decide who had been the strangest: Max or Doreen or Jason.

Smiling, Amy settled back on the cushions and tried to sort out her thoughts. First there was Max. She could understand his fit when she'd tried to leave him with his grandmother and the nanny; after all, both women were strangers to him. And, besides, she and Max hadn't spent more than three hours apart since he'd been born, so to suddenly spend a whole day apart would have been traumatic for both of them.

But in the end, Max had hurt her feelings by the way he'd attached himself to both Jason and Doreen. I'm glad he likes other people, she told herself, but still she felt some jealousy.

It had started at the art supply store, where Jason had driven them so she could buy whatever she needed for the job. As usual, Max started getting into everything, and out of habit, Amy told him no, to leave that alone and don't break that and don't climb on that and get down from there and—

"Does he talk?" Jason asked.

"When he wants to," Amy said, pulling Max down from where he was trying to climb onto a big wooden easel.

"Does he understand complex sentences?"

Amy pushed the hair out of her eyes and looked up at Jason. "Are you asking me if my son is intelligent?" She was ready to do battle if he was insinuating that because Max's father was a drunkard that maybe Max wasn't as bright as he should be.

"I am asking about what a two-year-old can and cannot do, and I—Oh, the hell with it. Max, come here."

This last was said with authority, and it annoyed Amy that Max obeyed at once. Even when she used her fiercest tone with her son, all he did was smile at her and keep on doing whatever she'd told him not to do.

Jason knelt down so he was at eye level with the tall toddler. "Max, how'd you like to paint like your mother does?"

"Don't tell him that!" Amy said. "He'll get paint all over everything and make such a mess that—" She broke off because Jason had given her a look that told her her comments weren't wanted.

Jason straightened Max's shirt collar, and the boy seemed to stand up straighter. "Would you like to paint something?"

Max nodded, but he was cautious; he wasn't usually allowed to touch his mother's paints.

"All right, Max, ol' man, how'd you like to paint the room you slept in this morning?"

At that Max's eyes widened; then he turned to look up at his mother.

"Don't look at me; I've been told to keep my mouth shut," Amy said, her arms crossed over her chest.

Jason put his hand on Max's cheek and turned the boy to face him. "This is between you and me. Man to man. No women."

At that Max had such a look of ecstasy on his face that Amy wanted to scream. Her darling little boy could not have turned into a man already!

"So, Max," Jason said, "do you want to paint that room or not?"

This time Max didn't look up at his mother but nodded vigorously.

"All right, now the first thing you need to do is plan what you're going to paint, right?"

Max nodded again, his little face absolutely serious.

"Do you know what you want to paint?"

Max nodded.

Jason waited, but when the child said nothing, he looked up at Amy.

"This wasn't my idea," she said. "*You* are going to clean him up after this."

Jason looked back at the boy and smiled. "Tell me what you want to paint."

At that, Max shouted "Monkeys" so loud that Jason rocked back on his heels.

"All right," Jason said, laughing, "monkeys it is. Do you know how to paint monkeys?"

Max nodded so vigorously that his whole body shook.

Jason took the boy's shoulders in his hands and said, "Now, I want you to listen to me, all right?"

When Max's attention was fully on Jason, he said, "I want you to go with this lady, her name is Doreen, and I want you to pick out everything you need to paint your monkeys. Big monkeys, little monkeys. A whole room full of monkeys. Understand?"

Max nodded.

"Any questions?"

Max shook his head no.

"Good. I like a man who can take orders. Now go with Doreen while I work with your mother. Okay?"

Again Max nodded; then Jason stood and looked at Doreen. She held out her hand to Max; he took it, and the two of them disappeared down the aisles of the art store.

"You have no idea what you've done," Amy said. "You can't let a two-year-old have carte blanche in a store. Heaven only knows what he'll buy and—"

Taking Amy's arm, Jason pulled her in the opposite direction. "Come on, let's get what you need and get out of here. At this rate the president will be here before the murals are started."

"Then maybe you should have ordered the supplies before I arrived. I did send a list to Mildred so everything would be ready."

"And the supplies were purchased," Jason said under his breath.

Amy stopped walking. "Well, then, why are we here buying more?"

Jason gave a sigh. "You wanted watercolors, so Doreen ordered sets with those tiny squares of watercolors in them."

"But I ordered gallons . . . Oh, my. How many of those sets did she order?"

"Let's just say that every schoolchild in Kentucky now has a brand-new set of watercolors."

"Oh," Amy said, smiling; then she couldn't help but laugh. "I hate to ask about the overhead projector."

"Did you know that when you turn a slide projector upside down that all the slides fall out?"

"No, I've never tried it. How do *you* know that that's what happens?"

"Because Doreen bought thirteen different brands of

them and couldn't find one that could be used 'overhead.' "

"I see," Amy said, trying unsuccessfully not to laugh out loud. "It's a good thing you're marrying her, or you'd be broke in another couple of weeks."

"Amy, I need to talk to you about that."

"Really?" she said. "I hope you aren't going to tell me anything bad, as it puts my work off when I hear bad news. And Arnie—Ow! What was that for?"

"Sorry, didn't mean to hurt you," he said as he released her arm. "You want to get what you need so we can get out of here?"

For the next hour and a half Amy concentrated on what she needed to buy for the huge art project ahead of her, and she couldn't help thinking how wonderful it was to be told that money was no object. It was luxurious in the ultimate to be able to buy the best brands of paint, the best brushes, the best . . . "This is going to cost a lot," she said, looking up at Jason, but he just shrugged.

"What else do you need?" He was looking at his watch, obviously bored and wanting to leave the store.

"Men," she said, which made him look back at her. "Or women." She gave him her most innocent smile. "I need at least three of whichever to help me paint."

"Taken care of."

"That was fast."

"You may have heard that I used to run a business and I often did things quickly."

"Oh? I do believe I heard something about that. So why did you—? Oh, no," she said, without finishing her thought.

Down the aisle, coming toward the cash register, was Max, Doreen following him. Only Max looked liked a young prince leading his elephant, for Doreen was laden with three carry baskets of goods and a paintbrush in her mouth. Only she wasn't carrying the brush across her teeth as any one else would have done it. No, Doreen had stuck the brush into her mouth so it was sticking out about eighteen inches.

She went past Jason and Amy, spit the brush out onto the counter, then dumped the three big baskets by the register. Only then did she turn to Amy, and say, "Your kid is weird"; then she walked away.

"Max, what have you done?" Amy asked, but Max put his hands in his front pockets and tightened his mouth in an expression that Amy didn't recognize as being just like one of hers.

But Jason recognized it and laughed.

"Do you want to buy all of this or not?" the bored clerk said.

"Sure," Jason said, just as Amy said, "No!"

"So which is it?"

"We'll take it," Jason answered, getting out his wallet to hand the young man a platinum American Express card.

But Amy was going through what her son had chosen to purchase, and she was beginning to agree with Doreen that, if not the child, the child's purchases were indeed strange. "Max, honey, did you buy one of every brush the store has?" she asked her son.

Max gave a nod.

"But what about your colors?" she asked. "What colors are you going to paint your monkeys? And what about the jungle? Are you going to make them live in a jungle?"

Before Max could answer, Doreen reappeared with four one-gallon cans of black acrylic paint and a stepladder. "Don't look at me," she said. "He only wants black."

When Max stood there with his hands in his pockets, his face defiant, Jason laughed more.

"Don't encourage him," Amy snapped. "Max, sweetheart, I think you should get another color besides black, don't you?"

"Nope," Jason said. "He wants black and he's going to get black. Now, come on, let's go. We have to get out of here before—"

"The president comes," Amy and Doreen said in unison, then laughed at Jason's scowl. Fifteen minutes later the back of Jason's Range Rover was filled and they were on their way back to the library.

And that's where Amy first met Raphael. He was about seventeen years old, and he had the anger of the world in his eyes, along with an unhealed knife wound on his face.

She took one look at the young man, then grabbed her son's hand and started out of the door, but Jason blocked her way.

"Don't look at me like that," he said. "He was all I could get on such short notice. The other painter was bringing his assistants, and this boy needs to do community service."

"Needs?" she said in a high-pitched voice. "Needs? Or do you mean 'sentenced to'?"

When Jason shrugged guiltily, Amy pulled Max to one side.

"You can't leave me," Jason said. "Just because the boy happens to look a little rough—"

"Rough? He looks like something off a Wanted! poster. How could you think of letting Max around him?"

"I won't leave you alone with him. I'll be here every minute. I'll carry a gun."

"Oh, now, *that's* reassuring," she said sarcastically. She didn't say any more because Raphael pushed past her and started down the library steps. When Jason grabbed the boy's arm, he said something in a language Amy couldn't understand; then, to her surprise, Jason answered him in the same language.

"Look, Amy, you've hurt his feelings, and now he wants to leave. But if he does leave, he'll have to spend several months in jail. Do you want that on your conscience?"

Amy could have burst into tears, for she knew when she was defeated. "No, of course not."

To her consternation Raphael gave a big grin, then walked back into the library.

"He never meant to leave," Amy said under her breath. "He was manipulating me."

At that Jason laughed, picked Max up, and took him back into the library.

And that was just the beginning, Amy thought as she ate the last of her muffin and stared at the fire. After that things were too hectic to pay much attention to any one thing. Once she got started with transferring her drawings onto the walls, she was too busy to think about being afraid of Raphael. All day long a steady stream of girls in ridiculously tiny bits of clothing trouped in and out of the library, all of them posing so Raphael could see them. But Amy had to give it to the young man: he kept his mind on his work and never once did his concentration falter.

Not so Amy, as her son seemed to have turned into someone she didn't know. He marched into the room Jason had said was his, Doreen trailing behind him, her arms full of bags of brushes, and closed the door.

And Amy hadn't seen him the rest of the day. Here she'd been worried that her son would fall into a traumatic fit if he was away from his mother for more than three hours, but now Amy was thinking that he'd been wanting to get away from her for his whole little life.

"Don't be jealous," Jason said from behind her. "Max probably recognizes that Doreen is his intellectual equal."

"I am not jealous!" she snapped. "And stop saying bad things about the woman you love."

Then, to add to Amy's annoyance, Jason didn't make his usual disclaimer about Doreen, but instead, said, "There are other things to recommend her," just so Amy could hear him. As he said this, Doreen was walking into the anteroom, and every male in the library stopped to watch her.

"Drop dead!" Amy said, then stuck her nose in the air and walked away, Jason chuckling behind her.

But Max didn't seem to miss Amy at all. In fact, they didn't see each other all day because Max used Doreen as his emissary.

"He wants to know what monkeys eat," Doreen said on her first trip out of the Land of Secrecy, as Amy had immediately dubbed it after Max had told Doreen not to allow anyone, including his mother, inside the room.

"What do I know?" Amy said over her shoulder. "I'm only his mother."

"Vegetation," Jason said. "Tree leaves."

Doreen went back into the room, but she came out again almost immediately. "He wants pictures of what monkeys eat."

When Amy opened her mouth to speak, Jason said, "Let me"; then he went into the stacks and came back with some books on monkeys and their habitat. One of the books was Japanese.

Doreen took the books into the room, but she was soon out again, one of the books in her hand. "He says he wants more books like this one. I don't know what he means, 'cause it looks like all the others to me."

"Japanese art," Jason said as he disappeared into the stacks again, returning with his arms laden.

As Doreen took them, she said, "He's a weird kid."

At four o'clock, Mildred showed up with three baskets full of food and told Amy she was taking her out to "lunch."

"Lunch was hours ago," Amy said as she studied the color of the face of one of the horses she was trying to paint.

"And did you have any?" Mildred asked.

Amy didn't answer, so Mildred took her arm and pulled her toward the entrance door. "But I—"

"They're men. They're not going to work if there's food around, so we have about thirty-seven minutes all to ourselves."

"But Max—"

"Seems to be in love with Doreen from what I've seen."

Amy grimaced. "How long were you watching us?"

Mildred didn't answer until they were seated in a booth in a coffee shop across the road, their orders placed, and drinks put in front of them. "I was only there for minutes, but Lisa Holding was in the library earlier to check out a book on abnormal psychology—actually she's engaged to the banker's boy, but she's got the hots for Raphael, so she went to see him—and she told her cousin, who told my hairdresser, who told me that—"

"Told you everything that's going on," Amy finished for her.

"Of course. We're all dying to know what's going on between you and Jason."

"Nothing is going on, really nothing. All the men in there are so hot for Doreen that all work stops every time she slinks in and out of that room. Even my own son—" Amy paused to take a breath.

"Jealous," Mildred said, nodding. "I know the feeling."

"I am *not* jealous. Will all of you stop saying that?"

"Jason told you you were jealous?"

Amy took a drink of her Coke and swallowed, refusing to answer her mother-in-law.

"When Billy was a baby, we were never apart for the

first year of his life; then my sister kept him one afternoon and that night Billy refused to let *me* put him to bed."

When Amy didn't answer, Mildred said, "So how are you and Jason getting along? Has he proposed yet?"

Amy didn't say anything but looked down at the club sandwich that had just been set before her. "I know this is a game to you, but I don't want to make a mistake like I made last time."

"You want to talk to me?" Mildred said softly. "I'm a good listener."

"I want to get to know Jason. I want to spend time with him. I made a big mistake the first time I got married, and I don't want to do it again."

She looked up at Mildred with pleading eyes. She wanted to talk to someone, but she was well aware that this woman had been Billy's mother. "I don't want to think what my life would have been like if I were still married to Billy. And one of the few things I know about Jason is that he lies well. He lied to me about being gay, about why he wanted to move in with me, and about why he needed a home. In fact, everything I knew about him was a lie."

She took a breath. "So now I've been told that he's been searching for me for two years, but what does he really know about me, about my son? And what kind of man is he really? Can he take a joke as well as play one?"

Mildred smiled at Amy and said, "With the kind of money Jason has, who cares what kind of sense of humor he has?"

"Me. I care and your grandson cares."

"You're a hard woman to please."

"No, I just want to get it right this time. This time I have to think about a man who will be a *good* father to my son. I don't want Max to get attached to a man, then have the man leave when the going gets rough."

"Or put something in a needle and get out that way," Mildred said softly.

"Exactly."

Mildred smiled. "You've grown up, haven't you?"

"Maybe. During the last two years I think I was able to find out who I am and what I'm capable of. I can take care of myself and my son if I need to. In fact, I can make quite a nice life for the two of us. And I'm proud and happy to have found that out."

Mildred reached for Amy's hand. "And I'm glad you aren't after a man for his money. So tell me all about Jason and Doreen. Tell me everything."

It was nearly six when Amy got back to the library to find a furious Jason.

"Are you going to take a two-hour lunch *every* day?" he said to her.

"If I feel like it," Amy said without blinking an eye.

"She was on the phone to her beloved fiancé," Mildred said. "Love like theirs takes time. I think he might come to see her next week."

. Jason's scowl deepened. "In the future, please conduct your personal life on your own time. Now, could we get back to work?"

Amy looked at her mother-in-law and couldn't decide whether to be pleased by her comment or exasperated.

Mildred felt no ambiguity about the situation. "Don't worry," she said, "you can thank me later." With that she turned on her heel and left the library.

So Amy went back to work, even working through the delicious dinner that Charles showed up with. "I owe everything to your son, who has the taste buds of a gourmet," he said over Amy's shoulder.

She glanced around to see everyone eating, Max ensconced in the middle, a plate full of food before him. He didn't so much as look up at his mother.

At nine o'clock, Amy decided that Max had to get to bed, whether he wanted to or not, and that's when she found out that the Abernathy Room door had been locked against her and other intruders. Annoyed, she tapped on the door, and Doreen answered.

"It's time he went home and went to bed," Amy said. "This is too late for him to stay up."

"All right, I'll ask him," Doreen said; then to Amy's further annoyance, she shut the door against her.

Seconds later Max came out, rubbing his eyes from sleepiness, and Amy felt guilty that she had allowed him to stay up so late. Outside, she strapped him in the car seat in the car Mildred had lent her and drove Max home.

And that's when the trouble started, for Max would not go to sleep. He was usually a good-natured child, but that night he was a demon. He screamed at the top of his lungs, and when Amy picked him up, he straightened out his arms and legs so rigidly that she couldn't get him into the bed.

At eleven he was still fighting, and Amy could not figure out what was wrong with him—and Max only screamed, "No!"

"I'm going to call Jason," Mildred shouted over Max's screams as she picked up the telephone.

"What good would that do?" Amy shouted back. "Please, please, Max, tell Mommie what's wrong," she said for the thousandth time, but Max just yelled and cried, his little face red, his nose stuffed.

"Anything, anything," Amy said as Mildred dialed the phone.

Within minutes Jason was there, and from the look of him he had still been working. He hadn't showered and his clothes had paint on them.

But Jason's presence had no effect on Max. "Poor ol' man," he said as he tried to take him from an exhausted Amy, but Max wanted nothing to do with him.

"I have an idea," he said at last. "Let's take him home."

"Home?" Amy said. "You mean we get on a plane at this time of night?"

"No, I mean his *real* home." Jason didn't give Amy time to say more as he took Max from her, the boy fighting him, carried him outside, and strapped Max into a car seat. By this time the child was too tired to fight, but he still cried.

Amy got into the passenger seat and watched in amazement as Jason drove them through town to . . . At first she couldn't believe her eyes. He pulled into the driveway of what had once been the derelict old house that she and Billy had owned. When she left, she knew that the property would revert to Mildred because she had co-signed on the mortgage, so Amy hadn't concerned herself about the house. She'd assumed that Mildred had sold it, maybe for the building materials, as it wasn't worth much else.

But now the house stood before her in perfect repair. It was what it should have been, beautiful beyond anything Amy could have imagined. Jason had clearly made it his home.

Inside, she didn't have time to look at much as Jason carried a tired, but still whimpering Max through the marble-floored foyer, through the living room, then down the corridor into the room that had once been Max's nursery. It was preserved intact, just as it had been two years ago, everything clean and tidy, as though the baby who used it would be back any minute.

All in all, Amy thought, it was rather creepy.

Jason put Max down, the child looked about for a second, then he relaxed, and finally, at long last, he went to sleep.

"He can*not* remember this place," Amy said. "He was just a baby when he left."

"No one ever forgets love, and he loved this house," Jason said.

And he loved you, Amy wanted to say but didn't.

For a moment Jason waited, as though expecting her to say something, but when she was silent, he said, "You know where your room is," then turned away and went to what Amy knew was the same room where he'd stayed when it was her house.

When she was alone, she went into what had been her bedroom. It was a far cry from what it had been when she lived in the house, and she knew that only a professional decorator could have made the room so beautiful. Even down to the fresh flowers, it was heavenly. Exhausted from her struggles with Max, she did little more than visit the bathroom, then fell onto the bed.

So now it was morning, Max was still asleep, and she guessed that Jason was still sleeping in the spare bedroom.

"And we forgot Doreen's furniture," she said as she finished her tea, then she stood and stretched. She needed to get dressed so she could get to work. The murals needed to be done before the president's visit, she thought, smiling.

In her bedroom she wasn't surprised to find clean clothes, just her size, in the closet. And when Max woke up, she wasn't surprised to find that Jason had already left the house.

CHAPTER NINETEEN

"DAMN IT TO HELL AND BACK," JASON SAID AS HE BANGED his fist on the steering wheel of the car. Just what did Amy think he was made of? He hadn't slept ten minutes last night for thinking that she was in the next room. But his presence didn't seem to have bothered her, for she slept heavily. Quietly, so he wouldn't disturb her of course, he'd checked on her and Max four times during the night.

So now he was driving to the library, it wasn't even daylight yet, and he faced days of working side by side with her. Yet every time he tried to tell her that he wasn't engaged, that he still loved her, she cut him off. Why in the world hadn't he tried harder to explain?

He'd better stop that or he'd go crazy. Sometimes it seemed that since he'd met Amy, all he did was regret his actions. Already he regretted hiring a juvenile delinquent to help paint the library. When Amy saw him and Jason saw her fear, he'd instantly regretted what he'd done. But then Raphael had tricked her, and . . .

"Oh, the hell with it," he said as he swung the car into the library parking lot. Maybe he should do what his brother advised him to do and forget about Amy. Maybe he should find someone else, a woman who would love him back. A woman who didn't run away rather than have to spend time with him.

When Jason entered the library, his jaw was set and he was determined that he was going to stay away from Amy and her son. Maybe it would be better if he went to the Bahamas for a while. He could return just in time for the opening of the library and—

No, he told himself, he was going to stay and fight like a man. Maybe what everyone said was right and he didn't know Amy at all. She certainly didn't *look* the same as when he'd known her before. Two years ago she'd been thin and tired-looking, and she had an air about her of helplessness that had appealed to him.

But this new Amy was altogether different. There was now an air of confidence about her. Yesterday she'd been quite clear about what she needed to paint the murals and who she needed and what was to be done.

"Mildred's probably right, and I only like helpless people," Jason muttered. "I'm sure that after I spend six weeks near her I'll realize that I never even knew her and that the woman I thought she was is a fantasy."

Smiling, he began to feel better. Yes, that was it. Before he'd spent just a few days with her and Max, and of course he'd liked them. As David pointed out they were in need of "fixing," like one of the little companies Jason used to buy then reorganize and sell for a fortune. Amy and Max were like Abernathy. And the fixer inside him wanted to sort them out and do something with them.

Now that he had that solved, he felt much better. But then he looked at his watch and wondered when the hell Amy was going to get there, because, damn it! he missed her.

No, he told himself. Discipline! That's all he needed. He needed the discipline of an iron statue. He was *not* going to make a fool of himself over Amy again. He wasn't going to pursue her, lie to her, trick her, or in any way try to make her like him. Instead, he was going to be all business. They had a job ahead of them, and he was going to do it, and that's all.

Right, he told himself, then looked at his watch again. What in the world was she doing?

When he heard her car pull into the parking lot, he smiled, then went into the office. He wasn't going to let her think that he'd been waiting for her.

"Doreen, dear," Amy said, as she handed half her sandwich to Max, "we forgot all about your furniture last night."

"Yeah, I know," she said, looking down at her sandwich as though it were as appetizing as paper. "I didn't think it would happen."

"And why not, honey bun?" Jason asked.

Both Amy and Doreen looked up at him with startled eyes.

"Are you losing confidence in me already?" Jason asked. "Even before we're married?"

Both women stared at him with their mouths hanging open.

"I was thinking, darlin', that since I don't have a lot of time . . ." Jason shifted the sandwich to his other hand and opened a newspaper that someone had left lying on the table. They were, after all, in a library. "How about this one?" he asked as he pointed to a photo of a big white farmhouse with a deep porch all around the front of the house. It was two stories with a full attic and three dormer windows across the front. Even in the grainy black and white photo the house looked cool and serene under the big trees that were at the sides and back of the house.

"You like it?" Jason asked as he took another bite.

"Me?" Doreen asked.

"Of course. You're the one I'm marrying, aren't I? Unless you've changed your mind, that is." With that he winked at Amy, who still hadn't closed her mouth. "You like the house or not?"

"It's beautiful," Doreen whispered, her eyes as big as the giant cookies Charles had brought in on a porcelain platter.

"Not too little? Too big? Maybe you'd like something more modern."

Doreen looked at Amy as though for advice.

Amy cleared her throat. "If that house is in good condition, it'll hold its value better than a new house," she said softly.

"So what will it be, love?" Jason asked.

It was Doreen's turn to swallow hard. "I . . . Uh . . . I, ah." Suddenly she blinked hard, as though she'd made a decision. "I'll take it," she said enthusiastically.

In the next moment, Jason picked up his cell phone and called the realtor's number. Amy and Doreen sat in silence while they heard him tell the man that he wanted to buy the house pictured in today's newspaper.

Jason paused. "No, I don't have time to see it. No, I don't care what it costs. You do all that, just bring me the papers and I'll give you a check." He paused again. "Thank you," Jason said, then turned the phone off.

"You can't buy a house just like that," Amy said.

"Sure I can. I just did. Now, shall we get on with the painting? What color are these saddles supposed to be?"

"Purple," Amy said, and she had no idea why she was annoyed, but she was.

Twenty minutes later a hot, sweaty man appeared

with papers, saying that there had to be a title search and it was all going to take time.

"Anyone living in the house now?" Jason asked.

"No . . ."

"For how long did the previous owners own it?"

"Four years. He was transferred to California and—"

"Then I'm sure the title is fine." Jason picked up a pen and paper, wrote down a number, then handed it to the agent. "Okay, then how about this figure to sell it and forget the title search?"

"Let me make a phone call," the agent said, and five minutes later he returned. "You got yourself a house," he said as he pulled a set of keys out of his pocket. "I think that under the circumstances you should have these."

Jason handed the keys to Doreen. "Now, what else do you need?"

As Doreen clutched the keys to her breast, she looked as though she was going to faint.

Of course no one had done any work while this was going on. And even Amy gave a bit of a smile.

At last I did something to please her, Jason thought, even if it did cost me six figures. And if it took giving a gift to Doreen to get a smile from Amy, then Jason was going to buy Doreen the whole state of Kentucky.

"I hate him," Amy said to her mother-in-law.

"Calm down and tell me again what he's doing."

They were in the library, it was late, and Max was asleep on the little bed that Jason had purchased for him and set up so he could sleep while his mother worked at night. Amy was sanding as she talked, taking the rough edges off a fresco of an elephant draped in gold.

Amy took a deep breath. "I have been here one whole week, we live in the same house, work together all day long, but he pays *no* attention to me. None whatever."

"I'm sure he's just trying to proceed slowly. He probably—"

"No," Amy whined. "The man doesn't *like* me. If you knew what I've done in these last few days . . ."

"Out with it. Tell me all." Mildred glanced over at her grandson and had the sneaking suspicion that he was awake. "I want to know everything that Jason has said to you."

"That's just it. He never says or does anything."

"Is that elephant supposed to be red?"

"Now look what he's made me do." Amy grabbed a rag and began rubbing, which did no good, so she painted over the red with gray; it was going to be a very dark elephant. Taking a deep breath, she tried to calm herself. "I thought he wanted . . . Well, that he was . . . You said . . ."

"That he was in love with you and wanted to marry you," Mildred said quietly. "He was. Is. I'd stake my hairdresser on it."

Amy laughed. "Okay, so I'm being overly emotional. It's just that, well, he's a good-looking man, and I . . ." She glanced at Max, who had his eyes suspiciously tightly closed. "You know that red peignoir set they had in Chambers's window?"

"The tiny one with all the lace?"

"Yes. I bought it, then made sure that Jason saw me in it. I acted embarrassed, but I could have been wearing my old chenille bathrobe for all he noticed."

Mildred raised one eyebrow. "What did he do?"

"Nothing. He drank some milk, then said good night and went to bed. He didn't so much as look at me. But then I'm no Doreen. She has curves that—"

"—are going to turn to fat in about three years' time," Mildred said, waving her hand in dismissal.

"Don't say anything against Doreen," Amy snapped. "I like her. And Max adores her."

Again Mildred looked at the child and thought she saw his eyelashes flicker, and there seemed to be a crease forming between his brows. "So tell me what my grandson is painting in that room."

Amy rolled her eyes. "I have no idea what's in there, since he won't let me see. Top secret. Secret from his own mother! And he won't sleep at home even if Doreen stays with him because he's afraid that if I'm here in the library alone, I'll snoop."

"And would you?"

"Of course," Amy said as though that were a given. "I gave birth to him, so why shouldn't I see his painting? It couldn't be worse than what I saw inside his diaper after he ate the abacus. And, no, don't ask."

Mildred laughed, especially since she saw that the crease was gone from Max's forehead and there was a tiny curve to his lips. Obviously, the child knew his mother well. "So what are we going to do about you and Jason?"

"Nothing. When this is finished, Max and I go home to . . ."

"To what?" Mildred asked.

"Don't say it," Amy said softly. "We go home to nothing, and no one knows that better than I do."

"Then stay here," Mildred said, and her voice was a plea from her heart.

"And see Jason every day?"

"See *me* with *my* grandchild!" Mildred snapped at her.

"Be quiet; you'll wake Max."

"You don't think taking him away from his only living relative besides his mother will wake him? Amy, please—"

"Hand me that can of green, will you, and let's talk about something else. I'm not running away this time; I'll just be going home."

But right now an apartment in New York City didn't

seem like home. With every day that she was in Abernathy, she was remembering things that she'd always
liked about the small town. At lunch she made Max
quit work and the two of them took a stroll through
town so they could eat their sandwiches under the big
oak tree at the edge of town. And as they walked, people called out to them to ask how the library was going
and they teased Max about his secret room.

"Home" was taking on a new meaning.

CHAPTER TWENTY

AMY DIDN'T TALK TO MILDRED AGAIN FOR A WHILE because for the next ten days she was so busy that she had no time to think about anything whatever. She was existing on little more than four hours of sleep a night, and she was glad that, somehow, gradually, Doreen had taken over the daily care of Max. Amy didn't know whether to be grateful or sad that her son took so well to being bathed by someone other than his mother, dressed by someone else and read to sleep by another woman. And she hadn't had time to sit down with Max and hear what he had to say about spending so much time away from his mother.

Somehow, Amy wasn't sure when or exactly how, Doreen had moved into the Salma house. And why not? Amy thought. It wasn't as though anything private was going on between her and Jason.

After Amy had been in town only two days, Cherry
Parker gave birth to a baby girl, and within two weeks
Cherry had organized her whole household so well that
she had her baby waking for only one feeding during
the night (which David took care of) and Cherry was
helping Jason to sort out the town of Abernathy in
preparation for the library's opening.

"I love you," Jason said once after Cherry rattled off
a list of things that had been done and were being done.

"Hmph!" Cherry said, but they could all see that she
was pleased by his compliment. She was wearing a
white Chanel suit, but strapped across her chest was a
huge scarf that had to have been made in Africa, and
inside, her newborn daughter was sleeping peacefully.

After Cherry returned to work, Doreen moved into
the house with Amy, Jason, and Max and began to look
after the little boy. By that time Amy had overcome her
jealousy and was just grateful. Every morning Doreen
saw that Max was fed whatever Charles had cooked
especially for him; then she took the boy to the library.
And each morning Max would take the key out of his
pocket and make a ceremony of opening the door to
the Abernathy Room, then disappear inside for the
whole day.

Amy did, however, have a fit of pique once when
Charles showed up and Max invited the chef into the
"secret" room. Thirty minutes later Charles came out,
his eyes wide in wonder, but his lips were sealed.

"Did the boy's father paint too?"

"I don't know," Amy said. "Why?"

"That boy got a double dose of talent, and I just wondered where it came from. Can I be here when the president sees that room?"

"Did you forget that you're catering for him?" Jason shouted from the scaffolding, where he was on his back painting the ceiling.

"Right," Charles said, then leaned forward to Amy to whisper, "How long has he been in this bad mood?"

"Since 1972," she said without hesitation.

Nodding, Charles left the library.

It was well into the third week that Amy began to see what was happening between her and Jason. It took her that long to get over her annoyance that he was paying no attention to her, and she was so busy with the painting that she hadn't had time to look and listen.

But by the third week they were all into a routine, and she began to see things. She wasn't the only one who had changed. Jason had changed too, but she didn't think he knew it. As the days passed, one by one, her objections to him were destroyed.

The first time it happened she hadn't paid much attention. A little boy, about eight, tiptoed into the library and silently handed Jason a piece of paper. Jason made a few marks on the paper, said a few words to the boy, then the child had left the library with a big grin on his face.

The next day the same thing happened, then the next. Each time it was a different child, sometimes two children; sometimes as many as three interrupted Jason as he painted.

One afternoon a tall boy of about sixteen came in, shoved a paper under Jason's nose and stood there with a look of defiance on his face. Jason wiped off his paintbrush, then went into the office with the boy and stayed in there with him for over an hour.

If Amy hadn't been up to her neck in painting, she would have been quite curious as to what was going on, but she had too much to do to think of anything but getting the murals on the walls.

It was after the sketches were up and all that was needed was days of fill-in work that she was sitting with Doreen and Max, eating the pasta salad and crab cakes Charles had made for lunch, when two little girls came in with papers and handed them to Jason.

"What is he doing?" Amy asked.

"Homework," Doreen said.

"What do you mean, homework?"

Doreen waited until she'd finished chewing. "He's Mr. Homework. He helps the kids out with their school-work."

"Doreen, so help me, if you make me beg you for every piece of information . . ."

"I think it started as a joke. At the pet store. No, at

the barbershop. Yeah, that's it. The men had nothing to do on a Saturday, so they started complaining that they didn't understand their kids' homework, so somebody said that if Jason really wanted to help Abernathy, he'd make the kids smart."

"So?" Amy asked, narrowing her eyes at Doreen. "How could Jason make the kids smarter?"

"I don't know, but the board of education says that our kids are a lot smarter now."

Amy wanted to ask more questions, since she didn't understand anything from what Doreen had said, but she had a feeling she wasn't going to get much more information from this conversation. Amy turned to her son. "So how are you doing in there? Can I see what you're painting?"

Max had his mouth full, but he gave a smile and shook his head no.

"Please," Amy said. "Can't I just have a peek?"

Nearly giggling, Max kept shaking his head no. This was a daily conversation, and Amy went to great lengths to think up persuasions and promises to try to get Max to let her inside the room. But he never came close to relenting.

It was the next day, when David came to the library to view the progress of the murals, that Amy managed to get David off into a corner. "What is this Mr. Homework stuff I've heard about?"

"Mildred didn't tell you?" David asked. "I would have thought she'd have told you everything and then some."

"Actually, I'm beginning to think that no one has told me anything."

"I know the feeling well. My brother has an open door to any child in Abernathy who needs help with his homework."

When Amy just looked at him, David continued. "It started as a joke. People in Abernathy were suspicious of Jason's motives for helping rebuild the town, and—"

"Why? He's a hometown boy."

David took a moment before he answered. "I think you should ask Jason about that one. Let's just say that they were a little concerned that he had some devious, underlying reason for what he was doing. So one day some men were talking and—"

"Gossiping in the barbershop."

David smiled. "Exactly. They said that if Jason wanted to do some good, he could help the kids with their homework."

"And?"

"And he did."

Amy looked at David. "What is it that you're holding back?"

"Would you believe, love for my brother? Jason had Cherry look into the test scores of Abernathy's children, and I can tell you that they were appalling. A town that's had as many out-of-work people as Abernathy has, has depression for dinner each night. Jason knew that it would do no good to give a pep talk to the people that they *should* help the kids with their schoolwork, so he hired tutors."

Turning, David looked at his brother's broad back as he helped Raphael with a painting. "My brother didn't hire dry, scholarly professors. No, he hired out-of-work actors and dancers and writers and retired sea captains and doctors and—" Pausing, he grinned at Amy. "Jason hired a lot of people with a lot of knowledge who wanted to share that knowledge. They came here and worked at the schools for three months. And afterward, quite a few of those people decided to stay here."

Amy was silent for a moment as she digested this information. "And he helps the children with their homework?"

"Yes. Jason said that I'd given him the idea. I'd said that there were 'other children.' " David's voice lowered. "I was talking to him about there being children other than Max."

"I see," Amy said, but she wasn't sure that she did see.

It was after that conversation that she began to watch Jason more closely. Over the past two years, when she'd been in New York trying to make her own way, she'd built up an image of this man in her head. She'd read all the articles about his philanthropy and she'd applied that to her own situation in which Jason had spent a lot of money on her and her child. She had concluded that Jason and his money were one and the same.

But giving of money and giving of yourself to help children understand long division were two different things.

It was after her talk with David that Amy quit trying to entice Jason. Instead, she tried to see him as he really was and not as she'd thought he was based on a few press articles and what she assumed he was like. As secretly as she could, she began to watch him.

For one thing, he complained all the time about how much everything was costing him, but she never once saw him turn down any bill. By snooping through some papers he left lying about, she found out that he owned the local mortgage company and that he had given low-interest loans to most of the businesses and several farms in the surrounding area.

Amy also saw that the formidable Cherry Parker seemed to have changed toward him.

As nonchalantly as she could manage, as though it meant nothing to her, Amy said to Cherry, "Is it just me or has he changed?"

"From black to white," Cherry said, then walked away.

One Saturday morning, Jason wasn't in the library and Amy found him at the school grounds playing basketball with half a dozen boys who made Raphael look like an upstanding citizen. "So how many boys like you has Jason taken on?" she asked Raphael later that day.

Raphael grinned at her. "Lots. We used to have a gang, but . . ." He trailed off, then went back to painting. "He thinks he can get me some more work like this," Raphael said softly. "He thinks I have talent."

"You do," Amy said, then wondered if Jason planned to paint the inside of every building he owned just to give these gangsters a job.

When Jason returned from playing basketball, Amy looked up at him. He was wearing gray sweatpants that were dirty, sweat-soaked, and torn. And she'd never seen any human sexier than he was at that moment.

For a moment Jason looked at her, and Amy turned away in embarrassment, but not before Jason gave her a knowing grin.

"Hey!" Raphael yelled because Amy had just drawn a camel's face on a princess's body.

"Sorry," Amy murmured and refused to turn back around to look at Jason.

Just a few more days, she thought, and a thrill of excitement went through her.

CHAPTER TWENTY-ONE

THE NIGHT BEFORE THE OPENING OF THE LIBRARY, ALL OF them except Doreen and Max were working in the library until three A.M.

"That's it," Jason said, and looked up at the others. "Tell me, do I look as bad as the lot of you?" he asked, his voice hoarse from talking so much in an attempt to answer the thousands of questions fired at him that day.

They all looked around. The library was as finished as it was ever going to be.

"You look worse than we do," Amy said, deadpan. "What do you think, Raphael?" After six weeks of daily contact, they had come to know each other well, and Amy marveled that she had ever been afraid of him. And Raphael had proven to be quite talented, both in art and in organization.

"Worse than me," Raphael said, "but then old men always look bad."

"Old?" Jason said. "I'll give you old," he said, then made a leap for the young man, but Raphael side-stepped, and Jason went down hard on the oak floor, and he cried out in pain.

Instantly, all of them were hanging over him. "Jason! Jason!" Amy cried as she put her hands on the side of his head.

Jason kept his eyes closed and a little groan escaped his lips.

"Call a doctor," Amy ordered, but in the next second Jason's hand shot up, grabbed the back of Amy's head, and pulled her mouth down to his for a long, hard kiss.

After a long moment she pulled away, although she didn't want to. And the instant they broke contact, Jason was up and after Raphael. Tackling him, Jason soon brought the younger and much smaller man down to the floor.

"Just didn't want to hurt you," Raphael said when Jason finally let him up.

Amy was standing in the shadows, her back to the group. She was still shaking from Jason's kiss, a kiss that hadn't seemed to mean anything to him.

As he always did, Jason drove Amy home and tried not to think about how lonely his house would be once Amy and Max were gone.

"One more day," Jason said. "And then it's over. You'll be glad, won't you?"

"Oh, yes, very."

Jason didn't say anything, but her words hurt. "Max will be glad to get back, I'm sure," Jason said. "He must miss his own room, one that isn't as babyish as the one he has here."

"Yes, of course," she said.

"And that man . . ."

"Arnie," she supplied.

"Yeah. No doubt he'll be glad to see you."

"Madly," she said, trying to sound lighthearted and happy.

"Amy—"

"Oh, my, look at the time," she said as Jason pulled into the driveway. "I bet Doreen is waiting up for us."

"Sure," he said. "I'm sure she is. Look, about to-night . . ."

"Oh, that," she said, knowing that he was talking about the kiss. "I won't tell Arnie if you won't. I'll just say good night here, and I'll see you in the morning," she said as she made her way up the porch steps. Minutes later she tiptoed in to see Max, to make sure that he was all right. He was sleeping so soundly that he didn't stir when she pulled the covers over him.

"I think maybe your grandmother is crazy," she whispered to the sleeping baby. Amy had promised Mildred that she'd let Jason make the first move.

"Until he tells you that he's not going to marry Doreen, you're to keep on telling him about Varney."

"Arnie," Amy had said.

Max rolled over in his sleep, and for a moment he opened his eyes, saw his mother; then a sweet smile appeared and he closed his eyes again.

To melt the heart, she thought as she looked at him. He had a smile to melt a heart. "And I am blessed at knowing you," she whispered as she kissed her fingertip, then touched it to Max's lips. Standing back, she yawned. Time to go to bed because tomorrow the president of the United States was coming to visit.

"Here's the first of them," Amy said as she put her hand on the paper rolling out of the fax machine; then as she read it, her eyes opened wide, first in horror, then in disbelief.

"Tell us!" Raphael shouted. "What does it say?"

With a face full of disbelief, Amy handed the fax to the boy. His knife wound had healed in the last weeks, and he looked less like a murderer looking for a victim.

Raphael scanned the paper, then let out a hoot of laughter and handed the fax to Jason.

Everyone who had worked on the murals was in the library huddled around the fax machine as though they were freezing and it was a fire. This morning the president had visited Abernathy, and now they were waiting for the clipping service to send through any reviews of what the president had seen. What was in these reviews could make or break Amy's career.

"A cross between Japanese art and Javanese shadow

puppets, with a bit of Art Deco thrown in," Jason read aloud. "Stunning, individual." He looked up at Amy in disbelief.

"Go on," she said, "read the rest of it."

When Jason said nothing else, Amy took the paper from him. "Basically, the article dismisses my murals as 'well executed' and 'appropriate,' but Max's work was . . ." She looked down to quote exactly. " 'Art with a capital *A.*' " Amy looked at her son sitting on a red bean bag chair and smiled at him. "And they are," she said. "They are magnificent."

They were in the Abernathy Room, the room that for six weeks had been locked against Amy as her son created in privacy. When Amy looked back on it, she knew that she had been prepared to console Max when no one was impressed with the black shapes that a two-and-a-half-year-old called monkeys. But when she'd finally seen the room, she was walking behind the president and she had been too stunned by the art on the walls to remember whom she was with.

"Holy Toledo," she'd murmured as she looked around the room, and her words seemed to speak for all of them, as no one else could make a sound. All the walls, the ceiling, and spreading onto the wooden floor was a shadow jungle. Huge, towering bamboo plants seemed to move about in a breeze that wasn't in the room but was in the pictures. Monkeys peeped out from the branches and stems, some eating bananas, some just staring, their eyes looking at you until you stepped back, afraid of being too close to these untamed animals.

"I've never seen anything like it," a short man in the back whispered, and Amy had already been told that he was an art critic for *The Washington Post*. "Marvelous," he said under his breath as he craned his neck this way and that. "And you painted them?" He managed to look down his nose at Amy even though they were the same height.

"No, my son did," Amy said quietly.

The little man turned surprised eyes toward Raphael, who was standing behind her. "This is your son?"

"My son is over there," Amy said, pointing to where Max stood near Jason.

For a moment the art critic and the president as well looked confused. She couldn't mean that Jason was her son, could she?

"Max, sweetheart, come here," Amy said, holding out her hand. "I want you to meet the president."

After that, all hell broke loose. The president's visit to Abernathy had been undertaken half for the sake of creating some good publicity, as he was on his way to another meeting about the Middle East, and half to pass out scholarly awards to the schoolchildren of Abernathy. Because of his ultimate destination, he was surrounded by journalists. And now, when they saw that this extraordinary room had been created by a very little boy, they started firing questions. "Young man, where did you get the idea for this room?" "Come on, now, tell the truth, your mother painted this room for you, didn't she?" "I think you'd better tell the truth about these monkeys, don't you?" "Just tell us the truth: who painted these pictures?"

Jason picked up Max and glared at the photographers. "If you'll excuse us, it's the artist's nap time. If you must badger someone with your questions, ask one of the adults." At that, he nodded toward Amy and Doreen; then he left the building, Max held protectively to him.

The journalists started shooting questions at Amy, since they knew that she'd painted the murals in the other room, but Amy directed them toward Doreen. "She knows everything. I wasn't even allowed inside the room to see what was going on."

Turning, Amy expected Doreen to be shy with the press or at the very least reticent, but she wasn't. Instead, she took to being interviewed and photographed as though she'd always lived in front of a camera.

So now, hours later, they were reading about what a triumph of achievement the "Shadow Monkeys" were, and Max was being hailed as a newly discovered genius.

"I always knew he was brilliant; it's just nice to have the world's verification," Amy said proudly, and they all laughed.

"Here it is," Jason said as the door opened and Charles entered carrying three magnums of champagne.

Behind him trailed four young chefs carrying great trays of food.

"Who is all this for?" Amy murmured, and Jason turned to her with a broad grin.

"I invited a few people to celebrate," he said. "I knew you'd be a triumph, so I planned ahead."

It didn't matter to Amy that her work had been dismissed and that in her heart she knew that she'd probably never be a great artist or achieve great success, but Max had accomplished both and would continue to do so—and that was enough for her. To have produced a child with the talent that Max obviously had was all that she could ask of life. Except, she thought as she looked Jason up and down, maybe she might like to have a father for her child.

"To us!" Jason said as he raised a glass in a salute; then his eye caught Amy's and his smile changed to one of intimacy, as though he could read her mind.

Behind the chefs came the man who owned the general store in Abernathy, and behind him came his wife and three children. They were followed by the hardware store family and the elementary school principal, then the four teachers at the school, then—

"Did you invite the whole town?" Amy asked.

"Everyone of them," he said. "And their kids."

Amy laughed and knew that she'd never been happier in her life than she was at that moment. It's too good to last, she heard a little voice say, but she took another sip of champagne and thought no more as music came from the outside garden and, to her astonishment, she found that a band had set up there and was playing dance music.

Smiling, she turned to Jason, who was watching her, and from the look on his face, he wanted her approval. She lifted her glass to him in a toast.

At one A.M. a fleet of cars arrived in front of the library to take everyone home. Jason had even given lists of addresses to the drivers so no one who'd had too much champagne had to worry about remembering where he lived. Doreen carried a sleeping Max out to one of the cars. She had already told Amy that she would put Max to bed and stay with him until Jason and Amy got home.

In an astonishingly short time, Amy and Jason were left alone in the library, and after the frivolity of the party the library seemed huge and empty. Amy sat down on one of the hard oak chairs by a reading table and looked up at Jason. The triumph of her son was still running through her veins, and it would for the rest of her life.

"Happy?" Jason said, standing in front of her, looking down at her with an odd expression on his face. He had a glass of champagne in his hand.

"Very," she murmured, looking up at him boldly. Maybe it was the soft light in the room, all those reading table lamps, but he looked better than he ever had before.

"You aren't a bit envious of Max stealing the show?"

"What a sense of humor you have," she said, smiling. "I have given birth to the greatest artist this century has known. Let's see my son top *that* one."

Jason laughed, and, before he thought, said, "I have always loved you."

"Me and every other female in this hemisphere," she said before she could stop herself.

At that Jason threw his glass against the wall, where it shattered into thousands of tiny shards. In one strong swoop, he grabbed Amy to him, pulling her out of the chair and up into his arms. Then he kissed her hard. But the kiss soon softened, and the moment his tongue touched hers, Amy's body went limp in surrender.

"So long," she murmured. "It's been so very, very long."

Jason held her to him, caressing her back, his fingers entangled in her hair. "So long since me or since . . . him?"

"There is no 'him,' " she said, her face pressed into his neck.

At that Jason pulled her away from him and held her at arm's length. "There is no Arnie?"

"Only the man who owns the potato chip factory."

It took Jason a moment to understand; then he pulled her back into his arms. "Me. I bought the factory and named it after my great uncle."

"What about Doreen?" Amy wanted to say more, but she couldn't think with Jason's hands on her body.

Jason grabbed her with all the pent-up passion he'd been holding back and kissed her with all his body. "I love you, Amy," he whispered against her lips. "I've loved you forever and will always love you. Doreen made up our engagement . . . she thought she was doing me a favor. I tried to explain."

Amy's sigh of relief said it all. She believed.

Jason pulled Amy even closer and looked deeply into her eyes. "Don't go, Amy. Please don't go away. Stay here with me forever."

What could she say but yes? "Yes," she whispered, "yes."

After that there was no more breath for words as they tore at each other's clothing, pulling and tearing, tugging, then giving great sighs of pleasure as each new bit of skin was exposed. When they were naked, they fell down on the mattress that Max had used for his afternoon naps, and when Jason entered her, Amy gasped in pleasure and disbelief—how could she ever have left this man? How could she—?

"Amy, Amy," Jason kept whispering. "I love you. I love you."

And all Amy could answer was, "Yes."

It was an hour later when they lay still on the mattress, exhausted, their arms wrapped tightly about each other. "Tell me everything," she said, sounding like her mother-in-law. "I want to know about all the women, about everything. What I see and what I feel coming from you are two different things. I want to understand, to know you, but I can't. I need words," she said.

At first Jason was reluctant to talk; after all, what man wants to tell a woman how much he needs her? But once Jason began to talk, he couldn't stop. Loneliness is a great tongue loosener. And it hadn't been until he'd met Amy and Max that he'd known how empty his life was.

"I'm sorry," she said, and the words were from her heart. "I'm sorry for your pain."

He told her how difficult it had been in Abernathy, how the townspeople had fought him. "I thought they'd be grateful, but they resented a New Yorker coming in here and trying to tell them what to do."

"But you were born and raised here," Amy said.

When Jason said nothing, she pulled away so she could look at him. "What is between you and this town? And your father?" she asked softly. "Not even Mildred would tell me what happened."

It was a while before Jason spoke. "Sometimes a person has to face his worst fears, and . . ." He took a deep breath. "You know that my mother died when David was just a baby."

"Yes. And I know that your father had to raise you two boys alone."

"That's his version of it," Jason said angrily, then stopped himself. "My father didn't have much time for kids, so after my mother died, he left us alone to fend for ourselves."

"Ah. I guess that means he left you to take care of David by yourself."

"Yes."

"But I don't think that's what you're angry at Abernathy about, is it?"

Again Jason took his time, as though he had to calm himself down before he could speak. "My mother was a saint. She had to be to be married to a cold bastard like my father. When she learned that she was dying, she told no one. She didn't want to be a burden to anyone, so she went to the doctor alone, kept the news to herself, and we kept on living like nothing was wrong."

As he paused, Amy could feel the tension in his body. "But one of the Abernathy gossips saw her in a café in a motel about thirty miles from here, then went home to spread the word that Mrs. Wilding was having an out-of-town affair."

"And your father believed the gossip," Amy said softly.

"Oh, yeah. He believed it so much that he got her back by jumping into bed with some hot little number from—" He cut himself off until he was calm again.

"I was the one who found out the truth. I cut school and hid in the backseat of my mother's car. I was in the waiting room of the doctor's when she came out. She made me promise not to tell my father. She said that life was to be lived, not mourned."

"I would have liked to have met her," Amy said.

"She was wonderful, but she got a raw deal."

"She had two children who loved her, and it seems that her husband was mad about her."

"What?!" Jason gasped.

"How did he take it when he found out that his wife was dying?"

"He never said a word about it, but after her death he locked himself in a room for three days. When he came out, he took on extra work so he was never home, and as far as I know, he's never spoken her name again."

"And you doubt that he loved her?"

For a moment, Amy held her breath. Maybe she'd gone too far. People liked to hold on to their beliefs and didn't like to have them contradicted.

"I guess he did," Jason said at last. "But I wish he'd loved us more. Sometimes I got sick of being my kid brother's mother and father. Sometimes I wanted to . . . to play football like the other kids."

Amy didn't say anything, but she could see the pattern in Jason's life. His father had taught him that making money was everything and that if you worked enough, you could block out pain and loneliness and all sorts of unpleasant emotions.

She snuggled against him, her flesh touching his, and she could feel that he was beginning to become aroused again. But he held back. "And what of your life? You seem to have done well."

It was on the tip of her tongue to tell him that she

had done very well, that she'd gone off and made herself a fortune, that she didn't need any man. But the words wouldn't come out of her mouth. It was time to tell the truth.

She took a deep breath to calm her pounding heart. "Yes, I've done well, but at first I was afraid that Max and I would starve," she said at last. "I did a very stupid thing when I ran away."

"Why didn't you call me?" he demanded. "I would have helped. I would have—"

"Pride. I've always had too much pride. When I found out what Billy really was, I should have left him, but I couldn't bear to hear people saying that I gave up just because I found some flaws in the man."

"Flaws?" he said in astonishment.

Turning on her side, Amy put her hand on his face. "My marriage to Billy was awful," she said. "I was miserable. I hated the drinking and the drugs, but I also hated that he was weak, and that he could sacrifice everything just so he could feel good."

"When you met him—" Jason said softly.

"He was in one of his sober periods. But I should have known. He made all sorts of remarks that later I remembered and knew that they had been clues to what and who he was. And when you came along, you seemed so perfect, but then I found out that you, like Billy, had a secret life, and I couldn't handle it. I ran. I just picked up my son and ran as fast and as far as I could. Can you understand that?"

"Yes," he said as he ran his hand up her bare arm. "It makes sense. You're here now and—"

"But it was so awful! I was so frightened and alone and—"

Jason turned her in his arms until her face was buried in his shoulder. "Shh, it's all over now. I'm going to take care of you and Max, and—"

"But everyone will think I've married you for your money. They'll say that I learned my lesson with Billy, so this time I went after a man with money."

Jason smiled into her hair. "I think it's more likely they'll say that I went after you. Did Mildred tell you that I had private detectives looking for you for over a year? They could find nothing. Yet all the time Mildred knew where you were." There was a touch of bitterness in his voice.

"But she didn't. She just found us a few months ago, and that was by accident."

Jason pulled away to look at her. "How did she find you?"

"She bought Max some Christmas presents because she said that she never gave up hope of seeing him again, and one of them was a children's book. She saw my photo in the back of a book I had illustrated."

"That simple," Jason said, then smiled as he remembered all the agony he'd gone through with the private detectives. "And what is your pen name?"

"My real name is Amelia Rudkin. Using Billy's name was just a courtesy to him, but I never bothered to change it legally. I was listed in the New York phone directory. I guess I never gave up hope that you would look for me and find me."

Jason tightened his arms around her. "I'm glad it happened. If you hadn't run away, I would have continued as I was. I'm sure I would have kept on working without stop just to prove to you that I could support you and—"

"But why would you need to prove anything to *me?*"

"Because you're the woman I love, the only one I've ever loved."

Turning, she looked at him. "But if Mildred is to be believed, the people of Abernathy have given you such a hard time that by all rights you should want the first plane out of here."

"I agree. They are an ungrateful, complaining lot, but, on the other hand, they treat me as a person. Mr. William, who owns the hardware store, told me that I'd always been hardheaded and I hadn't changed. Maybe it was that I was at last surrounded by people who weren't toadies that kept me here. If I raised an eyebrow at my employees in New York, they backtracked and said what they thought I wanted to hear. But here . . ." He smiled.

"Here they tell you what they think of you," Amy finished for him.

"Yes. Mildred told me day after day that I was the reason you'd left. She said that David and I had played such a nasty trick that any woman in her right mind—"

"Don't hint that *I* was in my right mind, to run off with a baby and no way to support him."

"Ah," Jason said, smiling, "but it's all come out in the end. At last Max will have a father. If you'll have me, that is."

"I'll take you if you want us," Amy said softly. "But I . . ."

"What?"

"Today has been a revelation to me, for today I've found out that my two-and-a-half-year-old son is not only a better painter than I am, he's smarter than I am. I'm afraid that I'm like so many other people and I couldn't see *you* for your money. But Max always saw what was inside you."

"Real smart kid," Jason said, making Amy laugh. "You think you'd like to have more of them?"

At that, Amy groaned. "Morning sickness, exhaustion, and, oh, no, not breast-feeding again!" When she saw Jason's face, she laughed. "Yes, of course I'd like to have more of them. Half a dozen at least. Think they'll have gray hair?"

But before Jason could answer, they were hit by a solid projectile that landed smack on Jason.

"What in—" he began as he tried to sort out arms and legs that seemed to be everywhere.

"You little devil," Amy said, laughing as she started to tickle her son. "You made Doreen bring you back, didn't you?"

For a moment Jason was a bit horrified at the thought

of what the child might have seen and heard, and he was also shocked at the lack of privacy. Little did he know that such adult things were gone forever.

But he didn't have time to contemplate his fate and the blessings of it because Max stood up and shot himself forward. Amy knew what was coming and protected her face with her arms, but Jason caught the full weight of the boy on his face.

"Monkeys!" Max squealed, then started bouncing on his new father's stomach.

F
DEV

Deveraux, Jude. *1A*

The blessing.

$22.00

DATE			

10-98